I0585373

The Crowning

BOOK I OF THE CROWNING SERIES

Nattie Kate Mason

Copyright © 2020 Nattie Kate Mason
All rights reserved.
ISBN Paperback: 978-0-6484853-0-8
ISBN Hardcover: 978-0-6484853-1-5
ISBN eBook: 978-0-6484853-2-2
ISBN Amazon Paperback: 978-1-7944569-5-2
Revised edition, published 4th August, 2019
Third edition, published 30th October, 2020

All rights reserved. No part of this publication may be
reproduced, stored in or introduced into a retrieval system, or
transmitted in any form or by any means without the prior
written permission of the author and publisher.

Cover illustration and design by Bethany Gilbert
Title page illustration by White Heart Design
Other interior illustrations by Creativeqube Design Studio

Revised edition copy editor: Chloe Hodge
Series: The Crowning, Book I

To my gorgeous daughter Lily
and my amazing supportive husband Joel,
Thank you for believing in me.
I love you both more than
all the stars in the sky.

Prologue

Queen Amealiana

Fifteen years earlier.

Atop the Alearian snow-capped mountains, Queen Amealiana Caston Brandistone of the Kingdom of Alearia, paced expectantly around her castle suite, pausing intermittently to centre her breathing as the tightening's occurred. She yearned for her nursemaid Lady Lilianna's impending arrival.

As tradition dictated, all offspring's birth names were to begin with the same first letter as their mother's and would be declared at birth in honor of the Mother and the Goddess, who brought them into the world. Queen Amealiana was no exception to the rule and following each birth she had declared the potential heirs' names, along with their gifting which she had foreseen through her prophetic visions.

Amealiana's strong seer gifting had been granted to her by the Goddess herself — passed on through her maternal bloodline.

The stormy sky, hardly a glimpse of the sun visible through the thick dark clouds, promised another blistering cold winter's day ahead; a bad omen of things to come.

Lady Margarette, the Queen's most trusted Lady's Maid; had garnished the sitting room table of the royal suite with delectable pastries, exotic fruits, and many aromatic soothing teas, unsubtly trying to tempt the Queen into eating something. Regretfully, even the Queen's favorite foods were not enough to entice her appetite to return, despite knowing the strength that she would need to draw upon in the journey ahead.

In her suite adorned with all the royal fineries, her Majesty the Queen, a gifted seer and sage, had uneasy feelings towards the impending birth of her twins. The Alearian people were aware of Her Majesty's pregnancy; however, her expectancy of twins was a secret only the Queen and her nursemaid shared. A surprise that Her Majesty was eagerly waiting to reveal to her husband King Titian Brandistone and the rest of Alearia, should all go well with the birth.

A gentle knock at the door drew the Queen from her thoughts and back to the present. Deep breaths through the next brief contraction, followed by a short affirmative nod from Her Majesty to her Lady's Maid, had the door opened to the waiting visitor.

Lady Lilianna stepped through the doorway, smelling familiarly of lavender and chamomile. The mature aged woman's calming scent and aura wafted towards the Queen, easing some of the tension she held in her shoulders.

Queen Amealiana shared a small smile as she beheld her faithful friend and nursemaid and excused her Lady's Maid Margarette from the room with a graceful wave of her hand.

The two women embraced with as much love as a mother and child, for Lilianna had played a large part in raising her Majesty from infancy as the sole Princess of the kingdom of Quillencia.

Beloved second-born of Queen Annalyse Amidon Caston and King Julian Caston, Queen Amealiana had inherited her strong sage and seer giftings from her mother. Much to her father's dismay, Queen Amealiana had not inherited any trace of his mind conqueror gifting.

Lady Lilianna gently pulled back from the Queen's embrace and dropped into a small curtsy. "Your Majesty, I forget myself, I am sorry to have kept you waiting. I came as soon as I received your summons."

"Arise Lady Lilianna, you do not curtsy for me," the Queen replied, gently shaking her head with that small smile still adorning her face. "It is I who owe you a world of gratitude for all you are and have done for me and my family."

The Queen gently took her precious friend's hand and guided her over to sit beside her in a wing-backed chair nestled beside the fireplace. She paused to take another centring breath.

"It is time Lilianna," the Queen spoke softly. "The tightening began during the night. The twins are coming."

Throughout the day and long into the evening, Lady Lilianna supported Queen Amealiana through the throes of labor, though her simple presence and calming nature was her most comforting gift to the Queen.

The Queen, gently assisted with the help of her friend, moved from the bathing room into the bedroom for the final stages of her journey.

The first babe, blond with crystal blue eyes, was born quickly into the loving arms of Lady Lilianna and guided straight onto her mother's chest for a warm embrace.

"Princess Anastasia," the Queen declared, "my sweet child."

As had occurred following each of the previous births of her children, the Queen beheld a vision of her daughter's future.

The young Princess Anastasia danced merrily on her seventh birthday, wielding her gift of fire as magnificently as her father, the King of Alearia.

The Queen pressed a kiss to the infant's head, as Lady Lilianna tucked a warm blanket over the babe and her mother.

The second child was birthed by her Majesty shortly afterward, also blessed with her mother's luscious blond hair and then placed just like her twin, directly onto her mother's chest by her nursemaid.

"Princess Annalyse," the Queen revealed.

Queen Amealiana's eyes glazed over as she was shown a vision into the future of her beloved second twin daughter.

"TAKE HER!" The Queen suddenly bellowed, staring at Princess Annalyse, all at once alert and straight-backed but still cradling her two newborns.

Lady Lilianna, taken aback by the Queen's request, quickly masked the shock on her face and reached for Princess Annalyse, silently wrapping the babe in a warm blanket and nursing her closely.

Queen Amealiana struggled to overcome the shock of her vision, for what she had foreseen had shattered her heart.

The Queen gravely shared her vision with her friend.

"My precious Annalyse, around the age of twelve, lay dead on her bed. Her long blond wavy tresses hung limp. Her eyes drained of all their glossy brown color, betrayed by someone in our kingdom..."

Queen Amealiana went onto explain how she was shown that her daughter would have had the potential to bring balance to her Kingdom with her strong gifting, but her life was more important than a kingdom or even the unbreakable bond of mother and child. Queen Amealiana knew what she must do and what she must ask of her most trusted and loyal friend.

"Take her Lilianna, you must trust if she stays here her life is forfeit. Take her to our home kingdom of Quillencia, raise her as your own in secret. Let no one know of this deceit. You must protect her with your life," the Queen sobbed, barely holding the pieces of her fractured heart together.

"When the time comes," Amealiana continued, "she will need to return for The Crowning Ceremony rituals beginning on her sixteenth birthday, as the Goddess requires. We must hope with all our hearts that no harm comes to her upon her return."

Lady Lilianna, understanding the urgency and severity of the Queen's vision, and trusting her own gifting as a sage and healer, took the baby to her mother for one final goodbye before she vowed to her Queen to protect and raise the newborn as her own.

Out of the hidden passageway in the Queen's chamber, with Annalyse concealed under her cloak, the nursemaid escaped the castle into the dead of night.

Only her Majesty and the Goddess herself were aware of the precious package she bore in her arms.

When the Queen felt she could cry no longer, she finished feeding her remaining daughter, wrapped her in a warm blanket, and attended to her own personal needs.

Exhausted and heartbroken, the Queen did her best to burn all evidence of the second child's birth in the suite's hearth, before summoning her trusted Lady's Maid Margarette.

Amealiana tried her best to plant a broad smile across her face, though it did not quite reach her eyes.

"Rejoice!" The Queen exclaimed, "the Goddess has blessed us with another precious Princess and final potential Heir of Alearia. Alert the King so he may come to meet his beautiful daughter Princess Anastasia Brandistone.

"Order the herald to proclaim a royal birth announcement on the castle steps, so the Alearian people may hear of their new Crown Princess Anastasia, a gifted fire wielder," The Queen finished.

If Margarette suspected anything amiss or questioned where Lady Lilianna had disappeared, she did not say. Her loyalty to the Queen was a mark of her integrity.

Queen Amealiana

It was a brisk winter's day and Queen Amealiana was taking an early morning ride on her prize stallion Ebony, given the namesake reflecting her deep colored coat. She rode through the Royal family's private estate, winding through the thick evergreen trees on the outskirts of the forest bordering their castle grounds, taking in the peace and tranquillity of her kingdom.

Queen Amealiana had lost her lustre for life over the years spent fraught with anxiety, plagued by her visions offering her only glimpses of the potential future, visions ever-changing based on the choices she and her loved ones made. The constant helplessness she felt from her inability to change the future was enough to leave her in a permanent state of hyper-alertness.

The morning horse rides had become as ritualistic as her evening worship of the Goddess before retiring to bed each night. No matter the frigid alpine temperatures of winter or blistering hot summers, Amealiana relied on these brief moments of solitude to collect her thoughts. A momentary escape from the day-to-day responsibilities that came from being Queen of Alearia, one of the three most influential Kingdoms of the realm.

Fifteen years ago, Queen Amealiana's youngest child Princess Anastasia was born. The knowledge of her twins' birth was a secret closely guarded, locked away in the depths of the Queen's heart. A secret only shared with her closest friend Lady Lilianna and the Goddess herself.

The Queen had not dared to contact her dear friend or attempt to locate her long-lost daughter for fear that her child may meet her demise if she were to return to the kingdom. The time had passed since her vision was prophesied to occur, but the Queen still feared the fates would punish her for her deceit and take what they believe was already predestined prior to her birth. Queen Amealiana refused to accept that fate. Her protective motherly instincts reminding her of the importance of remaining anonymous to her youngest child.

The Queen sent a whispered prayer along the winds to the Goddess, begging for her daughter's protection and blessing, wherever she may be.

Queen Amealiana cantered her horse back towards the stables, already having been out longer than usual to try and calm her nerves. Today was an important day for Princess Anastasia and she would compose herself for her daughter's sake.

The Queen had beseeched the Goddess that her dear child would enjoy this last special birthday before her next, which would mark the beginning of the Crowning Ceremony rituals.

As tradition and the Goddess demanded on the youngest potential heirs' sixteenth birthday, all gifted potential heirs would submit to the ceremony rituals. Following the Crowning Ceremony, an Heir would be chosen and crowned future King or Queen of Alearia. But today, marking Princess Anastasia's fifteenth birthday, should be a joyous occasion and Amealiana was determined to make it as such.

As she cantered into the stable and greeted the stable master with a polite nod, he bent into a low bow and the stable hand brought over a stool before assisting Her Majesty down from her horse. Amealiana savored this last moment with Ebony, picking up a brush from the nearby table and gently combing the horse's mane in farewell.

The Queen briefly thanked the stable hand for his assistance and turned to gracefully walk back up the curved cobblestone path towards the royal family's private side entrance to the castle. Taking in a deep breath, she strode through the centuries-old castle until reaching her royal suite.

Lady Margarette, the Queen's Lady's Maid, dropped into a curtsy before following her Majesty into her bathing chamber. No words needed to be spoken between the two women as Margarette was in tune to the Queen's need for a rejuvenating bath prior to joining the royal family for breakfast.

Lady Margarette was well accustomed to the Queen's morning routine, after serving her faithfully for the past 25 years since Amealiana first arrived in the Kingdom of Alearia.

At 18 years old, Amealiana, Princess of the Kingdom of Quillencia, arrived just days before she was to marry her betrothed, former Prince and Heir, now King Titian Brandistone of Alearia.

Lady Margarette assisted the Queen to disrobe before she settled herself into the porcelain bath, already filled with steaming hot water. It smelled sweetly of essential oils and fresh lavender, the soothing combination immersed in the water, designed to relax the Queen's soul before her busy day ahead of Royal duties and celebrations.

Her Majesty rested her head gently on the rim of the bath, her honey blond hair flowing delicately over the end. Lady Margarette began massaging tonics designed to strengthen and bring out the hair's natural shine into the long blond tresses, preparing it for styling. Queen Amealiana allowed her eyes to gently close, feeling the aura of a vision floating to the front of her mind.

Queen Amealiana was dancing in the palace ballroom arm in arm with her husband, King Titian. The floor was filled with people joyously dancing and celebrating her youngest daughter's birthday.

Her eldest son Prince Alexander, a talented shapeshifter whom inherited his gift through the paternal bloodline, waltzed nearby with Countess Valencia's daughter Lady Violet. The young woman was wearing a regal red satin gown, a daring color choice to be sure, but an elegant gown all the same.

The Queen found herself mesmerized by the couples' dancing, feeling as though perhaps a connection was developing between the pair before her very eyes, or perhaps it had already bloomed and the Queen had merely been too preoccupied to notice. Alongside her son waltzed her eldest daughter.

Princess Agnes was partnered with Sir Riley, the charming son of nobleman Sir Alfred Bernadine, who had indeed been fawning over the former these past few months. Clearly smitten with each other, they would have made a delightful couple if only love had a say in royal betrothals. Alas, the Princess was already promised to another, Prince Joseph from the Kingdom of Stanthorpe.

The Queen's attention quickly drew back to her son Alexander, who seemed to be suddenly short of breath, his skin becoming progressively mottled. Was he choking? Has he been poisoned or bewitched?!

A scream unleashed from the Queen's mouth as she ran to her son's aid, but just as quickly as he had lost his breath, his light began flickering out, his soul preparing to meet the Goddess.

The Queen caught her son as he collapsed lifelessly to the ground.

He was gone.

The Queen of Alearia screamed, her consciousness returning instantly to the present, her body shaking from head to toe.

The Queen struggled to regain control of her breathing as she began to process what she had foreseen.

'Why is this happening?' The Queen thought.

Suddenly scrambling to get out the bath, Lady Margarette held up a towel for her Majesty, quickly assisting her to get dressed.

Her Majesty frantically rushed to pull on her cloak as she slipped on her shoes, eager to find her husband the King and alert him of her vision.

'*Please Goddess,*' the Queen silently begged, '*save my son!*'

2

Princess Anastasia

Princess Anastasia awoke in her royal chambers to the sound of birds chirping amongst themselves, escaping the early morning chill on her balcony overlooking the gardens, sheltered from the cool breeze.

The Princess rang her bedside bell and her Lady's Maid, Charlotte, gracefully entered the suite bedroom from the side passageway door that led to the servants' quarters.

"Good morning Princess Anastasia, many blessings be upon you on your fifteenth birthday," Charlotte warmly greeted the Princess with a curtsy.

The maid then offered her charge a satin nightgown and placed a pair of matching slippers on the ground before her. Princess Anastasia accepted the gown and slippers graciously and thanked her nursemaid for her well wishes, before politely requesting that she prepare the bathing chamber for her.

Additional layers of clothing like the nightgown were merely ornamental luxuries for a talented fire wielder such as Princess Anastasia. The Princess could wield fire, heat water or adjust her body temperature to make herself comfortable without a second thought. Princess Anastasia's fire wielding gift was inherited from her father's paternal bloodline.

'*Praise and thanks be to the Goddess, who bestowed upon the first fire wielders their remarkable gifts,*' Anastasia thought to herself as she removed the chill from her gown with her gifting.

Strolling out onto the ornate balcony of her bedroom to watch the last of the sun rise, the Princess spotted her mother Queen Amealiana, returning from her early morning ride. Why her Majesty insisted on riding in the brisk early hours each day without possessing a fire wielder gift to keep herself warm, was a mystery to the Princess. She noticed keenly though, that the time outside seemed to bring her mother some inner peace, so the Princess had never thought to pry, not that she dared question her Queen Mother.

Queen Amealiana was a gifted seer and sage, truly blessed by the Goddess and beloved by her people. Though, the Princess often pondered how difficult it must be for her mother to see glimpses into the future whilst knowing it was ever changing, and having little input in the eventual outcome.

'*Both a gift and a curse*', that was how the Queen had once described her prophetic visions to her daughter many years ago.

The Princess wondered what the Queen had foreseen for her and the kingdom's future.

Turning to go back inside, the sky now tinged with a shade of pink, the Princess relaxed in the company of her nursemaid, excitement stirring in her heart for the celebration ahead.

Princess Anastasia gracefully walked into her bathing chamber, her favorite scents of rose petals and lilies greeting her on the way in. The bath was already full as requested.

With a flick of her hand steam began to rise from the water as it heated further to the Princesses desired scorching temperature, thanks to her gifting. The Princess thanked her nursemaid for her assistance before asking Charlotte to prepare her silk lavender colored day gown and matching jewels to wear for breakfast with her royal family.

Anastasia stepped into the luxurious tub, releasing a small blissful moan as the water enveloped her like a warm welcome embrace. The young Princess then savored what was sure to be the last calm and quiet moment in her busy day.

Princess Anastasia wandered down the hallway, her lavender gown trailing behind. Long honey blond hair hung in loose curls down to her waist. She passed various bustling palace staff attending to the preparations for her celebratory birthday ball that evening; each servant giving the royal a respectful bow as they crossed paths.

The Princess approached her families' private dining room, greeted with more well wishes and bows by the two guards stationed outside the gold leaf gilded, double-doored entrance.

The guards opened the doors for her, and the Princess approached her usual place at the table, eagerly looking forward to a delectable array of treats for her birthday banquet breakfast.

Prince Alexander, her brother, stood up from his chair to respectfully bow to his youngest sister as she entered the room. A servant helped Anastasia be seated and placed a napkin across her lap before walking back to his place by the wall.

Anastasia warmly greeted her awaiting siblings and gratefully accepted their well wishes and presents, which they happily passed across the table to her. In the midst of opening one of her gifts, Anastasia looked briefly around the room for any sign of the King and Queen's whereabouts.

"The King and Queen have been delayed my apologies, Anastasia. I passed our Queen Mother in the corridor looking frazzled," Prince Alexander informed her. "Mother said to apologize to you on their behalf, but our parents will not likely make it in time for breakfast. Urgent royal business is all she would say."

Slightly disappointed but used to the erratic royal life, Princess Anastasia sighed and then plastered a smile on her face, setting aside the beautiful emerald jewelled necklace she had been gifted by her brother.

"Oh, that is too bad… Thank you for the present Alex, it's lovely. Soo… Who is hungry? I'm starving and these chocolate croissants aren't going to eat themselves!" She giggled.

With that, the four royal siblings; Princess Agnes the weak gifted prophetic, Prince Alexander the shapeshifter, Princess Anastasia the fire wielder and Princess Alecia, another talented fire wielder, settled into comfortable conversation, enjoying the delicious spread of sweet and savory breakfast treats.

Following breakfast, Princesses Anastasia and Alecia, thick as thieves, exited out the back entrance of the castle for a morning walk.

The two sisters' close bond formed in their earlier years, when Princess Anastasia was able to commence training her fire wielding gift with her sister. Together, the siblings had mischievously been pushing the King and Queen's limits in subtle ways for as long they could remember.

Along their walk, they noticed an increasing amount of guards stationed around the castle grounds.

"I wonder why there are so many guards everywhere, the ball isn't until this evening," Princess Anastasia noted.

"I'm sure it's nothing," Princess Alecia replied, dryly disregarding her sister's worry, "just our parents being their usual overcautious selves."

Anastasia conceded that her sister was likely right. Nothing out of the ordinary ever occurred in Alearia, so she quickly shrugged off any concern she had.

As the young potential heirs continued their stroll, Princess Anastasia redirected their morning walk past the stables where the young stablemen were tending to the horses.

Anastasia had always had a not-so-secret sweet fondness for the stable boy Joel, who was a year older than herself. She often enjoyed making excuses to speak with the young man under the guise that she was merely there to visit her own horse Duchess. Anastasia blushed slightly as Joel gave a low bow and sly wink towards her as the two Princesses walked by. Alecia taking the opportunity to indiscreetly tease her sister about her suddenly flushed cheeks. Anastasia glared at her in response and quickened their pace, leading them towards the royal gardens for the rest of their walk.

"I know you like him," Alecia teased.

"I don't know what you are talking about," Anastasia responded.

"It is no use pretending darling sister," Alecia drawled, with a hint of mischief in her tone. "I know I tease you about him, but I've seen the way you gaze at each other. You're rather smitten with the stable boy, aren't you? You know the King would never allow his youngest precious daughter to marry the help. What is the fascination with him anyway? Sure, he's cute but what could he possibly offer you?"

"Oh, please Alecia," Anastasia replied sarcastically, "like you haven't been swooning over the young squire that assists you with your combat training."

"Well played sister," Alecia conceded, and the two sisters continued taunting each other and giggling like ordinary girls.

3

Lilianna

In the quiet rural village of Lavender Grove, on the outskirts of Quillencia, Lilianna was busy mixing and brewing various tonics and tinctures for use in her apothecary. The middle of winter brought with it some of the most debilitating health conditions the villagers saw all year and their stores were regularly running low.

After fleeing to the country where no-one would know her, Lady Lilianna abandoned her title, name, and profession, and assumed the role of the town's local apothecary healer, going by the name of Lily. The townspeople had accepted her story that she was merely a traveling healer looking to finally settle down in a small town. Neither had the townspeople questioned how the older woman had stumbled upon a young babe on her travels, presumably abandoned at birth and taken her in to raise as her own.

The quaint wooden white cottage Lilianna had purchased with her meagre savings was situated along the outskirts of the town, by the riverside.

Squeezed into the tiny bedroom were two single beds where she and her ward both retired at night. The cozy living room had a large bookshelf, a small dining table and seating.

In the evenings, the two companions could often be found relaxing in their two matching chairs by the hearth, resting their aching feet in front of the warm fire. The heat easing their tired muscles, after a hard day's work healing the sick and injured.

For fifteen years, Lilianna had guarded Queen Amealiana's secret and raised the oblivious young Princess Annalyse, whom Lily affectionately nicknamed 'Annie,' as her ward.

Annie was growing into an empathetic apprentice healer. She demonstrated a strong sage gifting, which Lily had taught the young girl how to wield and use to help others.

Lilianna was almost certain that Annalyse possessed another gift, a rare but often easily misused mind conqueror gifting. Lily suspected this based on the young girl's uncanny ability to make her heart's desires come true. The community found it particularly difficult to ever refuse the young woman and Annie never demonstrated any manipulative character traits.

'Annalyse's birth mother, Amealiana, had prophesied at her birth, that Annie would have the power to 'bring balance' to the kingdoms'. One might wonder if a potentially gifted mind

conqueror who possessed sage wisdom may be a force to be reckoned with.

'Equally balanced with power and wisdom, surely the young woman would not be seduced by the potential dark side of her mind conqueror gifting.' The old healer pondered but she kept her musings to herself.

Lily feared the young girl could be taken advantage of if her second gifting became public knowledge, and Annie's ancestry questioned if her second gifting became apparent.

The Quillencian Royal family — where Annie's maternal Mother heralded from — possessed the only known bloodline carrying the mind conqueror gifting. Lilianna had promised her beloved friend Amealiana, that she would protect her child at all costs, and to fulfill her promise it was imperative that Annalyse's identity remained a secret, even to the young Princess herself.

Lily's thoughts were interrupted when Annie entered the small kitchen, and placed the basket of aromatic herbs she had been picking beside her mentor. They would be added to the ointments the healer was already preparing.

Annie washed her hands with a sigh.

"Lily, why must we work so hard on my birthday? Why not come for an ice skate with me on the lake and then we can gorge ourselves on sweets until we feel near bursting," Annie exclaimed smiling at the elderly lady she adored.

Lily smiled, "my sweet girl that sounds divine, however, the sick will wait for no-one and my duty is here, serving our townspeople. Why don't we quickly finish up and after we see our final patients of the day, we shall go for an ice skate to celebrate, followed by consuming the delicious birthday cake I have baked for you."

Annie squealed with delight at the prospect of birthday cake and quickly hurried back to work, helping Lily prepare the various ointments they needed to restock their supply cupboard.

Annalyse

The fire in the hearth was rejuvenating. Annalyse stretched her feet out in front of her, dispelling the chill from the ice that had seeped into her skates.

Despite the miserable cold weather, Annalyse had never felt more content and happier than she did at that moment sitting beside her honorary mother figure. Annie and Lily had spent a wonderful afternoon ice skating and overindulging on decadent chocolate cake.

The two companions celebrated Annie's birthday on the winter solstice each year after Ms. Lily claimed she had a dream one year that the Goddess revealed Annie's birth. Annie wasn't sure if a dream was a good enough excuse to determine someone's birthday, especially if you had no way of confirming if it was true, but regardless of the date, it gave Annie a sense of identity and a way to measure the passing years.

Celebrating her fifteenth birthday with Ms. Lily made her feel like she was valued and that she mattered. When Annie was spending time relaxing by the fire with Ms. Lily, she felt that warm tingly feeling spread in her chest. She could forget that once she had been an abandoned baby, left in a basket that no-one wanted. Annie often wondered if a part of her was missing out in not knowing her birth family.

'Why didn't they want me? Is there something wrong with me?'

Thoughts like these often floated through her subconscious around her birthday each year.

'Unloved and unwanted', that is what the towns kids call me, teasing me because I do not have a 'real' family,' Annie thought sadly.

But today Annie would do her best to forget their taunting words and just be content with her life in that precious moment.

'For this is who I am; an orphan, healer's apprentice, sage and a granddaughter in spirit to my inspiring mentor, and I will own my identity.'

4

Princess Agnes

All Princess Agnes's life she had lived amongst a family of high achieving, immensely talented, gifted Royals. All the while, Agnes watched on from the sidelines with a mere whisper of prophetic gifting, craving more and waiting for her moment to shine.

'*Agnes the Ungifted,*' that was what the people called her.

Envy and jealousy had bloomed in Agnes's heart during her founding years when her siblings and the young nobility had teased her, laughing amongst themselves at the mockery of a potential heir with a near useless gift. Agnes's joy for life was quickly drowned by the seeds of hate and sorrow that grew intertwined in her soul.

In her earlier years, Agnes would stay up late each night praying to the Goddess to strengthen her prophetic gifting or bless her with another gift.

'If only I were a great sage and seer, like my mother. If only my father, the King, passed on his mighty fire wielder or shape-shifter giftings to me as with my other siblings.

'Why do you forsake me Goddess, to be just a useless lessor prophetic? My visions are rarely accurate, and my dreams are just that; wishes upon a star hoping to come true,' Agnes ruminated to herself.

Princess Agnes had forever felt like an outsider in her own family, merely there to make everyone else look good.

Agnes desperately wished she could shapeshift like her brother, Prince Alexander. Often fantasizing dark thoughts of turning herself into a mighty dragon, then burning the castle to cinders. Perhaps then transforming into a golden eagle who would glide upon the winds to a distant land where she could escape all the hurt and pain she felt inside.

'Those are fools' dreams and a waste of time to hope for something so impossible,' Agnes thought angrily.

In a constant attempt to gain favor with the King and Queen, Agnes sought out regular opportunities to shadow her parents at work so she could gain valuable insight into the art of ruling a kingdom. Agnes trained more aggressively in her combat lessons and studied more meticulously in her academic studies, than any other potential heir.

Agnes honed her body and mind into a finely tuned weapon.

'One day I will be crowned Queen, I will make sure of it.'

Eight years ago, on Princess Agnes's sixteenth birthday, all her dreams came true. The Goddess secretly awakened a second gifting in Princess Agnes that day. Unbeknownst to her family, this unanticipated secret gift was going to help her along the path to achieving her dream of being crowned heir.

As the eldest potential heir, Princess Agnes felt compelled to prove to her family that despite her perceived weak gifting, she deserved to be crowned Heir of Alearia.

One year from today she would have her chance, when all potential heirs would compete for the Crown. The Alearian royal siblings were known for being fiercely competitive, always boasting about why they each felt they were more suitable to be crowned Heir. No one ever considered that *'Agnes the Ungifted'* would stand a chance of claiming the seat of power in the Crowning Ceremonies.

Agnes had spent the last six months scheming potential ways to eliminate her competition with her newest gifting, and nothing would get in her way.

It was the eve of Princess Anastasia's fifteenth birthday ball. Agnes's Lady's maid had just positioned the final amethyst comb in the Princesses unbound, sandy blond hair.

Her emerald ball gown, embellished with jewels, glistened in the light as she gracefully exited her room and made her way to the ballroom for the celebration. Sir Riley would be accompanying her to the ball tonight as usual.

Sir Riley was a handsome naive young man. The secret moments the young pair passionately shared in the palace gardens at events such as tonight's, offered Agnes a delicious escape from acting like the perfectly behaved Princess her family needed to believe she was.

Sir Riley was certainly clueless enough not to realize that she had been using him all this time as a pretty accessory to wear and discard as she saw fit.

Tonight, Princess Agnes planned to get one step closer to ensuring what she believed to be her Goddess-given-destiny.

'Why would the Goddess have awakened in my soul a second, much more powerful, devious gifting if she did not intend for me to use it?

'I am a mind conqueror, a weapon hidden in plain sight. Nothing will get in my way of becoming Queen.

'Soon, I will make my first move, and no one will see it coming.'

Queen Amealiana

In the grand ballroom, Queen Amealiana sat on her throne upon the dais, dressed in a flowing, golden embroidered gown and wearing a crown adorned with priceless jewels. The Queen attempted to mask her utter terror and fear with a fake, tight-lipped smile and a gentle nod of acknowledgment to her noble guests as they passed on their well wishes and thanks.

Earlier that day, her Majesty's vision had rocked her to the very core. Not since the birth of her youngest child, had she foreseen a vision that caused her so much fear. Worst of all, she knew in her heart that she could not whisk away her only son into endless hiding to protect him as she had chosen in secret to do at Princess Annalyse's birth.

With an evacuation plan out of the question, the King and Queen had no choice but to continue with the planned event, though they introduced as many extra safety precautions for the evening as possible. The hope being that they may avert any harm coming to their beloved son Prince Alexander.

The King and Queen had discussed her vision for hours on end in whispered terror amongst each other. The most likely scenarios they had come up with were that someone would either try to poison the Prince or bewitch a spell upon him.

'What motive would there be to harm my son, other than Alexander is the only shape-shifting potential Heir?' Amealiana mused. *'My dear son, is favored to be crowned Heir amongst the people but that does not warrant a death sentence!'*

One thing the rulers both agreed upon, was that Prince Alexander was not to know of the potential threat. They did not want him forever living in fear of a potential attack on his life.

The Monarchs would do everything in their power to protect him. The Queen's most trusted Chef Antony was charged with taste testing samples of the food before it was to be served at the ball. The Queen had ordered guards be posted alongside the banquet tables to ensure none of the food was tampered with.

The King's personal guard Roman was trusted with inconspicuously protecting the Prince for the night, never being further than a couple of feet away from his side.

To avoid any further speculation or questions regarding the additional security measures put in place around the Prince, her Majesty had also appointed guards to watch over her other children should the potential threat turn to them.

The Queen had also summoned the highest-ranking healers in the kingdom to attend the ball should the worst befall and their emergency services be required.

The birthday celebration ball was going better than expected, with no signs yet of anything untoward. The Queen even managed to relax a little, trying her best to enjoy the evening for the birthday girl's sake.

Her daughter Princess Anastasia approached the Queen on the dais to thank her for the wonderful birthday party, begging Amealiana to join her for some sweets and wine. The Queen allowed herself a few moments reprieve from overseeing the ball to accompany her daughter to the royal family's designated table, where they indulged on decadent chocolate cake — the Princess's favorite — accompanied by sweet dessert wine.

"Mother, is something troubling you?" The young Princess Anastasia inquired. "Forgive me for asking, but you seem distracted this evening. Is anything the matter?"

"Everything is just fine my dear Anastasia, just a slight headache bothering me, nothing to worry about," the Queen lied. "Why don't you go ahead and ask one of the nice young gentlemen here to dance or go and find your sisters. I am sure there is some mischief you and Alecia could be getting into while I am conveniently looking the other way," Queen Amealiana dared her daughter, with a cheeky smirk across her face.

The Princess grinned broadly at her mother, any concern she had vanished. Anastasia hugged the Queen, thanked her again for the party and disappeared off into the crowd, no doubt in search of Princess Alecia.

Once again gazing over the masses from her throne upon the dais, the Queen watched her children immersed in the celebrations. Princess Anastasia and Princess Alecia were indeed mischievously flirting with a couple of the young noble men's sons.

Princess Agnes was dancing blissfully arm-in-arm on the ballroom floor with Sir Riley. Dancing nearby, as alarmingly her vision had shown her earlier that day, was her son Prince Alexander dancing with the sweet Lady Violet.

The Queen breathlessly turned to the King sitting beside her and alerted him to the unfolding events. The King calmly ordered the guard stationed beside him to alert the other guards to be extra vigilant in monitoring for any danger, and to summon the healers to prepare themselves to act on a moment's notice. The King then turned to his Queen and asked her to dance so they may more closely monitor the situation.

The crowd parted for the King and Queen, allowing them ample room to dance near their offspring Princess Agnes and Prince Alexander.

'Please Goddess, let this not be a self-fulfilling prophecy and protect my son,' the Queen silently prayed.

Queen Amealiana watched her son closely whilst dancing seemingly adoringly with the King. There appeared to be no signs of danger; the Prince was enjoying himself, absolutely smitten with his dance partner.

The Queen turned to check on her daughter Princess Agnes who suddenly had a concerned look on her face, tilted in the direction of her son. Agnes's eyes were beginning to glaze over.

'Is Agnes foreseeing the future? Does she know if what is going to happen? My daughter's visions have never been reliable, could they have improved? Have we done enough to stop the prophecy?'

The Queen began to feel her pulse rise, and her chest tighten from anxiety as she heard the noise she had been dreading. The Queen, already fearing what she would see, turned to her son who was suddenly short of breath and clutching his own throat.

The Queen let out a gut-wrenching scream as she pushed herself out of the King's arms and hurled herself towards her son. She was just in time to catch him as he began to collapse to the ground just as she had foreseen in her vision.

Prince Alexander's skin turned from blue to sickly pale as the last of his life drained away. There was nothing she could do. She had failed to protect her son.

The healers ran across the ballroom to try and resuscitate the young man, but nothing worked, their healing powers somehow unable to revive him. The Queen felt her heart shatter into a million pieces.

"Goddess why have you taken him!" The Queen screamed in between heaving breaths, tears streaming down her face.

Amealiana began hyperventilating, the ballroom suddenly too small. All around her, people stood stunned or crying in disbelief.

The King fell to his knees in despair.

The Queen felt as if the world was spinning around her. Her vision suddenly grew dark as she collapsed over her son's cold, lifeless body.

5

Princess Agnes

The castle was eerily quiet.

Black mourning banners hung around the halls and exterior in remembrance of Prince Alexander, whose unexpected passing had broken the hearts of everyone in the kingdom.

The King had ordered that a small team of guards be stationed at every castle door and gate. A necessary precaution to keep the royal family safe from the unknown threat, he declared.

Only the Goddess and Agnes knew what had truly occurred last night at Princess Anastasia's birthday ball.

Agnes trembled in the privacy of her bathing chamber; the warm water unable to take the edge off her nerves. A murderer, that's who she was now after everything had gone so wrong at the ball.

Princess Agnes had only planned to disable the Prince's connection in his mind to his shape-shifter gifting. Agnes believed that if she could have rendered the favored potential heir incapable of accessing or controlling his gifting, he would have become ineligible to compete for the crown.

Jealousy had driven the eldest sibling to take drastic measures in her mission to be crowned Heir and future Queen.

Using her mind conqueror gifting, Agnes had sifted through the Prince's brain, searching for that vital shape-shifter gifting connection. It had been more difficult then she had anticipated, and her attempt to sever Alexander's connection to his gifting had rapidly gone disastrously wrong.

Agnes tried to slow her breathing as she felt her guilt swelling, causing her chest to feel excruciatingly tight.

'It was an accident,' the Princess tried to reassure herself. 'I didn't mean to do it.'

But it did no good. Agnes knew she had allowed her power to seduce her. Just as Princess Agnes was severing the Prince's connection to his gifting, she felt the urge to keep going, to probe a little further into his mind and see what else her powers could do.

It was then that Agnes recalled lightly tugging on the part of Alexander's brain that controlled his breathing, and curiosity swelled in her, wondering what it would feel like to hold someone's life in her hands.

Before Agnes could think twice about what she was doing, she had ripped a hole in his brain, preventing the Prince from voluntarily breathing. She tried to fix her mistake, but there was no way to heal her brother.

He was dead and it was her fault.

Princess Agnes was an untrained mind conqueror dabbling with magic she did not fully control or understand. Power had seduced Princess Agnes and caused her brother to perish.

'What kind of a person kills her own family?' she thought.

Elspeth, her lady's maid, knocked on the door to Princess Agnes's bath chamber.

"Princess Agnes, forgive my intrusion," she spoke softly through the door, "but the Queen and King have summoned you urgently to the throne room."

Agnes froze in terror.

'The Queen must know it was me!'

Queen Amealiana

Upon her throne, beside the King of Alearia, the Queen sat bravely masking the endless sorrow and grief she felt. Queen Amealiana had scarcely been able to leave her private suite whilst she mourned the loss of her only son. The second beloved offspring she had to say goodbye to, unbeknown to the kingdom.

Prince Alexander was a kind boy, a perfect gentleman. He was always looking out for his sisters and working diligently to train his gifting.

Alexander's passing had hit the Queen the hardest. The Matriarch's grief was compounded by the immense guilt that she felt from foreseeing her son's demise and being unable to prevent it. The guilt was a heavy burden she would carry deep in her soul until the Goddess deigned it time for her to be reunited for eternity with her precious son in the After World.

Queen Amealiana was struggling to stay strong and be brave for her living children and the people of Alearia. She felt as if her heart had been ripped in two, and one half had drifted away with Alexander to the After World.

Between periods of mourning and anxiety, Queen Amealiana had ruminated over the events of the previous night.

'What did I miss? What else could I have done? Why has this happened?'

All thoughts leading her onto other questions she needed answered. *'What about Agnes? Has her gift of prophecy truly awakened and if it did, what did she see in her vision?'*

All avenues of investigation needed to be carried out for the Queen to feel any closure regarding the Prince's death, and that included finding out what Princess Agnes knew.

After much discussion, the King and Queen had decided to address the matter with Princess Agnes and therefore she was summoned to the throne room for interrogation.

Princess Agnes

Princess Agnes anxiously made her way to the throne room. having quickly thrown on a comfortable dark velvet winter day dress with matching overcoat to keep out the chill in the hallways.

Elspeth, her lady's maid, had also managed to quickly brush out the Princess's tangled hair from the bath and apply a small amount of makeup, so she appeared presentable for the King and Queen.

Upon Agnes's arrival at the entrance to the throne room, the guards stationed on either side of the door bowed in respect before opening the door and announcing her arrival. The Princess entered the room sombrely and greeted her parents with a low bow.

"Good morning your Majesties. I came as quickly as I could, I apologize for the delay," Agnes stated sincerely.

The King and Queen nodded their heads in acceptance of her apology, the King electing to take the lead in this difficult discussion with their daughter.

"Good Morning Agnes, thank you for coming. I'm sure you are wondering why we have summoned you for such an official meeting," King Titian began.

Princess Agnes nodded, keeping her face neutral whilst trying to avoid the urge to run out of the room and escape whatever conversation was about to reveal.

"The Queen and I are deeply saddened by the passing of our son Prince Alexander. It is to your benefit as much as ours that we meet today to discuss our concerns regarding the events that unfolded last night," King Titian summarized.

"Yes, your Majesty. I too miss Prince Alexander terribly. Anything I can do to help I will gladly do it," Princess Agnes claimed, hoping her parents couldn't sense the rising panic in her voice.

"The reason we have called you here is due to something that was witnessed last night, just prior to the Prince's tragic passing. The Queen will elaborate," King Titian stated.

Agnes didn't know how she was still standing, barely able to hold a straight face and stop herself from fleeing the room and escaping whatever disastrous end she was about to meet.

'They know it was me,' Agnes thought. *'It's all over, I'll hang for what I have done.'*

"Princess Agnes, I fear there is something you are withholding from us and the kingdom," Queen Amealiana stated.

Agnes's chest felt so tight that she thought she may die; her palms sweating. Her eyes couldn't help but dart to the palace guards standing at attention along the throne room walls.

'This is it; they know I killed him. My life is over. If only they understood it was a mistake. I didn't mean to kill him, the power just momentarily consumed me,' Agnes internally fretted.

"Is there anything you would like to say, Agnes, before I tell you what I strongly suspect?" Queen Amealiana asked.

"No, your Majesty. I am sorry but I am afraid that I don't know what you are talking about," Agnes denied, stuttering over her words and partially revealing her guilt.

"I know your prophetic gift has strengthened. I saw the change in you. Your eyes glazed over just before Alexander died. You foresaw his death just before it happened, didn't you? We need to know what you saw so we can figure out who did this. We need to know who harmed our beloved child!" Queen Amealiana begged.

Agnes's heart really did feel like it had stopped, and she let out a sigh of relief once the shock had worn off.

'They don't know it was me, they only believe I foresaw his death in a prophecy! Gosh, I couldn't dream up a better alibi for myself. Praise the Goddess!' the Princess thought with relief.

"I'm sorry your Majesties, I should have come to you earlier about my vision," Agnes lied. "I wasn't sure if what was revealed to me was true given my poor gifting history. Please forgive me for not telling you sooner. Yes, I did foresee my brother's death."

"Then who did it? Who killed Alexander?" The King exclaimed as he rose from his chair.

"It was..." Agnes found herself at a loss for words.

'What do I say? I can't blame someone else, can I? Do I just pretend that I am not sure what happened and deny everything? I don't want to die. If only they would understand I didn't mean to kill him and then they could know the truth. But they must never know. I will not tell them the truth. I must be strong even if the guilt is eating me alive.'

"Agnes, did you not hear me? Who was it?! If you know anything, you must tell us!" The King pressed on, the suspense clearly getting the better of him.

"I do not know your Majesty. I am sorry. It's all a blur to me now. I really am sorry," Princess Agnes whimpered, hoping the lie would convince the King and Queen to concede defeat and dismiss her from the meeting.

The King sat down, taking a deep breath to calm himself.

"Very well Princess," the King spoke more calmly. "But if I find out you are withholding anything from us, you will be held accountable and face the consequences of lying to your King and Queen. Do you understand?"

"Yes, your Majesty," Agnes meekly replied, barely able to contain her relief that she had not been found out.

"Agnes," the Queen said, walking down from the dais to hold her daughter's hand. "If there is anything else you remember or need to tell us, please come and speak with me no matter the time. I am glad to hear your gifting has developed, praise the Goddess. Perhaps you may make a strong potential heir after all."

With that final statement, the Queen squeezed her daughter's hand affectionately and exited the room silently, the weight of the world appeared to be pressing down on her shoulders.

Princess Agnes turned back towards her father and bowed before requesting to return to her suite. Her request was granted with a slight nod of affirmation from the King, his heavy gaze burying into Agnes's soul as though he knew without a doubt that his daughter was hiding something but could not yet prove it.

Princess Anastasia

Snow fell silently over the castle grounds. A pleasant start, to what was sure to be an exceedingly difficult day for the royal family.

Princess Anastasia was helped by her Lady's Maid into her black mourning gown for Prince Alexander's funeral. A delicate black matching veil laid over her head.

'One would hate to show any signs of grief in front of the kingdom's people. 'We can't have that nonsense occurring', the King would say!

'The world would end if the kingdom saw us acting like normal people in mourning with broken hearts, crying over the loss of a loved one. We must wear a veil and hide all evidence that we are capable of feelings too,' Anastasia thought with fists clenched.

The Princess hated funerals. She hated all the overdone pageantry and the townspeople crying as if it was their relative that had passed away.

It had been a week since Prince Alexander's death and the time of mourning would officially end after he was laid to rest. Alexander would have wanted them to live their lives to the fullest. So, in his memory, the black mourning banners would be replaced non-traditionally with golden ones at sunset, in acknowledgment of the Prince's love for life and his new endless peaceful existence in the After World, free of pain and sorrow.

As of tomorrow, the castle would return to its normal routine, living the life that the Prince would have wanted them to enjoy.

Despite Princess Anastasia's dislike for funerals, she dearly missed her older brother and took comfort in knowing that Alexander was now safe with the Goddess, enjoying eternal peace and happiness.

"If Alexander had a say in today, he would tell us to scrap the ceremony rubbish, lose these ridiculous mourning veils and wear our favorite clothes. He would want us to dance the night away drinking copious amounts of wine, laughing as we shared our favorite memories of him. It would be just the family. No one else would be permitted to attend and intrude upon our family bonding time, not that we would ever be allowed to do anything like that. Kingdom first, family second, that's the unwritten law amongst royals," Princess Anastasia vented to her Lady's Maid Charlotte.

"Right you may be Princess, however tradition and ceremony will help Alearia to heal. It is the way of our kingdom," Charlotte reminded the Princess.

Remembering her place, she added, "Please forgive me, Princess, for speaking out of turn. I know you are grieving and missing Prince Alexander dearly."

"No apology necessary Charlotte, you have been my friend in this palace most of my life. You can speak plainly with me from time to time. It's quite refreshing to have someone challenge me on occasion, though I still strongly dislike all this ceremony carry-on we must go through for the kingdom. For the most powerful family in Alearia, there sure are an endless number of rules and expectations placed upon us Royals," Princess Anastasia replied with a sigh.

"Right you are Princess. I wish you the strength of the Goddess as you face today. All the best Your Highness, and may the Prince enjoy the endless bliss of the After World, Goddess bless his soul," Charlotte spoke gently as she curtsied for the Princess and left the room.

Anastasia took a deep breath and savoured the few precious, quiet moments she had to herself before the funeral ceremony began.

Princess Agnes

Sitting on a pew beside her sisters, Princess Anastasia and Princess Alecia, Agnes felt like an impostor at her own brother's funeral. By law, Agnes was a traitor to her own family and the crown.

As a way of coping with her grief, Agnes justified her brother's passing to herself as, *'a mere accident, a casualty of war in the battle to be named Heir and future Queen. Accidents happen,'* she told herself. *'I didn't mean to end Alexander's life, even if I did enjoy the feeling of holding his life in my hands'.*

It had been days since the King and Queen had summoned Princess Agnes to the throne room for questioning, and she had not spoken to or heard from them again until today. The Princess believed their lack of communication was a sign that she had been ruled out as a suspect and she chose to shake off any remaining guilt she had felt to refocus on her end goal of becoming heir.

'The time for mourning is almost over. Wouldn't Alexander want me to forgive myself and refocus on working towards my goal? Live life to the fullest and all that nonsense,' Agnes pondered to herself.

Tomorrow, Agnes planned to start training her mind conqueror gifting more thoroughly to prevent further accidents. Princess Agnes was determined she would achieve her goal of being crowned heir.

Today, however, she would play the role of the dutiful Princess. She would mourn the loss of her brother whom she had held some affection for, but she would also forgive herself.

Agnes had made her peace with what had happened, and she would move on with her life. Nothing was going to hold her back from what she wanted, and she would not look back. So, Princess Agnes sat beside her sisters, partook in the ceremony rituals, listened to the eulogies and did what was expected of her.

Tomorrow, would be a fresh start for her. Tomorrow Agnes would begin secretly training her second gifting and she would keep training just as she had always done until her mind conqueror powers were another finely tuned weapon in her arsenal.

7

Princess Anastasia

It had been one month since Prince Alexander's funeral and life, for the most part, had returned to normal. Princess Anastasia missed having her brother around. Alexander was constantly up to mischief, always pulling pranks on the palace staff in one animal form or another. Princess Anastasia had often confided her secrets to him and found his over-protective brotherly instincts entertaining when it came to her courting boys.

Anastasia fondly remembered when Alex was around ten years old, how he had snuck into a dinner party disguised as a mouse. Alexander then quickly transformed into a snake right upon the dining table where twenty noble guests and the remaining royal family were seated. Poor Lady Bloomington had a heart attack.

The Queen Mother had banned her brother from all future royal engagements for a whole month after that stunt until she deemed he had earned his penance.

It was another brisk morning in the training arena. Thankfully, the worst of winter was finally behind them and the early signs of spring were beginning to show.

Princess Anastasia began her morning warm-up alongside her sister Alecia. Both potential heirs were eager to let off some steam and lose their thoughts in the predictable daily training routine.

The fire wielding sisters had been feeling spooked by recent reports circulating, that several people in the kingdom had suddenly lost their ability to wield their giftings.

The healers couldn't identify the strange events cause but theorized it may be a foreign magic disease. The condition, likely easily transmissible, evidenced by the erratic nature of its occurrence, indiscriminating in gifting or person.

The healers were working hard to find a cure, but thankfully none of the royal family had contracted the illness. The presence of such an unknown disease, however, placed everyone on edge, especially Princess Anastasia and Princess Alecia.

'What if I or Alecia contract the condition? We wouldn't be eligible to compete in the crowning ceremony. Neither of us would be crowned heir.'

Keen to forget the endless Royal issues, especially this new magic disease beginning to infect the kingdom, Anastasia and Alecia threw themselves into training, trading stress for perspiration.

"Watch out!" Princess Alecia yelled, whilst hurling a cheeky fireball at Anastasia while her back was turned.

Anastasia took a quick sidestep to her left, still facing away from her sister. The fireball missed her by a hairsbreadth.

"Show off!" Alecia exclaimed.

"You'll have to do better than that sister, even if sneaky behind-my-back moves are probably the only way you'll ever land a hit," Anastasia cockily teased.

"Very un-Princess like behavior indeed, trying to hit your poor defenseless sister while her back is turned," Anastasia continued just as she hurtled a volley of fireballs towards Alecia in retaliation.

Alecia threw herself to the ground, rolling into a somersault to escape being hit by the flurry of fire.

"Defenseless?!" Alecia blurted out. "You are almost as gifted as I am! It's not as if you aren't my biggest threat in the upcoming heir crowning competition, I mean *ceremony,*" she chided her sister.

"Who? Me!" Anastasia feigned shock. "You mean to tell me our dear sister Agnes doesn't stand a chance with her apparently newly strengthened 'prophetic' gift?" she mocked.

The girls both burst into laughter.

"Come on sister, enough wasting time chatting, we both know Agnes is a joke! Now let's fight!" Alecia declared, hurtling a wave of fire towards her sister.

Anastasia grinned, instantly throwing her own firewall up to block her sister's attack. The girls practiced wielding their fire gifts for hours together. Both Princesses enjoyed the temporary reprieve from royal duties and the adrenaline singing through their bodies as they let themselves be wholly immersed in the intense power of their giftings.

Exhausted but content, Princess's Anastasia and Alecia walked sluggishly after their training session through the palace grounds and back up towards the castle, talking as they strolled.

"I feel like I could sleep for a week," Anastasia sighed. "Your fire wielder gift is strengthening so quickly I can hardly keep up with you," she praised her sister.

"Nonsense Tash! You give me a run for my money every time we train together, and I wouldn't have it any other way," Alecia rebutted.

"Alecia, where do you think Agnes goes all day?" Anastasia pondered aloud changing the subject. "Why doesn't she train with us anymore? Obviously, she can't wield fire like us, but she could at least give the impression she cares about the competition ahead and physically train with us."

"No idea sister, maybe she thinks she is beyond training. Maybe Agnes thinks her precious prophetic gift will be enough for her to be crowned heir. Perhaps she's just given up. We've never been close to her. Maybe she's finally realized how much of a dead weight to the family she is, and forfeit her right to compete for the title of heir," Alecia cattily mused.

"Yesterday I saw Agnes sneak out of the castle towards the city. Where do you think she went? Do you think she's sneaking off to meet Sir Riley at his family estate? What a scandal that will cause, if she continues with that disastrous romantic interlude once her engagement is formerly announced to the other young man," Anastasia gossiped.

"Do you really want to know what I think sister?" Alecia asked.

Anastasia keenly nodded in affirmation.

"I don't care where our sister is going," Alecia stated matter-of-factly, "and I do not care what she is doing. Going out into the city is reckless with this magical disease spreading. Hopefully, she catches the condition and she will officially be out of the potential heir race for good."

8

Princess Agnes

The streets of Alearia were disconcertingly quiet. The townsfolk, all hiding away in their homes, afraid that the so-called foreign mystery disease would strike them next and leave them powerless. Usually, the streets were bustling with people from the night markets, couples out for romantic strolls beneath the moonlight and young people in a passionate embrace in the alleyways.

Princess Agnes pulled her dark hood tighter over her head, ensuring that her identity remained a secret.

Earlier that evening, to be certain that her family didn't suspect anything amiss, Agnes had arranged for a royal carriage to take her to Sir Riley's estate near the center of town, where she was to be their guest for dinner.

In the city proper, nobles and successful merchants lived near the city centre and Castle Brandistone. Whereas farmers, labourers and other low-level workers lived in the mountainous region surrounding the city.

Feigning a headache during the meal, Princess Agnes apologized to her hosts and excused herself from dinner, claiming she would ask the doorman to call her carriage to take her back to the castle for an early night's rest. Agnes then went to the ladies' room near the back door to the mansion, pulled on her cloak and silently exited out the back door.

Agnes crept through the garden, keeping to the shadows to avoid being seen, and walked straight into town through the back garden's wrought iron gate.

Princess Agnes now walked casually through the winding cobblestone streets, her head hanging low to avoid detection. Across the alleyway she heard a fiddler playing in a nearby tavern, where an intoxicated rowdy crowd could be heard singing along to the tune the musician played.

'*Drunks,*' Agnes thought to herself, '*easy targets for the picking.*'

Agnes crossed the road and entered through the side door of the pub. A burly middle-aged gentleman stumbled into her as he tried to exit the establishment, before painting the cobblestone road with his most recent meal. Disgusted, Agnes ventured deeper into the tavern.

'Praise the Goddess he didn't spill his guts on me or I would have made him pay,' Agnes fumed to herself.

After pulling up a stool by the bar, Agnes placed a silver coin upon the countertop and requested the barman get her a pint of the house ale. The drink was watered down and tasted like it had been brewed in a dirty back alley tub, but it would serve its purpose for the night.

Agnes dared a quick glance around the tavern, looking for a suitable target. A drunk middle-aged man with a thick girth and rough facial hair, she decided would do nicely.

'Agnes picked up her pint of ale and weaved her way through the crowd headed towards where the drunk was rowdily conversing with a lady of the night.

'Pathetic,' she thought to herself. *'People like him don't deserve a gift from the Goddess. Maybe this will teach him a lesson for such deplorable behavior in public.'*

Princess Agnes leaned against one of the nearby walls and took a small sip of her ale and began to tap her foot in time with the music. To anyone who took notice of her, she would appear as though she was just another stranger out for a quiet drink after a busy day's work.

Once Agnes felt comfortable that her cover was believable enough and no one was paying her any attention, she rechecked her target's whereabouts, pulled her hood down further and began to train her gifting.

Slipping back through the streets and hailing down a carriage, Princess Agnes began the journey home.

'*Another success,*' Princess Agnes thought with a sinister smile.

'*Slipping into his brain was almost too easy. Severing the connection to his gifting had been as easy as breathing. Perhaps next time I'll pick a harder target with a more complex gifting.*

'*I wonder if it is possible to steal gifts. It seems a waste for these worthless nobodies to possess giftings that I do not have. Maybe I should probe around someone's brain and try...*

'*On the bright side, now everyone believes this so-called magical disease has spread across the kingdom, my cover story is firmly established. Thanks to my hard work, preparation, and mind conqueror training, no-one will question when the mysterious illness infiltrates the castle.*

'*I'm sure my darling sisters would love to know what it feels like to be powerless like I was for so many years. It would wipe that smirk right off Alecia's face if she knew just how powerful her eldest sister truly was.*

'*Of course, my mother may again foresee harm coming to her poor children and attempt to protect them. I expect as much after seeing the extra security measures that were put in place for Anastasia's ball. The King and Queen must certainly realize by now that they are dealing with something far more menacing and unpredictable then they could have ever imagined — that no amount of extra guards can prevent.*

'*I am more careful these days, my skills more accurate, and I have managed to resist the urge to meddle with people's life force whilst I have busily worked on their brains. I will not make the same* mistake I made with my brother. This time I will merely focus on nullifying their powers, so they are ineligible for the crown.

'I must be careful not to draw too much attention to myself, or the Queen and King will become suspicious and I will give myself away. Soon it will be time to enact the next step in my plan to becoming crowned heir.

'I will become Queen, and nothing will get in my way.'

9

Queen Amealiana

The days were arduous, though the weather itself was pleasant enough now that spring was beginning to bloom. The endless stress of being Queen was taking its toll on Amealiana. An everlasting migraine etched away at her ability to fully function.

Yesterday, the Queen had personally visited the infected people who had sadly lost their giftings, to pass on her encouragement and offer her sympathy. A hard fate indeed for these people to come to terms with, no thanks to the magical disease spreading around the kingdom.

All infected citizens were being held in quarantine in the city's hospital, though none showed any signs of sickness. The mode of transmission remained unknown, making the quarantine enforcement vital. No clear links had been drawn between the infected people which was particularly strange given how quickly the disease was reportedly spreading according to the healers.

Twenty people were now infected, ranging in age from ten to sixty-seven, both male and female. So many unknown factors remained despite the greatest healers in the land working tirelessly to try and find a cure for the people.

Queen Amealiana was beginning to theorize that perhaps something, or more specifically someone, was behind the disease.

'But who could it be? What is their motive? What would anyone gain from rousing fear amongst our people? Where are their giftings going? Is someone stealing them for their own or do they still exist somewhere within the person's soul? Countless questions with no answers.

'I had always believed that a person's gifting was linked to their soul. In theory, if their giftings were completely gone, they would perish to the After World. Surely it isn't possible for one to go on living once such a core part of themselves had been taken away,' the Queen mused.

Suddenly the Queen had a revelation.

'If my theory is right and there is still some of the Goddess's gifting in each of those affected by the disease, there must be a way to renew their giftings. Could their gifts be re-trained or revitalized from the seed that remains inside them, keeping them grounded in this life?

'Rather than the healers focusing on how the infected people lost their giftings, maybe they should try to determine how to find that last speck of power within them and nurturing it, retraining it,' Queen Amealiana thought hopefully.

'I need to do more research. If there is a chance that I am correct, then I will need to summon the healers and discuss my theory with them.'

The Queen spent what little spare time she had researching in the many castle libraries, searching through old history books and journals. This evening her Majesty sat by one of the many library's fireplaces in a comfortable red velvet wing-backed chair, her feet elevated on a matching plush footstool.

The Queen was wearing a casual maroon colored day dress with a thin woollen blanket draped across her lap. Her lack of formality in such a public area, was a true sign of how much the stress was bothering her.

Amealiana combed through a weighty volume with a leather embossed cover, titled; '*The History of Power*'. She was searching for information on similar magical diseases or any mention of people losing their gifts by other means.

The Queen sighed deeply as she finished scanning through the book, again finding nothing to aid her in the search for answers.

Annalyse

The sky was crystal clear today, a beautiful spring day. The blooming flowers along the river created a rainbow of color.

After a long, hard, busy winter of treating patients under her mentor's supervision, Annalyse was permitted a day off by Lily. Her mentor unsubtly hinted that she should use the day wisely to try and make friends whilst she enjoyed the stunning weather.

Annalyse packed a small satchel with food for her lunch, a couple of coins, a book, a small blanket for picnicking and a water skin.

The young apprentice healer conveniently overlooking her mentor's suggestion that she go and 'make friends'.

The young men and women of the town had always whispered about Annie behind her back. They found her peculiar and avoided her like the plague unless they ironically needed her apothecary skills.

No, 'making friends' was not a good suggestion.

Instead, she started to hike through the forest with the aim of spending the morning reading in the sun, with nothing but the blissful sound of a waterfall for company.

After several months of constantly caring for sick people, which she enjoyed for the most part but found incredibly draining, Annalyse needed some time to herself. Reading in nature sounded like bliss to her right now. After a particularly busy winter healing season in the Apothecary, a quiet day enjoying nature was exactly what Annie needed.

On the final trek along the river, approaching the bottom of the waterfall, Annalyse overheard a group of male mercenaries conversing boisterously by a campsite they had made.

Just great', Annie thought to herself. *'All I wanted was one day to myself. I've hiked for hours for nothing.'*

Beginning to turn around and walk back the way she came, Annie stepped on a tree branch, causing a loud cracking sound and alerting the men to her presence.

"Who do we have here men? Looks like a lost young woman. Shouldn't we be chivalrous and offer to help the lady out?" One of the burly men yelled to his drunk friends.

He had a tattoo of a snake down his neck and short, thick black facial hair. The man's tone and turn of phrase triggered Annalyse's sage gifting, alerting her to the danger she was in.

If she were to run, they would surely catch her and if she screamed, no one would hear her, this far out in the forest. Annalyse had to think on her feet and get out of there as quickly as possible.

"I am sorry gentlemen," Annie began, trying to hide the fear from her voice, "but I seem to have hiked a bit further ahead of my group than I intended. We weren't aware any one was up here at the falls. We were just headed here for a picnic. That's fine though, we'll find another place to have our lunch. If you would please excuse the interruption, I will be on my way back to my group to tell them the falls is already occupied. My apologies and good day to you," Annalyse responded turning around and beginning to walk away from the group calmly.

"Not so fast little lady, I'm just trying to be friendly. Why don't you come and sit by the fire with us and share some of our lunch? We have plenty to go around and you're welcome to stay around for dessert," the same burly man sleazily suggested, beginning to follow her a few steps into the woods.

"No thank you, I really wouldn't want to be a bother. I must be getting back to my friends or they will be wondering where I have gone," Annalyse called behind her, increasing her pace to broaden the distance between herself and the stranger.

The mercenary's comrades returned to their drunken revelry, not paying any attention to the conversation playing out between Annalyse and their friend.

"Hold on lady," the man said in a more forceful tone as he quickened his pace to catch up with Annalyse.

He grabbed her arm from behind, causing her to spin around to meet his gaze.

"Let me go so I can be on my way. My friends will be here any moment wondering where I am, and they will not be impressed that you are manhandling a lady," Annalyse lied in an assertive tone.

"I just want to get to know you kitten," he replied, pretending to sound offended that his honor had been called into question.

Then, raising his other hand, he gently caressed her cheek.

"We are going to get to know each other better kitten. It has been a while since a pretty young thing like yourself has stumbled upon one of our camps," the burly man stated.

Whilst attempting to pull her arm out of his grip, Annalyse threatened, "you will unhand me sir or I will scream, and my friends will come running to find me!"

The man let out a sinister laugh in reply.

"I don't think that's going to happen," the man responded matter-of-factly. "Do you know why I don't think that's going to happen?" The brut momentarily paused for dramatic effect. "Because there is no one coming to save you. No fake friends are coming to defend your honor," he declared, pulling her behind a big oak and pushing her up against the tree.

Then Annalyse felt her mind shift, as her heart began to race, her hands suddenly clammy. She felt her vision blur and unexpectedly she found herself in the horrid man's mind, looking back at herself through the ghastly man's own eyes.

His disgusting thoughts washed over her as she suddenly realized, *I'm reading his mind. How can this be happening?'*

Then as quickly as she had entered his mind, she found herself back in her own body, staring, wide eyed, at the stranger looking her up and down.

Using one of his hands, he forcefully pinned her own above her head against the tree, his free hand started to slide up her top.

'*This cannot happen, he will not have me!*' Annalyse swore to herself.

"Stop! Take your hands off me and leave me alone!" Annalyse screamed.

The man's friends ignored her struggles, pretending they couldn't overhear what was going on. But as soon as the words were out of her mouth and mind, Annalyse felt the man's hands leave her body.

Fear bulged in his eyes as he lost the ability to control his own actions. His arms were suddenly stiff as a board by his side, completely immovable despite his best efforts to regain control of them.

"What witchcraft is this?!" The man bellowed, "men, help!"

Completely confused as to what was happening and hearing the men coming to see what the fuss was about, Annalyse quickly composed herself and started to sprint away.

She ran faster than she thought humanly possible, dropping her bag in the process, adrenaline pumping through her veins, conscious of the group of men who were now in pursuit of her.

Seeing a cave she recognized nearby, Annalyse hurled herself as fast as she could towards its entrance.

'*Why is this happening? What did I do? Why did that man stop? Did I do that? No, that's not possible Annie! You're losing your mind! Focus Annie! Think! How are you going to get out of this alive?'* Annie stressed.

She ran through the cave entrance and into the dark, judging by the sound of muffled footsteps, her pursuers were falling a little further behind. Feeling a glimmer of hope by the slight advantage she had on the men, Annie increased her pace, searching frantically for a place to hide.

Further and further into the cave Annie ventured, until the cave floor and walls began to feel slick with a thin film of moisture and mud.

'I must be getting close to a water source,' she mused to herself.

'Think Annie, where are you? How are you going to escape?'

Annie could hear the men were slowly gaining on her once more, their footsteps echoing throughout the cave. She realised she must have slowed her pace whilst thinking.

Ahead, Anne could see light filtering in through the cave and what sounded like a river. Pushing herself harder, she slipped on the slick floor, panicking as the men gained on her, about to catch-up to her at any moment.

Suddenly, she spotted a gap in the cave ceiling, too small and high to fit through, but offering enough light so she could better assess her surroundings. The men were now close enough that one of them had spotted her, giving the group the confidence to increase their pursuit despite the slippery conditions.

Fearful of what they would do to her if they caught her, Annalyse continued racing as fast as she could through the cave. It was then that she spotted the canyon in the cave and the churning river flowing into it.

'*Goddess protect me,*' she prayed, throwing herself into the water, the river deeper and the current much stronger than she anticipated.

Annalyse was pulled deep below the water's surface by the current and down the canyon waterfall in a matter of moments. She tried desperately to swim towards the water's surface. Kicking her legs and pulling her arms as hard as she could until she finally breeched the surface, taking in a great gulp of air before she was pulled back under the water again.

Annie had no idea if she would live through this but if she were going to meet her end, she could at least find comfort in the fact that it wasn't at the hands of those mercenaries. They were long behind her now, wherever she was.

Annie felt the current easing slightly, and used her last burst of energy to breech the water's surface taking another deep gasp of air and fighting to keep her head above the water. The cave ceiling was barely two feet above the surface of the river and Annie frantically searched for anything she could grab a hold of to keep her head above the water, before having the realization that there was no-where to escape to.

Not yet willing to accept her fate, Annie swam as best as she could along with the current for what felt like hours, trying to keep her head above water as much as possible as she was carried throughout the caves narrow waterway channels.

Finally, she spotted light ahead.

'*Hang in there Annie, that must be the cave exit ahead. You only have to last a few more minutes,*' she told herself.

Unexpectedly, the current started to quicken again as Annie approached the mouth of the cave. A short moment of relief was met with sheer terror as Annalyse beheld the edge of a mighty waterfall that she was fast approaching.

Annie's heart felt like it was going to explode in her chest. Her lungs ached. She tried her best, but struggled to swim against the current as pure exhaustion overwhelmed her body.

Unable to fight it any longer, the young girl slipped under the water again just as she was pulled by the current over the waterfalls edge.

Lilianna

The hour was late, and Annie had still not returned to the cottage. Lilianna paced around the house, obsessively repositioning objects on the bookshelf — anything to keep her hands and mind busy.

Annie had never missed dinner before, and she had certainly never stayed out late at night before.

Lilianna suspected Annie had gone hiking, based on the casual pants and thin long sleeve top she was wearing when she left the house. Lilianna knew she wouldn't have packed more than a water skin and light lunch for the hike.

'What if something has happened to my poor girl? What if she's injured and stuck out in the forest? With no way of calling for help, she would be completely helpless, and all I'm doing is cleaning the blooming house!

'Something is not right. My gifting is singing to me that something has happened. Could Annie be in danger or worse... Has the prophecy finally come to pass?

'What if she's dead?

'I cannot fail Annie and I will not fail Queen Amealiana, who trusted me with her whole heart to protect her child.'

Lilianna could no longer shoulder her worries; her inner eye told her that her ward was in trouble, and she could not stand to wait around any longer.

The mature aged healer threw on a coat and hastily packed a shoulder bag full of water skins, dried meat, bread, bandages, various herbs, tinctures, and potions.

Lily lit a candle and encased it inside a lantern to protect the flame from the wind. Stepping out into the cool night, Lily cursed herself that she could not fit a blanket or change of clothes for Annie in her satchel.

'Don't get ahead of yourself Lil; Annie is likely fine, you're just being paranoid,' she tried to reassure herself, but in her soul, she knew that wasn't the case.

Wherever Annie was, Lilianna was sure she needed help, and the healer could only hope that she could find her ward before it was too late.

Through the forest she trudged, stepping over fallen trees and following the river through the forest towards Annie's favorite retreat by the waterfall.

Lilianna had been walking for what felt like hours, her fear growing with every passing minute. There had been no signs of dear Annie, so onward Lily continued.

Off in the distance, Lily spotted a fire and camp set up at the waterfalls base. A rowdy group of men could be overheard drinking heavily and cursing unhappily about something she could not decipher. Lilianna wrenched off her coat and quickly threw it over the lantern to hide its soft glow, careful not to give away her position.

Annie had been here, of that much Lily was sure. But she could see no sign of the young girl in the camp.

After weighing up her options, Lily refused to give up. She hid her belongings behind the tree to enable her to move more freely and quietly.

On silent feet, the healer crept around the outskirts of the camp with only the moonlight to guide her, careful to keep her distance. She wanted to get close enough to better hear the groups conversation but was careful to stay out of the campfire's light.

Hiding behind a big fern bush, Lilianna squatted amongst the shadows and listened.

"... One minute I was getting in the mood for a nice intimate... *conversation*," the gruff looking man said with a smirk.

His drunken mates elbowed each other, cocking their eyebrows as smirks painted their faces, knowing exactly what sort of *conversation* he had in mind.

"The next second," he continued, slurring his words occasionally. "My hands are off her and my arms are pinned down by my sides - I couldn't bloody move! It was like the cursed witch cast a spell on me and then she flipping ran away! I can't believe you didn't catch her, there's bloody six of you and one of her," the same man swore.

The men turned uneasy at the accusation, a few suddenly finding their boots mighty interesting.

"We may not have caught her George, but mark my words, she's as good as dead, if she isn't already. We all saw her jump into that cave river. No one could survive that current. Who knows where her body ended up? Probably fish food by now is my guess," one of George's gang declared rather proudly. "Anyway, I need a piss, I'll be back."

The man then began stumbling into the woods, headed straight for Lilianna.

With her deepest fears confirmed, Lilianna quickly fled from her hiding spot through the shadows and back towards where she had stashed her belongings. Praise the Goddess that she remembered exactly where she had put them.

The healer quickly backtracked, careful not to stray far from the river that would guide her way home. The last thing she needed was to get lost wandering in the dark. Thankfully, it was a full moon, so the forest wasn't too difficult to navigate without the use of her lantern, which she kept covered with her coat.

About ten minutes into her trek back towards home, Lilianna spotted something odd caught in a low branch and walked up to investigate. To Lily's horror, she realized it was Annie's shoulder bag, completely full of all her supplies. Meaning that whatever had happened to her had likely occurred before she had a chance to have her lunch, which could have been up to twelve hours ago if she had to guess. Pure terror filled Lily's heart.

'The bag confirms it... Annie would never go anywhere without supplies. What if these men found her as they said, and she has fallen in a river in only the Goddess knows where! The water up here is near freezing in the peak of summer and it's only spring. What if she knocked her head? What if she has drowned? What if she is dead?'

Lilianna sent silent prayers to the Goddess for guidance for herself and protection for Annie if Goddess willing, she was still alive.

Lilianna, finally deeming herself far away enough from the men that it was safe to use her lantern. She pulled on her cloak to stay warm and continued looking for Annie throughout the night.

Deep sorrow filled Lily's heart, tears silently trailing down her face as the night wore on and she started to lose hope. As the night sky gave way to dawn, Lily, completely exhausted, reluctantly followed the main river the rest of the way home.

Arriving back at her cottage, one last strand of hope had her searching the house and finally their bedroom in case her beloved ward had returned overnight, and it had all just been a bad dream. But Annie was nowhere to be found.

12

Princess Agnes

Princess Agnes was beginning to go stir crazy, pacing around the palace halls. As a protective measure, the city was in lockdown by order of the King and Queen. The temporary order now in place to keep the Royal family safe and prevent the supposed magical disease from spreading around the Kingdom.

It had been a whole week since Agnes had ventured into the city to train her mind conqueror gifting. The tension of not using her gift was building inside her, giving Agnes an arduous migraine and a wicked temperament.

Thanks to some quick thinking and handywork on the Queen's mind, Agnes not been called in for further questioning and no evidence against her had revealed itself.

It appeared the few safety precautions Princess Agnes had placed upon the Queen had worked just as she intended, giving Agnes a sense of security. Another devious idea she had to cover her tracks.

One night at dinner, Agnes slipped into the Queen's mind while sitting beside her at the table. It took her a while to break through the protective mental shields the Queen had in place. However, once Agnes successfully breached the Queen's mental defences, it was a simple matter of searching for the route of her prophetic gifting and blocking her from foreseeing any visions of herself.

Agnes highly suspected the Queen's visions regarding the magical disease, whilst still present, were now limited to only foreseeing the damage she had caused rather than the cause of the disease itself.

Exploring the Queen's mind and ordering her not to suspect anything amiss, was a simple way to take the edge off her power but had not managed to relieve the pressure of Agnes's building migraine. She needed to find a way to train her gifting without raising suspicion before the pain in her head became unbearable.

Finally, Princess Agnes resorted to joining her siblings in their morning physical training exercises to distract herself from her pounding headache.

"Agnes, are you OK? You seem tense," her sister Princess Anastasia asked.

"Tense, or maybe highly strung is a more appropriate term?" Princess Alecia teased.

"Shh, be nice!" Anastasia tutted Alecia.

"Look, girls I'm just here to train. My head is killing me! I don't have time for your sass Alecia, and I do not want any trouble from either of you. So, if you don't mind, I'd like to train on my own for the remainder of the session," Agnes responded in frustration, making to walk away.

"Well, that's not any way to talk to your darling sisters, Agnes," Alecia taunted, stepping in her eldest sister's way and blocking off her path.

"Anastasia was merely trying to show you some sisterly concern, though I don't know why she bothers..." Alecia cackled.

"Still..." Alecia shrugged, a wicked smirk across her face. "It must not be easy being the only sibling with no chance of becoming heir. What is it they call you in the town's streets, 'Agnes the Ungifted?' A title like that would turn anyone sour. As for the supposed 'strengthening' of your prophetic gifting, I don't believe it for a second! One lucky prophecy does not make you a seer!" Alecia taunted her. Agnes felt her blood beginning to boil as a scowl crossed her face.

Alecia turned arrogantly on her heels, "Come, Tash, let us move onto fire wielding training. One can only run so many laps before she feels positively un-gifted," she cackled, walking away from Agnes, taking Princess Anastasia with her.

Princess Agnes was fuming on the inside, but bit back her retort. She was sick to death of her sisters talking down to her, Alecia especially. They had teased her about her gifting ever since their fire wielding giftings awakened from a young age.

Anastasia was not so bad, but Agnes had big plans for Alecia.

'The time to act is coming, just be patient, don't let her get to you!' Agnes reminded herself. *'Alecia won't be feeling so cocky after I wipe that smug smile off her face.'*

Princess Anastasia

In the training arena, Princesses Anastasia and Alecia trained their fire wielding gifts until their stomachs growled and their bodies ached. Each day Anastasia trained, she could feel her gift develop and could see her power growing, along with her level of control.

Anastasia felt uncomfortable antagonizing her eldest sister Agnes. Alecia, however, made tormenting their sister a sport.

Alecia was like the other half of Anastasia's soul. Their bond was so tight that Anastasia felt obligated to go along with Alecia's bullying. She did not want to risk falling out of her sisters' favor, though teasing their eldest sister did not sit well with her. It wasn't Agnes's fault that she was born with a weak gifting. It could have easily happened to herself or Alecia. Perhaps she would have been closer with Agnes if they shared the fire-wielding gift together. Regardless, musing would not change anything.

13

Lilianna

Lilianna had managed a couple of hours of broken sleep before giving up on the idea of rest altogether. After quickly bathing, Lily re-dressed in some clean, comfortable hiking clothes and restocked her water supplies, before setting off into town to see if anyone would help her form a search party for dear Miss Annie.

Appallingly, most of the townspeople laughed her off when Lily expressed her concern for her ward.

"She's a young girl! Don't fret about her Ms. Lily, you have much more important things to do with your time. She is probably just up to no good somewhere with some young man," Sir Rodrick of the reigning house of Lavender Grove replied when she requested his aid.

"I'll tell you what Ms. Lily, if she doesn't return by tomorrow, I'll arrange a search party."

"That would be much appreciated Sir Rodrick, however, I fear harm may have already befallen my ward. I fear without help, her situation may quickly become dire if it hasn't already. Please Sir, can you spare anyone to help me search the forest, even just one man and a small boat to search the waterways would be of great help," Lilianna pleaded.

"I'm sorry Lily but you will have to wait until tomorrow. The girl is likely fine, and we cannot waste our resources on a run-away young woman with a crush," Sir Rodrick insisted.

The elderly healer thought she would try another tactic, seeing as polite requests and formality were getting her nowhere.

"Well, Sir Rodrick, what a shame it will be when I am unable to attend to the sick in the town's only apothecary because I must search the woods all alone. Annie is like a daughter to me and I will not risk her safety waiting idly by. Since you are unable to offer any resources, it seems I must be moving on to begin my search. Good day, Sir," Lily assertively stated before turning to walk away.

"Wait, Ms. Lily, my daughter is sick. I need you to tend to her today before her condition worsens," Sir Rodrick pleaded.

Turning back towards the noble, Lily looked him in the eye and responded, "your daughter is deeply important to you, just as Annie is to me. I'm sorry Sir but I must put my family first and look for her, unless of course you have changed your mind and can find a team at short notice to look for her on my behalf."

The noble realized he had no cards to play if he wanted Lily's help.

"Fine," he muttered. "I will ask the fishermen to search for her while they are out and about today. I will also arrange for a couple of my men to search the forest on horseback for the young girl this morning. But after today, if there is no sign of her, you will return to the apothecary and resume your work. You mustn't neglect your responsibilities to this town Lily. Now I would greatly appreciate if you could tend to my daughter, please, before you head out on your search today," Sir Rodrick informed her.

With a small satisfied smile, Lily replied, "certainly Sir Rodrick, thank you for your help. Bring your daughter to the apothecary straight away and I will do my best to heal her."

It was getting late in the morning, but Lily had finally finished tending to Sir Rodrick's young daughter Annabelle.

Lily utilized a combination of remedies and her own healing gift to soothe the girl's upset stomach, bring down the high fever and re-hydrate her body.

After the healer had finished washing her hands, she quickly sat down to eat a small lunch to regain her strength. Using her healing gifting was very draining, so she had to be careful to look after herself. Every time Lily healed someone with her gifting rather than her tinctures and tonics, a little piece of her life was taken in exchange for the gift of health she had bestowed upon the recipient.

The cost of her gifting had led Lily to prematurely age, her health given willingly in exchange for that of her patients. The Goddess's way of keeping the balance, healers believed.

Lily usually reserved her healing powers for dire emergencies, knowing the personal cost to her own wellbeing. Today, however, she was keen to resume her search for Annie.

Lily considered the frivolous use of her healer gifting to treat something as trivial as a stomach bug a small but necessary sacrifice to speed up the treatment process.

After finishing her lunch, Lilianna set off into the woods to continue her search for Annie. Lily retraced her steps back up the river and into the forest to where she believed she had found Annalyse's shoulder bag.

Surely enough, after scouting the area from last night, Lilianna found a small scrap of beige fabric from Annie's top that must have snagged on a tree branch. Then she recalled what one of the men last night had said; *"We may not have caught her George but mark my words, she's as good as dead, if she isn't already. We all saw her jump into that river in the cave and no one could survive that current."*

'They chased her into a cave and then into a river. But where is the cave?' Lily ruminated.

Lily continued to walk in the direction the piece of material was pointing until she found another scrap of her shirt on a tree about fifty yards away.

'Like following a trail of breadcrumbs in a fairy tale,' Lily mused.

Looking around for any further evidence of Annie's presence, Lily spotted a cave entrance in the base of a mountain.

'Cave entrance' seemed a generous title for the fallen down boulders making a natural archway leading into a tunnel in the rock. The entrance tunnel opened into caverns in various places.

It was difficult to see, but the tiny shards of light finding their way into the cave was enough for Lilianna to feel comfortable to continue her search.

As she walked through a tunnel, the mature healer noticed the walls and floor were becoming slick with mud. Evidence of boot prints through the mud indicated people had recently passed through.

Lilianna hoped that the trail of footprints was a good indication she was on the right track, but at the same time, she found her heart beginning to race. Lily paused for a moment to process what the accuracy of the man's story could mean for poor Annie.

'Annie, I will find you. I will not stop until I do. Just hang in there my sweet girl,' she promised herself and her ward.

Walking further down the tunnel, Lily began to hear rushing water in the distance. Dreading what she may find, Lily took a few deep breathes to prepare herself mentally. Finally seeing a thick shaft of light up ahead illuminating a small cavern, she beheld a river and her heart sank.

Approaching the river, she could see a dozen footprints by the edge of the water, as if people had indeed stopped by the river to watch it, or someone.

The current was raging.

At the end of the small cavern was a canyon dropping at least twenty feet into where the river continued its path. The ceiling of the cave near where the canyon dropped was barely a foot above the surface of the waterfall.

'If Annie has fallen in this water, with this current and that drop... What if she hit her head falling in? What if she ran out of

energy to swim? What if she drowned?' Lilianna fell to her knees in despair.

Her voice cracked and strained under the weight of her anxiety as she prayed.

"Goddess, please, please hear my prayer! My dear Annie, she is all that I have. I have given up my whole life gladly to protect her, please, I beg you! Please let her live, and I will do anything you ask! Please, Goddess, let her be alive," Lily prayed, barely holding together her last shred of sanity.

Lilianna didn't know how she could go on if Annie was no longer a part of her life.

Since a newborn, Lilianna had raised Annie and loved her as her own. Out of respect for her friend the Queen, Lily had never allowed herself to be called Annie's mother as she knew she wasn't, but she loved her ward as if she were her own flesh and blood. Lilianna's heart felt as though it had broken in two seeing the river in the cave.

'How could my dear Annie have survived this?' Lily worried.

There was no way to get into the lower cavern except through the water and Lily knew at her age it would be physically impossible to swim through the water and try to find her ward. She herself would likely perish if she tried, and that would not only doom herself but also the town who relied on her for her healing skills.

Lily felt completely helpless.

Never in her life had she felt this much worry and heartbreak. Lilianna didn't know how she would ever find happiness in life again if Annie wasn't with her to share it.

'If Annie has already been taken by the Goddess, I do not know how I could possibly go on. I have lived a full long life, praise the

Goddess. Maybe if Annie is truly gone, it is the Goddess's way of summoning me to the next world as well.

'Perhaps the Goddess is giving me permission to embrace the endless peace and happiness that the After World has to offer. I could spend eternity with my Annie, knowing that in the After World we would be forever safe.

'No need to hide or live in fear. We could be at peace together,' Lilianna thought with a broken heart.

Lilianna knelt on the cave floor for what felt like hours, praying and sobbing.

'I feel as though I have failed her.'

A tiny seed of hope that her ward might be miraculously still alive somewhere kept Lilianna praying, begging the Goddess, to protect Annie.

From the cave floor, tears streaming down her face, Lily beseeched the Goddess to allow her and Annie have a few more precious years together in this world.

The cavern was bathed with subtle moonlight filtering in through the natural skylight of the cavern. The temperature had dropped by at least ten degrees since dusk.

Lilianna knew she should start to make the trek back to her cottage, but knowing it would be empty when she arrived, she couldn't bear that final confirmation of hope lost.

Lily knew the chances had been slim that she would have found Annie at all let alone in good health. It was just as likely the searching horsemen and fishermen had not been able to find her either.

Tomorrow the town would carry on as though nothing had happened. Lily would be expected to resume her duties just as Sir Rodrick had bargained with her.

The mature healer was not yet ready to face the likely reality of Annie's passing, so she stayed on her knees praying in the cave with all her heart.

Finally, with the cold seeping into her bones, the cave too dark to see clearly in front of her. Lily set off with the last of her supplies in her shoulder bag and started the long trek back through the damp cave, towards her quaint cottage.

'My cottage will never feel like a home again without my darling girl,' Lily mourned.

"I love you, Annie, with all my heart," she spoke to her ward.

Wherever the young Princess was, Lily hoped she could hear her.

14

Queen Amealiana

The night was still, a million stars scattered across the endless sky, not a whisper of a breeze.

Queen Amealiana stood in the tallest tower of the castle, looking out over the land in the direction of her home kingdom of Quillencia. A part of her soul felt as if it had been torn from her.

The lifeline connection the Queen only just realized she shared across the kingdoms with her long-lost daughter was strained. Barely a thread of the mother-daughter bond remained, and it filled the Queen with more unimaginable despair.

'Something is wrong. Something is terribly wrong,' Queen Amealiana knew in her heart, without a doubt.

Her prophetic gift sung. The Princess's birth prophecy —her greatest fears – may finally be coming to pass.

"Stay strong my sweet darling girl, wherever you are. Hold on! I love you with all the remaining fractured parts of my heart and soul. Please forgive me for not being there to protect you! I will come for you! Please hold on my love. Goddess protect Annalyse." The Queen spoke to her daughter, hoping the stars and the Goddess would deliver her message to her.

"I love you, Annalyse. Hold on my love, I will come as soon as I can."

15

Lilianna

The crescent moon had reached its peak. Midnight was upon the land of Quillencia.

Lilianna approached her small village, her cottage just in view, light filtering out of the windows. Lily could hear hurried voices coming from her home but could not make out a single word that was being spoken.

The healer picked up her pace to see what all the fuss at this Goddess-awful time was about. She hoped and prayed no one was in labor. Lily felt mentally and physically destroyed after such a hard couple of days running on very little sleep. The healer could not bear to put on a brave face and support a woman through such a life-altering journey.

Lily quickly reached her cottage, stopped at the front door and took a deep breath before entering.

"Thank the Goddess you are here Ms Lily! We found her, and she needs your healing desperately!" Stanley, a fisherman exclaimed, rushing to meet Lily at the front door to help her with her coat and bag.

Lily stood in shock by the door, taking in the scene in front of her.

All the lanterns were alight in the cottage, and bustling about was the fisherman's wife, Marcy, running around the house in search of only the Goddess knows.

Before the burning hearth, laid upon a bed of pillows, blankets piled high, blood seeping through the blankets in a few places, was Annie. Her skin dangerously pale, she lay unconscious, but praise the Goddess, her ward was alive.

"My Annie," Lilianna breathed disbelievingly.

The healer ran over to her precious ward and threw herself across Annie's limp body. To embrace her loved one, smell her, feel her slowly beating heart, feel the shallow rise and fall of her chest, was a dream come true.

"Thank you, Goddess! Thank you, Stanley! Thank you for bringing my precious girl back to me," she sobbed.

Suddenly the adrenaline kicked in and Lily's healer gifting awakened. Lily sat back, reluctantly pulling away from her ward to allow herself to properly assess the situation.

'She's too cold, far too cold, her skin far too pale. Breathing is shallow and rasping. Pulse faint. Small bubbles leaking out the side of her mouth. Lacerations to the scalp, legs, and arms.

'She's likely had been bounced around by the current in the cave, earning the lacerations from sharp river rocks or the cave itself. How is she still alive?' The Healer assessed.

"Where did you find her?" Lily asked Stanley desperately.

"Annie was down by the edge of the Black Lands river," the fisherman supplied. "The poor girl had washed ashore and was unconscious face down in the dirt when we found her. Cold as ice. I thought she was dead, but then I heard the rattly breathing and thanked the Goddess."

Lily's face paled further, her eyes darting between her beloved Annie and her rescuer.

"The men and I wrapped her in blankets," Stanley continued, "and brought her back on the boat and straight to your cottage. When we couldn't find you, we tried our best to keep her warm and bandaged up her wounds as best we could. I'm sorry Lady. Marcy, my wife, has been running around replacing the bandages and blankets as often as possible. We figured cold, wet, bloody blankets wouldn't help warm the poor girl up. Just as you got here, Marcy was looking for more but I'm afraid I think you've run out," Stanley finished regretfully.

'Holy Goddess, how much blood has my poor Annie lost to warrant replacing likely six to eight blankets, apparently all soaked with blood. The poor girl should be dead, how is this possible? Goddess, with all my heart, thank you!' Lily processed.

"Thank you, Marcy and Stanley, for all of your help! Now I have one last favor to beg of you please," Lily sombrely requested.

Lily knew how much life-force healing power she would need to exchange to save Annie's life, if it would even be enough, and she could only hope and pray the Goddess would heal the rest.

"Marcy," Lily spoke softly, directing her gaze at the fisherman's wife, "you would do anything for your own children, wouldn't you?"

"Yes, Ms Lily, they are my life. I'm afraid I don't understand what this has to do with Annie," Marcy replied uncertainly.

"All healing has a cost — a price that must be paid in exchange. It is the Goddess's way," Lily replied softly. "Annie means the world to me. I am exhausted and have little energy in me right now. If I waited another day to heal her, I may have enough remaining strength, but Annie does not have any time to spare. So, you must understand why I need to do this for her. After I have healed her, she will still need a lot of rest to recover. Can you please look after her for me? Can I trust you to take on this important responsibility?" Lily begged Marcy to understand.

Marcy's face paled as she took in Lily's words and what they truly meant. Tears welling in her eyes.

"I promise you, Lily. I will do what I can, I will look after her for you."

"Thank you, Marcy. I mean that with all my heart. I am eternally grateful. Could you please do one last thing for me, Marcy?" Lily sadly asked, tears of grief spilling over.

Marcy nodded in affirmation, struggling to contain her own tears.

"There is a letter behind the portrait of Annie and I in our bedroom. Can you please make sure she gets it? It is extremely important Annie gets that letter. It is my final wish Marcy. Can you do that for me please?" Lily begged.

"I will Ms Lily. I will care for Annie and I will make sure she receives the letter when she awakes. I will also make sure you are honored and cared for, once all has come to pass," Marcy solemnly swore to the healer.

"Thank you, Marcy. Thank you," Lily managed to say between sobs.

"Take care, my friends," Lily spoke earnestly. "Tell my dear Annie that I love her with all my heart, and I do not regret one moment of precious time we had together."

"I will tell her Lily. Goddess bless you," Marcy sincerely responded.

Lily turned her attention back to Annie and lovingly smiled towards her ward, knowing in her soul, that there was no greater gift she could give her honorary daughter.

Annie would recover from this and go on to live a fulfilling, long and blessed life.

Tears gently trickled down Lily's face, no longer from sadness but happiness for her beloved Annie and the long life she would have ahead of her.

Lily picked her darling up from her bed of pillows and carried her into their bedroom, tucking Annie under the thick handmade quilt on her bed.

Lily went and put on her favorite navy, soft velvet dress, removed her treasured family heirloom necklace and tucked it into Annie's closed left hand. Lily then crawled into Annie's bed and lay down beside her, drawing the Princess into a loving embrace.

"I love you my dear precious girl. With all my heart, I love you, Annie," Lily whispered to her charge.

Lily sent out a silent prayer to the Goddess for strength, and released her healing energy into her ward, healing every part of her until there was nothing left for Lily to give.

She gave all of herself to save her precious Annie. When she had nothing left to give, the Goddess took Lily's soul by the hand and carried her into the endless peace and happiness of the After World.

16

Queen Amealiana

It was the early hours of the morning and Queen Amealiana awoke with a start. Her Majesty had fallen asleep in the tower, praying reverently to the Goddess for Annalyse's protection.

She clutched her chest, gasping for breath. Her heart felt like it had been ripped apart and re-built.

Her Majesty reached inside her soul, searching for the tether to her daughter, terrified that she wouldn't be able to find it. The Queen feared she was too late to save her daughter and tears poured out of her eyes as she searched frantically for that thin strand of bond they shared. Locating the very frail connection in her soul,

Amealiana found herself in complete disbelief as she felt the bond growing stronger by the second. Relief washed over her.

"Praise you Goddess! Thank you!" Amealiana roared to the sky in overwhelming gratitude.

The Queen didn't know what the guards would make of overhearing her scream at the stars at such an ungodly hour, but she didn't care. Princess Annalyse, her long lost daughter, was going to live.

"Thank you, Lilianna. I am eternally in your debt," the Queen promised her oldest, dearest friend. "Wherever you are. We will see each other soon, I promise."

17

Marcy

Marcy entered the healer's quaint cottage bedroom at sunrise and found Lily lying in bed, arm draped protectively across her ward.

Even in death, Lily was still caring for her loved one.

Lily's face appeared completely relaxed and at peace, as if she couldn't imagine a better way to leave this world then through sacrificing herself to save her dear ward, Annie.

Healing had a cost, Lily had told Marcy, and she had gladly paid the price.

Marcy and her husband helped to move Lily from the young ward's bed to her own, tucking her in gently and placing a bouquet of flowers on her chest.

Lighting a candle and placing it on the bedside table, Marcy prayed Lily's soul would be taken to the After World where she would never again know pain or suffering.

Stanley excused himself to go and attend to their own children, leaving his wife alone in the room to watch over Lily and Annie.

Marcy pulled up a chair beside Annie's bed, took the young ward's right hand in her own, and began praying over her, beseeching the Goddess to finish Lily's healing work in the girl.

Several hours passed.

News of Annie and her selfless mentor had spread quickly around the village. Bunches of freshly picked flowers had been laid around the healers' cottage by the many townspeople who had wanted to honor their blessed healer.

Mourners had gathered respectfully by the riverside, under the shade of the overhanging trees behind the white cottage, praying for Lily's soul and for the continued healing of their town's apothecary-in-training.

Lily was the pearl of the town — their selfless healer who had dedicated the past fifteen years of her life to serving her people through every birth, illness, and death, asking nothing in return. She was the first healer in several generations to have chosen to serve their small rural town, and the people were eternally grateful.

At some point during the morning, Marcy, completely exhausted, rested her head on the edge of Annie's bed. Marcy, still holding the young girl's hand, had fallen into a restless sleep.

Now midday, Marcy awoke, feeling Annie's hand pulling out from beneath her own. The prayers of the townspeople softly filtered in through the bedroom window.

Annalyse

Annalyse awoke in her bed; Lily's special homemade quilt that she treasured draped over her, the room basked with sunlight.

Annie could not recall how she had found her way home, or how she came to be alive in her bed. Her last memories were of being thrown around the river current; the cold and exhaustion overwhelming her, the world fading away.

Annie recalled having a strange dream that her soul was caught in limbo, but then the Goddess appeared before her, whispering '*the debt has been paid*,' before returning her soul back to her body.

"Lily," Annie spoke raspingly, "where are you?"

The young girl's head was pounding, her body stiff and aching. It was then that Annie noticed someone holding her hand, but to her surprise, it wasn't her mentor.

Stunned at first by the strange woman in her room, Annie then looked down to her left hand where she felt something smooth. Beholding her mentors beloved family heirloom necklace in her hand, Annie turned to see Lily resting in the bed next to hers.

"Who are you and why is Lily asleep? Is she OK? Is something wrong?" Annie rasped desperately.

Then Annie's gaze dropped to the flowers resting on Lily's chest and her heart broke, fear overwhelming her in an instant.

The stranger took Annie's hand in her own again and gently squeezed it in reassurance.

"Annie, my name is Marcy, I am fisherman Stanley's wife. My husband found you on death's doorstep on the riverbank and brought you straight here where we cared for you," she spoke solemnly. "Lily had barely rested since you disappeared, she tried looking for you everywhere. She loved you very much, she wanted you to know that."

Scared, in shock and denial, Annie abruptly responded:

"What do you mean she *wanted* me to know. How do you know? Why isn't she waking up? What happened to her?!"

"Annie, when we brought you back to the cottage you were barely alive. You must believe me, Annie, Lily said there was no other way. That all-healing magic had a cost and she would gladly pay it so that you may live."

Marcy paused for a moment to collect herself, though Annie did not miss the shine of her eyes as she tried to hold back tears.

"She gave up her remaining years in this world to save you my darling," Marcy continued sadly. "She said to tell you that she loved you very much, and she had never regretted one single blissful moment of her life with you. You were her family Annie. Bringing you back into this world was the last gift of love she could give you. I am so sorry for your loss. Lily was a wonderful woman," Marcy spoke gently, tears finally escaping down her cheeks, even as she tried her hardest to fight them.

Annie pulled her hand away and dropped it onto the bed.

Disbelieving tears welled in her eyes.

Annie pushed herself up into a sitting position, her body screaming with pain from the effort. Ever so slowly, she moved herself to the edge of the bed. Marcy supportively wrapped an arm around Annie's back to help steady her.

Annie placed her dear mentor's family heirloom around her neck, tears now freely spilling for her eyes. Annie allowed Marcy to assist her to stand, before she unsteadily walked the couple of steps over to Lily's bed, and just as she began to collapse, Marcy was there to catch her.

"I need some time alone with Lily please," Annie whispered.

The fisherman's wife nodded in understanding and helped Annie to sit on the edge of her mentors' bed. Marcy then silently pulled a letter from her pocket addressed to Annie from Lily and placed it gently on the bedside table and left the room, giving Annie the privacy she needed to grieve.

As soon as Marcy was out of the room, Annie pulled back Lily's own embroidered quilt and crawled into bed with her. Annie held Lily tightly in her arms and let her tears flow freely.

Annie's gift filled her aching heart with peace. She had long suspected Lily's gift was taking its toll on her, and her sage wisdom reassured her that her honorary mother would have gladly given her life to save her.

Lily was an incredibly selfless, generous woman until her very last breath. Annie just wasn't sure if she had enough strength to keep living without her dear Lily there to share all life's fleeting, precious moments. But Annie would not let her mentor down.

Annie vowed to her only friend that she would not waste her precious last gift of love and life.

Annie held Lily tightly, taking in her soothing scent of herbs and lavender, treasuring these precious last moments hugging her loved one.

"I love you, Lily, with all my heart," Annie whispered in her guardian's ear. "I couldn't have asked for a more caring, loving, generous role model to raise me. You are my world and I thank you from the depths of my soul, Lily, for all you have done for me. I love you, mum."

18

Princess Agnes

The sun was high in the sky, another glorious spring afternoon. Princess Agnes decided to explore the castle grounds to help relieve some of the tension built up in her head from holding back her gifting.

'Enough is enough, I will not go on living like a caged animal. I must use my gift before my head explodes! Today is the day the 'magical disease' infiltrates the castle...' Agnes thought mischievously to herself. '

'Now if I could just find a target... Someone unimportant... Someone whose role would demand they had to leave the castle grounds despite the lockdown. Or perhaps someone coming into the castle would be a less suspicious option.

'Hmmm.... think Agnes.

'Who can you use? Who has a useful enough gift that it would be worth stealing?

'A healer! A healer would make me indestructible. If I could heal myself and control the minds of anyone who stood in my way, I would be an unstoppable weapon. My sister's fire wielding gifts would mean little to me during the Crowning Ceremonies if I could instantly heal myself if I fell prey to them. Of course, that likely won't be an issue once I have severed the connection to their gifts. Still, a little extra insurance is a good way to solidify my chance of becoming Heir, and I will be crowned Heir. Now I just need a healer.'

Around the corner from where Princess Agnes walked, she predicted a guard would be stationed on watch.

"I do believe I feel suddenly unwell..." she snickered to herself.

Slowing her steps to an unsteady pace, Agnes silently rounded the corner of the garden hedge that was previously obscuring any view of her and pretended to faint.

Not fifty feet away from where she fell to the ground, supposedly unconscious, just as she predicted, a junior guard by the name of Bernard was stationed.

"Help!" Bernard yelled, seeing the Princess fall but unable to get there in time to catch her.

He sprinted to the Princess's side, checking for signs of life. Praise the Goddess, thankfully he could hear her breathing and her color was good.

Bernard thrice rang the bell he kept hanging on his belt, to notify anyone within hearing distance that there was a medical emergency. Anyone who heard would know as per protocol to send for one of the town's healers urgently.

Bernard lent over the Princess, careful of where he placed his hands, and scooped the Princess up into his arms.

Hastily the guard began walking back towards the castle, calling for help as he made his way, carrying the Princess gently in his arms.

Agnes pretended to rouse from unconsciousness in Bernard's arms.

"What happened? Where are we going?" she whispered in feigned confusion.

"You fainted Princess. I have alerted the guards to call for a healer, and we are on our way to the infirmary. You are going to be fine," Bernard formally responded, quickening his pace at the obvious awkwardness he felt touching a Princess.

Agnes let her eyes flutter closed again for dramatic effect allowing her body to go limp once more in the guard's arms. The guard stiffened in fear, noticing Agnes's supposed drift into unconsciousness again.

'*Perfect*,' Agnes thought. '*Everything is going just as planned.*'

The infirmary was empty that afternoon. Everyone except Agnes was being careful not to be sent there, lest they be considered at risk of falling prey to the dreaded 'magical disease.'

Normally a team of healers were stationed permanently in the castle. However, the King and Queen had ordered they be transferred to the hospital in the city to help care for the victims of the magical disease.

Princess Agnes had been laid on the bed in the royal family's private wing of the infirmary.

The main infirmary quarters were utilized as needed by the castle staff and any visiting guest that may need medical assistance. The royal infirmary wing was reserved for immediate royal family only.

The room itself was freezing, as the fireplace had not been lit in the quarters since the healers had departed for the city.

One of the castle maids who had witnessed the Princess being carried into the infirmary, hurried to get the hearth alight and to open the curtains to flood the room with natural light.

Agnes feigned regaining consciousness and turned towards the maid. "Pardon me Miss, but what happened? Where are the healers?" Princess Agnes softly spoke.

The maid hurried over to the Princess's bedside, dropping into a curtsy.

"Princess Agnes, forgive my intrusion. I am Winifred, one of the castle general maids. I did not witness what happened. I only saw Bernard carry you in here and rest you on the bed about five minutes ago. He said you fainted and have been unconscious since, my Lady. A healer is on her way from the main hospital he said. Bernard is stationed outside your door now, as a safety measure. Can I get you anything Princess?" Winifred asked nervously again dropping to a curtsy.

"Thank you, Winifred, for your help. Could you perhaps bring me some tea and broth, I feel quite weak," Agnes lied, her voice seemingly frail.

"As you wish Princess. I will be back in a moment with your tea and I suspect the Queen will be in shortly to check on you. I overhead Bernard asking a guard to alert Her Majesty," Winifred politely responded before curtsying and exiting out the servant's passage.

Princess Agnes waited for what felt like an eternity for the main door to the Royal Infirmary wing to open again. Agnes was terrified her mother, the Queen, would come in and know something was amiss.

Queen Amealiana was sage gifted after all, not just a talented prophetic. The Queen's instincts were usually right about most things and that had caused Agnes to be particularly cautious with how she proceeded in her plan to become crowned heir. Agnes needed to ensure the Queen remained oblivious to her intentions to eliminate her siblings from the competition.

The doors opened inwardly, Agnes holding her breath, waiting to see if the Queen was indeed coming to investigate.

'Praise the Goddess it's the King!' Princess Agnes thought with relief upon seeing her father accompanied by a healer enter the room.

Walking over to the Princess's bedside, the King briefly eyed over his daughter, looking for any signs of illness or trouble. But he could find nothing overly troublesome.

"Agnes, the guards said you were ill and brought to the infirmary for treatment. How are you? What happened? The guards were originally trying to locate the Queen to notify her of your decline in health, and when they could not locate Her Majesty, they informed me of your circumstances," The King informed her. "The Queen left the castle this morning, headed for Quillencia to attend to an urgent family matter. It appears not all the palace guards or my own family it seems, were informed. Praise the Goddess you appear well enough though."

Agnes felt relief wash over her. The Queen had been called away and now she would be completely oblivious to her eldest daughter's faux illness.

'*Nothing could be more perfect,*' Agnes thought to herself, fighting a smirk whilst still trying her best to appear bedridden.

"I'm terribly sorry to worry you, Your Majesty. I'm sure I'll be fine in no time. I was just out for a walk in the garden and the next moment I woke up in here. The maid said I fainted. I honestly don't remember, but I do feel rather weak. Maybe I didn't drink enough today. It is a rather unseasonably hot day outside," Agnes reassured the King.

"Not to worry Agnes, these things happen. The healer is here now so she may as well assess and treat you. I'm sure you'll be feeling better soon," the King replied before thanking the healer for her help and leaving the room to attend to his royal duties.

"Good afternoon Princess," the healer greeted her with a curtsy. "My name is Florence and I am one of the royal family's designated healers, though I have been working in the hospital recently, helping the unfortunate victims of the magical disease. Can you please describe to me exactly how you feel, in as much detail as possible? May I assess your vitals please, during your physical assessment?" Florence asked.

Agnes replied, "physical assessment won't be necessary Florence. I'm sure I will be fine. I just feel lightheaded; my brain seems foggy and my limbs weak."

"Very well your Highness. Most likely you are suffering from dehydration as you say, or your blood iron levels could be reduced, which could make you feel this way. Have you felt especially fatigued recently?" Florence replied.

"Yes, I have been rather tired lately," Agnes lied. "Could you perhaps refresh my blood iron supply while you are here?"

"Of course, Your Highness, as you wish. Normally I would prescribe oral remedies and leafy green vegetables to bring your blood iron stores up to their optimal level. However, as it is important for you to get back to your many royal duties as soon as possible, I can heal you with my gift if you prefer, Princess?" Florence offered.

"That would be much appreciated, Florence. I need to attend a meeting shortly in the throne room," Agnes thanked the healer.

"My pleasure Princess Agnes. If you could please allow me to hold your hand Princess, I will begin," Florence replied as Agnes offered the healer her dainty hand. "You may feel slightly warm for a moment as I use my healing gift on you." Florence continued, as she held the Princess's closest hand and closed her eyes to concentrate.

Now is my chance, while her eyes are shut, and she is preoccupied!' Agnes excitedly thought as she slipped gently into the healer's mind.

Agnes searched quickly throughout Florence's mind. Her mind was unlike any other she had ever seen. All the neurons where her healing gift was active, were lit like millions of bright stars guiding the way around her mind.

As Agnes approached one of the healing cells, she latched onto it with another thought, like she would a piece of sand with tweezers, and drew it into her own mind. As Agnes drew the healing cell from Florence's brain with her own gifting, she noticed that it was easily able to regenerate itself, however, a neighboring cell shrivelled up.

'All magic has a cost,' Agnes remembered being taught once in a class on the history of giftings.

Agnes quickly withdrew from Florence's mind and looked inside her own for that tiny healing spark she had stolen. Praise the Goddess, she found it hidden deep inside her mind.

To Agnes's disbelief, the cell looked like it was multiplying into many more cells and at the same rate it was growing, it was killing off pre-existing mind conqueror gifting cells.

It was as if the healing cells were trying to rid her of her mind conqueror gift, in exchange for obtaining the healer gifting.

Agnes began panicking. She didn't know what to do.

Agnes was terrified the healing cells would disastrously affect her mind conqueror gifting. Thinking quickly, she ordered her remaining mind conqueror gifting to capture the healing cells and send them from her mind, back into the healer.

Praise the Goddess her quick thinking worked, however, the cost to Agnes had been astronomical. Over a quarter of her mind conqueror giftings power had been affected by the healing cells, weakening her gifting severely.

'What have I done? Goddess I beg you, forgive me for my arrogance. Please renew my mind conqueror gifting!' Agnes silently

begged the Goddess, but it did no good. Agnes would have to live with the consequences of her greed.

"Princess Agnes are you OK? You look like you've seen a ghost!" Florence remarked.

Agnes was drawn out of her thoughts into the present. Trying her best to mask her horror, Princess Agnes stuttered, "Sorry, the healing just surprised me," she replied bluntly. "How do you feel?" Agnes asked curiously.

"No need to apologize, Princess. I feel wonderful, it is as if the Goddess has renewed my strength as reward for my service to you. You should feel better soon," Florence replied pleasantly.

"Praise the Goddess. Thank you for your help Florence. I will make my way back to my room to rest. You may go back to your work," Princess Agnes dismissed the healer.

Florence, sensing the Princess's sudden need for privacy, curtsied before leaving the room. Agnes made her way back to her suite, and dismissed her Lady's Maid, insisting she needed to rest. Then she threw herself upon her bed and mourned the partial loss of her gifting. *'How could I be so careless? Pull yourself together, Agnes! This is but a small setback. I will be Queen. I will just have to eliminate my competition before the Crowning Ceremony. Pick yourself back up and get on with it,'* Agnes ordered herself.

Tomorrow is a new day and Agnes was determined to make it count.

19

Annalyse

The first light of day was beginning to creep above the horizon, on the second day following Lily's passing. As Quillencian tradition demanded, Lily's body would be burned upon a pyre at sunrise. The burning ceremony would allow Lily's body to be cleansed of sin by the flames, and any remaining ties her soul held onto in this world would be free to ascend to the After World.

The townspeople were gathered by the river behind Lily's cottage, preparing to say their final farewells to their friend and healer. A pyre had been erected by the riverside the previous evening, by the many men of the town who wanted to honor Lily's memory through their gift of service.

Annie had spent the night preparing her dear friend's body with fragrant oils, being careful not to spill any on Lily's favorite velvet gown which she had washed, pressed and redressed her mentor in.

A knock came at the door. Shortly afterward, Marcy let herself in and joined Annie by Lily's bedside.

"She looks so peaceful," Marcy warmly remarked.

Annie nodded in recognition; she had not spoken since that first day when Marcy had told her of her beloved friends passing. Annie knew that she would need to speak at the funeral ceremony and had been trying to find the words all night so that she could give her friend the proper farewell she deserved.

Sir Rodrick, his noble son Derek, and Stanley the fisherman entered the room taking up positions by the far bedroom wall, heads bowed respectfully.

"It is time for us to honor Ms. Lily with the funeral ceremony. Are you ready for us to begin Annie?" Marcy asked gently.

Annie took a deep breath and nodded in affirmation.

"As I mentioned yesterday, we will carry dear Ms. Lily to the pyre. If you feel able, you can give a eulogy and then the priestess will lead us in prayer for Lily's soul before the town's fire wielders assist Lily to fully pass into the After World," Marcy spoke softly so only Annie could hear.

Annie again nodded in confirmation and knelt beside Lily, placing a kiss upon her honorary mother's cheek.

"I will always love and remember you, Lily," Annie whispered into her mentor's ear.

Marcy nodded her head towards the awaiting gentlemen to signal they were ready to proceed. The three gentlemen and Annie gently carried their dear healer, wrapped in her embroidered quilt, outside the cottage and laid her gently on a bed of soft pillows upon the flat top of the Pyre.

Annie embraced Lily and pressed a firm kiss to her forehead, before placing a bouquet of fresh wildflowers upon her loved one's chest. When Annie was ready, she turned around to face the awaiting crowd of townspeople.

'Goddess, please give me the strength to bring honor to my dear Lily through this eulogy," Annie silently prayed.

Annie took a deep centring breath, tears trickling silently down her cheeks, reflecting the overflowing well of grief she felt inside.

"People of Lavender Grove, thank you for coming this morning to honor our friend and healer, Ms. Lily." Annie, the young fifteen-year-old apprentice healer, spoke to the crowd with a level of wisdom and maturity beyond her years.

"It was my greatest privilege," Annie humbly spoke, "to live and work every day with such a generous, empathetic, woman. Ms. Lily was the kindest, most genuine person I knew. She lived a full and selfless life until her very last breath. Lily treated everyone with respect and dignity. She was always there for us in our times of need, whether as a listening ear, or helping our people through birth, illness, or death.

"Recently Ms. Lily reminded me of a valuable life lesson. She said: *'a gift of service and generosity is as rewarding to give, as it is to receive'*. Lily considered her healing gift, not a gift to squander or preserve but to share with those in need. A gift for the people, not merely herself. That was how she considered her Goddess-blessed gift.

"My life will never be complete without her, and I'm sure many of you will share the same sentiment. A piece of my soul feels as though it has been ripped away to join her in the After World so we would not be parted. I owe Lily my life and my eternal gratitude. She was more than a mentor; she was like a mother to me.

"I promise you, Lily, before our townspeople, that your final sacrifice will not be wasted. I will treasure this life you have blessed me with. We as a people will continue your work and your life will live on here in our hearts. I will always remember you, Lily, and I will never stop missing you. Goodbye for now, until we are reunited in the loving embrace of the Goddess in the After World," Annie bravely spoke from the heart.

Tears gently flowing, Annie turned back to where Lily lay peacefully and gave a deep bow of respect to her loved one. Behind her, the whole town followed her lead, bowing deeply in respect for their treasured healer.

Annie bent down to press one last kiss to her mentor's forehead, and walked away towards the riverbank to reverently watch the remaining ceremony.

The town priestess stepped forward and led the people in prayers for their beloved healers' soul, concluding the funeral rites by blessing Lily's body with the sacred water from the spring at the Priestess' home temple upon the mountain of Galicia.

The Priestess nodded her head towards the town's four awaiting fire wielders. They positioned themselves in a diamond surrounding Lily and dropped to their knees, heads bowed, the community following their lead.

After a minute of silence, the fire wielders led the crowd in a song of blessing for Lily as they released their gifts upon the pyre, cleansing Lily's body and soul.

"Goodbye, mum. I love you," Annie whispered to the sky.

Then Annie turned to take a walk along the riverbank to honor her mentor in her own way.

She strolled along the path where they spent most of their spare time enjoying nature together. Something mentor and ward would sadly never be able to enjoy together again.

Lily's unopened letter to Annie was tucked safely in the pocket closest to her heart. One day, when Annie felt she needed Lily's guidance the most, she would read the letter and savor every word.

Until then, preserving her mentor's final passing words, Annie kept the letter safely by her heart like a secret treasure no one else knew about.

20

Queen Amealiana

Across the ever-changing terrain of Quillencia, the Queen of Alearia rode on horseback, accompanied by six of her most trusted personal guards. The Queen and her company traveled from one far away village to the next, in search of a healer by the name of Lilianna, whom the Queen told her men was likely accompanied by a young, blond female ward.

It had been a fortnight since they had left the kingdom of Alearia. The Queen kept the secret of whom they truly searched for closely guarded in her heart for her young daughter's protection.

The guards had been ordered by her Majesty to try and remain as inconspicuous throughout their search as possible. The party of seven travellers were dressed in plain clothes, forgoing the pageantry of armor and palace uniforms, in favor of more informal attire to avoid detection.

The kingdom of Quillencia was Queen Amealiana's birth kingdom. Her Majesty did not worry that they would be in danger if their identities became known, for the kingdom of Quillencia treasured their royal family. However, she felt that a Queen personally searching for one common healer would seem suspicious, and potentially hold up their search.

'Whoever designed riding pants for women is truly Goddess sent! I detest horse riding in a gown. It is always so horribly awkward to climb on and off a horse, whilst preserving one's dignity in a dress. Riding a horse in a gown is not nearly as comfortable as these.'

"A Queen in pants - whatever would the King think of me,"the Queen chuckled to herself.

The Queen's guards were beginning to become a little restless, despite their loyalty to her Majesty, but the Queen did not hold it against them.

'So many nights spent sleeping in bedrolls beneath the stars would make anyone short-tempered,' The Queen thought to herself. *'We are getting closer though, I know it! The bond between Annalyse and I is growing stronger by the day. Please Goddess, let that be a sign she is nearby. Goddess, please guide us to my daughter.'*

The Queen's head guard, Tomlin, rode up alongside her.

"My Queen, it will be dark soon. If you agree, I recommend we stop and make camp for the night by the river up ahead. There you could bathe if you wished, and we can water the horses. If we depart for the next town by sunrise, we could be at Lavender Grove by lunchtime to resume our search for the healer. If it would please you, perhaps we could grab a warm meal at one of the local establishments while we are there. I'm sure it would help raise the men's spirits. A nice hot meal and a mug of ale usually has that effect," Tomlin smiled sheepishly.

"I wholeheartedly agree Sir Tomlin. We shall make camp and before we begin our search of Lavender Grove, we can stop at an inn for a nice hot lunch. I personally wouldn't mind a glass of wine as well," the Queen joked with her guard.

Tomlin grinned from ear to ear at the Queen's casual ease in which she spoke to him.

The Queen enjoyed travelling with her guards, she never complained and was all too happy to sleep in a bedroll. Amealiana was most certainly a beloved Queen of the people, and her men considered it a great honor to serve her.

The small group, led by Tomlin, directed their horses to the river to set up camp for the night. It was guard Lawrence's turn on watch, so after briefly watering his horse, he set off to search the surrounding area.

Lawrence was entrusted to monitor for any potential threats to the Queen and secure the area. Any sign of danger, and the plan was for Tomlin to quickly evacuate the Queen to their predetermined rendezvous point. The remaining guards would stay to eliminate the threat, which usually involved taking on a group of bandits. Nothing the Queen's elite personal guards couldn't handle. The guards not-so-secretly relished the opportunity to jump into a sword fight. Any chance they could get to take on a group of no good miscreants, was a welcome change from the monotony of riding through forests, searching town after town, or standing guard at the palace.

Of course, the Queen knew all too well about her guards' mischievous sides, but she pretended not to notice their eagerness to jump into a fight. She found their antics to be quite amusing. If they only targeted criminals, she didn't mind how many miscreants they happened to *stumble upon*.

In all fairness, Queen Annalyse and King Julian of Quillencia, were likely grateful for their service to the kingdom, weeding out the criminals, even if it had become more for sport than noble intentions.

Queen Amealiana fondly recalled to mind the last occasion her men *coincidently* located a group of thieves trying to steal livestock from a farm. "Boys will be boys," the Queen chuckled to herself, whilst assisting the men to collect wood and kindling for the campfire.

21

Queen Amealiana

Queen Amealiana sat at a table nestled in the far corner of The Sir Rohan Inglebert Inn in the small town of Lavender Grove.

The patrons' view of the Alearian Queen was obscured by her guards. A protective measure, Tomlin had assured Her Majesty. The Queen's head guard always remained by her side when they were in public.

A bar fight was the last thing the Queen felt like witnessing today, so she prayed to the Goddess that her guards could resist the urge to rile up any trouble during their meal.

They rode into town in record time this morning. The guards were clearly keen for their promised hot lunch and ale.

"This particular establishment," the Queen recalled to her guards, "was aptly named after that famous knight you all seem to idolize, who hailed from this part of Quillencia. Who I also remember had a fondness for strong liquor from memory? '*Sir Rohan the brave*', isn't that what you call him?" The Queen asked her men with raised eyebrows.

Tomlin and Lawrence almost choked on their ale from laughter. The other guards, not used to hearing the Queen make jokes in front of them, offered an awkward chuckle. The guards had been retelling stories over the campfire each night about the Knight's bravery, but mostly bragging about Sir Rohan's uncanny ability to swoon the ladies even whilst being drunk as a skunk.

"Typical that my guards would idolize a man with such outstanding suave with the ladies," the Queen continued as she rolled her eyes for added effect.

This time Tomlin did choke on his beer, and the remaining guards all turned to him and began bellowing with laughter.

"Forgive us, Your Highness, we are not worthy of your company," Tomlin joked in return.

The others gaped at his brashness.

"Quite right you are Tomlin. I don't know how I ended up with you lot as my most trusted guards. It surely isn't for my youthful looks, that's for sure," the Queen sassily mused.

Bellowing laughter once again roared around the table. The Queen and her guards had never in the past had a chance to casually engage in banter. She could tell her guards greatly appreciated the brief reprieve from formality. So, they all sat back, relaxed and enjoyed themselves over steaming lamb stew and ale.

A full to the brim glass of red wine was brought over for the Queen as specifically requested by Sir Tomlin.

'Thank the Goddess for wine!' The Queen smiled contently to herself.

After finishing their meal, the Queen thanked the barman for his service. Amealiana made a habit of doing this at all the establishments they visited, and it was also a great opportunity to enquire about information on Lilianna.

"Dear Sir, thank you for your kind hospitality, the food has warmed our hearts and stomachs," The Queen smiled.

"You are too kind Lady. Wait a minute, don't I recognize you from somewhere? You look remarkably familiar," the barman stated before a spark of recognition crossed his face and he dropped into a low bow.

"Forgive me, Your Highness, I am honored by your visit. I apologize for not recognizing you earlier or I would have welcomed you into our private dining area."

"Rise, Sir," The Queen responded quietly, leaning forward. "Your discretion would be greatly appreciated."

Amealiana straightened and subtly looked around to see if anyone had noticed the overly formal interaction.

"I apologize again Majesty," The Barman whispered.

"Not to worry," The Queen responded in her usual pleasant tone. "Is there somewhere we could go to speak more privately Sir?"

"Of course! You and your companions are welcome to come into our personal family dining room if that would suit your needs? It would be our honor to host you. My name is Blaney, by the way. Excuse my lack of introduction earlier," he said sincerely to the Queen.

"Right this way, Your Majesty," Blaney spoke softly as he motioned for Queen Amealiana and her comrades to follow him through the door to his private residence.

"Thank you, Blaney," The Queen graciously replied, following the gentleman into the lower level of the Inn.

Tomlin walked alongside her, always on the lookout for any sign of danger.

Queen Amealiana sat at the head of Blaney's family table. Sir Tomlin took the chair to her right and the remaining guards adopted standing positions around the room and outside the door, keeping watch.

Blaney excused himself briefly, to arrange for his oldest son to serve at the bar. He also requested his wife Marionette, join them and serve their guests tea and dessert.

The Queen thanked the couple for their kind hospitality and took a small bite of the delicious orange cake Marionette had served her.

"This cake is divine Marionette, thank you ever so much," The Queen spoke appreciatively.

Marionette curtsied and modestly bowed her head, cheeks blushing.

"It is an honor to serve my humble cooking to you, Your Majesty," Marionette replied graciously.

The Queen smiled genuinely before moving along from pleasantries to the matter at hand.

"Marionette and Blaney, would you happen to know of any healers that live in this region, more specifically a lady by the name of Lilianna? We believe she is likely living with a young ward," the Queen inquired.

"Your Highness, I am sorry, but I do not know any healers by that exact name. A couple of weeks ago, our town's only healer Lily, tragically passed away. We are all greatly saddened by her passing. Lily blessed all of us through sickness and health. Now that I think about it, Lily did happen to be training a young female apprentice. Could Lily, possibly be the woman you are looking for? Though, I am sorry to say, your trip has been wasted if she is," Marionette regretfully informed the Queen.

The Queen's heart seemed to shatter and repair itself all in the space of a few milliseconds. A mixture of grief, and then hope, filled her soul and she attempted to maintain her composure.

"The healer, Lily, passed away recently you say? May I ask how?" The Queen inquired, her voice shaking slightly.

"I'm not entirely sure, I'm sorry Your Highness. Word around the town is she sacrificed her remaining life force and healing gift to save her young ward, Annie. Lily had raised the young lass since she was a baby. She found her abandoned in the forest one day, so the story goes and took her in to raise as her own. It's a terrible loss for our town. Lily was our only healer, the literal heartbeat of Lavender Grove in times of birth, illness, and death," Marionette responded, her eyes watering from emotion as she fondly remembered the healer.

The Queen's heart stopped dead in her chest.

'Annie! Could it really be that I have found her? But if it is Annalyse, then that means my dearest friend has faded into the After World. My precious daughter may be somewhere close by, but my poor friend is gone. I will never share another moment with dear Lady Lilianna,' Queen Amealiana internally processed.

"Are you alright Your Highness?" Marionette asked.

Her Majesty was pulled back from her thoughts.

"Yes, sorry Marionette. I was lost in thought. The young ward Annie, do you happen to know anything else about her, where she might live for example? I would very much like to speak with her," the Queen asked casually.

"Certainly, your Majesty. Annie mostly keeps to herself when she isn't working in the apothecary. She assisted Ms. Lily with the birth of our last child. He is almost one year old now. A quiet thing Annie is. The young people in the town, unfortunately, seem to give her a hard time about her heritage. Nothing wrong with being an orphan if you ask me. Annie has been nothing but polite and conscientious to us. The young apprentice has been very well trained by Ms. Lily, Goddess bless her soul. She lives not far from here, in a little white cottage by the river. I could take you there if you like?" Marionette kindly offered.

"Thank you for the offer, but if you could please give my guard, Tomlin, the directions, we will head over there shortly. We wouldn't want to inconvenience you any more than we already have," the Queen politely declined her offer and gestured to Tomlin sitting next to her.

"On second thoughts, you wouldn't happen to have any spare rooms available for the night, would you? Preferably two adjoining rooms to stop my guards losing their minds over security concerns?" Queen Amealiana joked.

"Certainly, Your Majesty. Unfortunately, none of our rooms are adjoining but you are welcome to use our three-bedroom private residence here. My husband, children and I can sleep in one of the family guest rooms for the night. It's no trouble at all," Marionette warmly offered.

"We would be eternally grateful. Thank you for the lovely offer. Lawrence, one of my guards, will stay behind while we go out to meet young Annie, to make sure the residence is secure and then have a rest. Poor Lawrence hasn't slept for a couple of days. The poor man had the unfortunate job of being on night watch all last night and I dare say he is desperately in need of sleep," The Queen smiled, gesturing towards the guard standing closest to her who nodded his head appreciatively.

"Thank you, my Queen, you are too kind. If it's no trouble, Ms. Marionette, and Mr. Blaney, that would be greatly appreciated," Lawrence agreed.

"Certainly, Lawrence. Then it is settled. It will be an honor to host you all. I will have my son Johnathan feed, water and house your horses in our stable. My wife can see to any personal needs you may have Your Majesty," Blaney assured her.

"Would you like me to prepare a hot bath for you before you set off for the afternoon, Your Majesty?" Marionette asked.

"That sounds divine. Thank you very much Ms. Marionette, I greatly appreciate your thoughtfulness," Queen Amealiana replied.

22

Annalyse

It was an overcast spring afternoon. Lavender Grove had been blessed by the Goddess last night with a heavy downpour of rain, and Annie was busy working in the garden collecting herbs for her tinctures and potions. It was also the perfect time to plant vegetable seedlings whilst the soil was soft and moist.

The rain had caused the river level to rise, so the melodious rushing of water winding through the river rocks was helping to soothe her soul. Annalyse heard the front gate creak open. Releasing a sigh, she rose from her spot in the garden, picked up her basket of herbs and quickly headed inside through the back door to wash her hands.

'A healer should always have clean hands and be well presented,' Lily had drilled into Annie from a young age.

'Please Goddess, let it be nothing urgent. My workload hasn't eased since Lily's passing. I desperately need a day to myself soon. I feel emotionally and physically exhausted. But as Lily always said, 'duty must always come first.' The people of Lavender Grove need a healer, and I will do my best to fill that gap. It's what Lily would have wanted,' Annie thought to herself.

A knock sounded at the door, pulling Annie from her thoughts. She quickly took off her gardening apron, smoothed out the creases in her apothecary uniform and went to open the door for her patient.

"Hello, my dear, my name is Amealiana. May I come in?" The confident, middle-aged stranger asked.

The young apprentice looked curiously at the woman. The woman seemed remarkably familiar, but Annie could not place where she could have possibly ever met someone as elegant at this lady before.

"Good afternoon madam, please come in. My name is Annie. May I ask, is it you or one of your companions that is unwell?" Annie asked, noting the two men standing by the front gate.

"I must disclose to you that I am only an apprentice apothecary. Sadly, my mentor passed away recently, and I was not able to complete my training," Annie concluded.

"We are all very fortunately in good health. Weary from our travels but thankfully in perfect health," Amealiana responded politely.

"I'm afraid I don't understand how I could possibly be of help to you if you are all thankfully well. I'm not in trouble for anything, am I? Lily left me this house in her will, you can check it for yourself," Annie said a little too defensively.

'Remember your manners Annie!' she internally tutted herself.

"I am sorry Lady. What I meant to say was, if you are not unwell, is there anything else I can help you with?" Annie quickly tried to recover.

"No need to worry at all my dear, it is I who may be able to help you. Do you mind if we talk privately? Over a cup of soothing chamomile tea may be best," Amealiana requested.

"Certainly, madam. Please come in, though I cannot think of any way you could help me, but I would be happy to talk with you over a cup of tea," Annie replied.

"Splendid, lead the way. My companions will wait outside for me if that is fine with you?" Amealiana asked.

"Of course, My Lady. Shall we?" Annie motioned for her guest to enter. "Please make yourself comfortable by the fire while I make us a pot of tea."

"Thank you, Annie," the lady responded gracefully entering her home, before pausing to look at some of the sketches on the walls of Lily and Annie together.

'Very strange indeed,' Annie thought to herself whilst heading off to the kitchen to prepare their tea.

Queen Annealiana

The Queen stood in awe of a beautiful sketch of Lilianna and Annalyse. The artist had captured a remarkable resemblance to Lily.

It was evident to the Queen that Annie had no idea who she was or why she had come. The Queen's heart sung with joy and nervous butterflies fluttered in her abdomen.

Upon seeing Annie for the first time in almost sixteen years, all the Queen wanted to do was fling her arms around her daughter and never let go. Staring at the sketch in front of her where Annie would have been no older than five or six, the Queen realized with sadness how much of the young girl's life she had missed.

The Queen knew she must tread lightly, if Annie genuinely believed she had been abandoned at birth. She would likely have many mixed emotions towards her mother once she knew the truth.

'Oh, my sweet child, I am so sorry for the pain I have caused you,' The Queen silently apologized to the image of her younger daughter before her.

Annie re-entered the sitting room and placed a pot of chamomile tea, two floral porcelain teacups with matching saucers and a plate of freshly baked cookies upon the table.

"Lady, is something the matter?" Annie inquired. "Excuse me for prying, but I am a sage, blessed by the Goddess, you see. My gift makes me more in tune to other people's emotions," Annie said softly.

Amealiana turned to face Annie, pride and awe shone across her face. Amealiana sat down in a high-backed red velvet chair opposite Annie.

"A talented healer apprentice and sage. Your mentor must have been immensely proud of you," Amealiana spoke softly.

"Thank you for your kind words. Amealiana, may I inquire where you are from? You seem strangely familiar, though I do not recall ever meeting someone quite as elegant as you," Annie stated a little awkwardly. "I'm sorry, that came out all wrong, please forgive me."

Amealiana chuckled softly to herself.

"It is quite alright my dear. Truth be told we first met a very long time ago. Your mentor Lilianna, or Lily as you know her by, was my closest friend and confidant. I owe her the world," Amealiana explained gently.

"I'm sorry, I'm afraid I am confused. Did you come to pay your respects to Lily? As per our tradition in Quillencia, Lily was released into the After World on the second day after her passing through the Holy Goddess blessed fires." Annie felt the tears welling in her eyes as she explained the ritual to the Lady.

"I know how hard it must have been for you to say goodbye to someone you love so much. I myself have faced the same heartache. I wish I could have been here to say goodbye to my friend Lilianna and to help you through your grief. Lily was a wonderful woman, the most selfless person I have ever met. She was truly a gift from the Goddess," Amealiana spoke earnestly, tears forming in her own eyes.

Annie offered Amealiana a handkerchief and reached her arm across the side table to take her hand and comfort her.

"If it would help you, I would like to hear your story. Sometimes when we share our pain, it can allow us to begin to heal," Annie wisely offered the stranger.

"That is very kind of you Annie. More kindness from you then I deserve, I'm afraid to admit," Amealiana replied, making eye contact with her daughter for the first time since her birth.

She treasured the moment, but also felt deep remorse for the pain and confusion she was about to cause her beloved child.

"I am sure that whatever you came to talk to me about, you came because you felt it was the right thing to do and I would like to hear your story."

Amealiana smiled warmly, holding Annie's gaze. The Queen took a deep calming breath and began to tell her story.

"I was born in the kingdom of Quillencia. I inherited my own sage and prophetic giftings from my mother, and my parents arranged my marriage to a noble in Alearia. Over the years we fell in love and were Goddess blessed with three wonderful children. I thought our family was complete until the Goddess deemed to bless me with twins. Only your mentor Lily and I knew I was expecting twins. It was a special secret we shared together, and I couldn't wait to share the joyous news with our family after their arrival into the world.

"I didn't understand at the time why the Goddess had guided me to keep the twins' birth a secret. My family knew I was expecting Anastasia, but to this day they still do not know about her living twin. It sounds horrible I know that I would keep one of my children a secret all these years but let me explain.

"On the day of the twins' birth, Lady Lilianna came to assist me. She was truly a messenger sent from the Goddess that day. After the birth of the first twin, Anastasia, I foresaw her full life ahead of her, wielding fire like her father with such joy. After the second child's birth, I sadly did not foresee her gifting but instead foresaw her death to occur at the hands of someone she trusted. Whom that person was that wished harm upon my dear sweet child, I still do not know.

"After I foresaw this vision, I couldn't bear to have my beloved baby meet that fate, so I begged Lilianna to take my child, raise her as her own and protect her all her life." The Queen paused her story to squeeze her daughter's hand as she foresaw recognition set upon her daughter's face.

"Are you trying to tell me that whilst I believed I was unwanted; I truly had a family that I belonged to? That you are my mother?" Annie's voice broke. "Are you saying that all of these years, Lily raised me knowing that I belonged to someone else? She gave up her life to protect me…" Annie spoke through tears.

"I am sorry Annie, but it is all true. Lilianna was my closest friend and I could trust no one else to keep you safe and raise you in a home of love. I knew she would nurture you and raise you into an amazing young woman, just as I see before me. Every day I regret the time we have missed together, but I thank the Goddess every day that you are safe.

"Recently I felt our bond grow taut and thin. I knew you were in grave danger. I thought I may be too late to save you. Then that same night I felt the bond strengthening again. I thanked the Goddess that she saved you. I had a strong feeling Lilianna likely had something to do with your healing, though it wasn't until I spoke with the Inn's owners that I realized the truth. That strong sense I had of your precious life being saved, was due to my beloved friend sacrificing her life to save you. I wish it could have been me. If I had been blessed with a healing gift, I would have sacrificed myself for you without a second thought. I am so sorry for your loss my dear Annalyse," Amealiana spoke honestly to her child.

"Please forgive me, Annie, for all of it. I am so sorry. I have never stopped loving you. Please believe me," Amealiana begged.

Annalyse

Annalyse dropped her hand from Amealiana's and sat back in her chair in disbelief. Her sage gifting told her that Amealiana was telling the truth, but her gut told her this was not the whole truth. Her whole life was being turned upside down for the second time in as many weeks and Annie wasn't sure she could handle any more life-altering news. '

Breathe,' she told herself as she closed her eyes to think. '*Just breathe... Be in the moment. I am stronger than I know. Lily always said so. I can keep going. I can get through this one more landslide. Just breathe. In and out, that's it. Slow deep breaths. Oh, how I wish I could run into Lily's arms and she could make it all better. She would tell me to trust this woman. Trust my gift.'*

Annie opened her eyes to find tears streaming down the woman's face.

'Amealiana has my eyes,' Annie realized. *'We share the same hair color. In fact, now that I look at her, the resemblance is astonishing! No wonder I recognized her; this woman is an older version of myself.'*

Annie's inner confusion turned to awe as she realized, - the woman before he was her long-lost mother. The person she had dreamed of being reunited with her whole life. The mother whom Annie had believed hated her and abandoned her, had in fact given her up for a chance at a better life. For the chance to live a full life with her closest, most beloved friend.

"Mother?" Annie whispered, both a question and a prayer.

"It's me, my darling Annalyse. You are my daughter. My beloved child," Amealiana said proudly, renewed hope shining in her eyes.

Amealiana stood up from her chair and walked around the side table towards Annie, who was holding her breath. Amealiana leaned down to kneel before her daughter.

"I love you my dear Annalyse, with all of my heart. I love you," Amealiana declared to Annie as she leaned forward and embraced her daughter in the first hug they had shared in almost sixteen years.

Annie and Amealiana held each other tightly, tears of happiness trickling down both their faces.

"I love you too mum," Annie whispered in Amealiana's ear.

23

Annalyse

The sun was setting. Gorgeous shades of pinks, purples, and oranges filled the endless sky. The temperature was rapidly dropping as the sunlight began to fade.

Annie and her mother, Amealiana, had spent the last hour toiling side-by-side in the garden. The pair worked vigilantly, picking the remaining herbs and flowers that were needed to make Annie's various apothecary ointments and lotions. The stores were running considerably low since Lily's passing, as Annie tried to keep up with double the workload.

Annie was currently busy in the cottage kitchen preparing vegetable soup by candlelight to share with Amealiana for dinner. Annalyse had invited her mother to stay for the evening meal before she would return to her accommodation at the Inn for the night.

Annalyse had briefly considered asking her mother to stay for the night, but offering Lily's bed to her felt like a betrayal to her mentor. Annalyse felt like she was riding a never-ending emotional wave. She had so many questions clouding her thoughts.

The young apprentice's sage gift told her there was much more to the story than Amealiana was letting on, but Annie trusted her mother enough to believe that she would do the right thing by Annie and tell her what she needed to know in good time.

'After all, Amealiana hasn't lied to me yet, unless you count almost sixteen years of anonymity as lying,' Annie thought to herself sarcastically. *'That's not entirely fair of me... She was only doing what she believed she needed to, to keep me safe. I shouldn't begrudge her for putting my interests above her own.'*

Amealiana walked into the kitchen from the washroom with unparalleled grace.

'How does she manage to make herself seem so effortlessly elegant, even whilst gardening?' Annie mused to herself with a small smile.

"That smells delicious Annalyse, thank you for all your hospitality. I am sure it has been a long day for you," Amealiana empathized.

"Thank you. Will your companions be joining us for dinner, or are they just going to continue awkwardly guarding the front of the house all evening as well?" Annalyse questioned jokingly whilst also hoping to subtly probe some more information from her mother.

"Ahh... you noticed that, did you? I am terribly sorry about my companions. They are just a little 'overprotective' of me, shall we say. I will ask them to leave, please excuse me for a moment," Amealiana responded diplomatically as she quickly exited the cottage door.

Her mother's evasive response only raised more questions for Annie.

'Are they guards?' Annie pondered. *'They sure seem like guards... But if Amealiana needs guards then who is she? Think Annie, think... For starters, I am apparently a twin... well, honestly, that explains why I have felt like a part of me was missing all these years! It literally has been! My sister's name is Anastasia. My sister... Well that certainly sounds strange since I've spent my whole life thinking I was an orphan!*

'Focus Annie... Anastasia would be almost sixteen years old since we share a birthday. Oh! That reminds me! I need to ask Amealiana when my actual birthday is! Actually... No, I don't... If Lily was present at my birth she would know exactly when I was born. Her so-called 'dream' about my birth wasn't a dream at all! I was born on the Winter Solstice! For as many questions as I have, it is finally nice to know for certain my actual birthday - Praise the Goddess for small mercies.'

"Sorry for keeping you waiting, the gentlemen have left now," Amealiana announced, pulling Annie from her musings.

"Not a worry at all. Shall we have a picnic dinner on the rug in front of the hearth? Lily and I used to enjoy doing that on cooler nights. The fire is already burning. Or if you would prefer, we can sit at the table," Annie asked.

"An inside picnic sounds lovely Annie. I don't think I've ever done that before," Amealiana replied thoughtfully.

The two ladies made themselves comfortable sitting on pillows in front of the crackling fire, eating their soup in silence, both enjoying the easy pace of the evening. The fragrant smells of the soup wafted around the sitting room.

After they were finished eating, Amealiana took their bowls out to the kitchen and brought back two new cups of steaming hot chamomile tea. Amealiana offered a cup to Annie, who graciously accepted before moving to settle down in one of the sitting room chairs. Amealiana, taking her lead, sat in the opposite chair next to the hearth. Lily's old chair...

This doesn't feel right,' Annie mused, feeling conflicted over her mother sitting in her mentor's chair. *'I am not replacing Lily,'* Annie reassured herself. *'It's only a chair, it is not the end of the world. Lily would scold me if she knew I was having such ridiculous internal debates of who sits in which chair. Pull yourself together Annie, move on."* Annie attempted to give herself a pep talk.

"It's getting late Amealiana, would you like me to walk you home after we finish our tea?" Annie asked, before deciding to take a gamble and add on; "I wouldn't want to cause your guards any worry."

Amealiana visibly stiffened in her chair before schooling her face into an elegant smile.

"Annalyse... I know your sage gifting is probably causing you strife right now. I dare not lie to you as you will know the truth if I do. Would you like me to tell you what you are no doubt waiting to hear?" Amealiana offered.

'Both a challenge and a choice, that is what she is offering me. But am I ready to hear what she has to say? She is right of course, if she tells a lie, I will know. The truth always comes out I have learned. It is only a matter of when. But am I ready for the truth? Will I ever be ready for the truth?' Annie mused to herself, weighing up her options and the potential consequences of that choice.

"I would like to hear what you have to say," Annie finally offered.

Queen Amealiana

The Queen stared deep into Annalyse's eyes and smiled knowingly.

"You are more like me than you know," Amealiana fondly noted. "Your sage wisdom can feel like both a gift and a curse. Sages are blessed by the Goddess with understanding; the ability to see things objectively and without emotion, to discern right from wrong. It also prevents us from fully experiencing those human emotions such as grief for very long, as we can see the point of what has occurred.

"Your gift is likely the reason that even though you have suffered such a recent tragic loss, you were able to accept Lily's death. You know in your heart that Lily's sacrifice was her own choice to make. Thus, making your journey of healing a little easier.

"Yes, you probably still miss her dearly and you probably still feel like a part of you is missing. But your sage wisdom gives you the peace-bringing knowledge that Lily is in a happier, peaceful place. You know, thanks to your gift, that Lily's wishes would be for you to not waste your life grieving what could have been. So, if I am not mistaken, you have likely continued to carry out her work since her passing."

Annie subtly nodded her head and gestured for her mother to continue.

"At one stage you would have doubted your ability to keep going without her. But your gifting has helped you understand her passing and your grief so that you can move through the mourning at a quicker pace than most. Why am I saying all this? Because even now your gifting is telling you that you know I am speaking the truth, even if you don't feel ready to hear it. Your gifting is the reason you were so easily able to accept my claims as your mother when most girls your age would have likely thrown me out the door for making such outrageous claims. Your gifting will help you through what I am about to tell you, I promise." Amealiana reassured her daughter.

"It is as though you can see right through me. As though you know me and understand me even better than I do!" Annie stated in disbelief. "Will my gift become so strong, that like you, my gift of discernment becomes so instantaneously accurate? What could you possibly say that would be more mind blowing then, '*I'm your long-lost Mum!*'," Annie stated bluntly, still processing what the woman had so far revealed about herself.

Annalyse closed her eyes, allowing her gift to calm herself before taking several deep breaths. After re-opening her eyes, she gazed into those of her mothers. "I am ready to hear what else you have to say."

Amealiana nodded, then took a deep breath of her own to prepare herself for what was to come.

"Annalyse, when I told you I was born and raised in Quillencia, that was true. However, I did not have a normal upbringing. I am the second born child in my family. I am of noble blood, and as you have likely guessed from my guards' presence, I was betrothed to a Prince of another country. Our marriage was agreed upon to establish strong ties between our kingdoms," Amealiana began.

Annie could do nothing but stare at her mother and clutch her cup of tea. "There is more to this story," Annie stated matter-of-factly.

"My husband and I had four other children, as I have already mentioned. My beloved son was a shape-shifter. He had such a kind soul. His gifting was possibly even stronger than his father's. Sadly, your brother, Alexander, passed away on the night of your fifteenth birthday. I am still unsure how it happened. I foresaw a prophecy of his death that morning and I tried everything to prevent it from occurring, but fate claimed him. Goddess bless his soul; he and Lilianna will be reunited in the After World where I am sure they will take care of each other.

"Lilianna was my midwife for all my children's births. Lilianna helped raise me as a child — that is how far our friendship dates back. I am eternally grateful for her endless help and service to our family. Your eldest sister, my first-born Agnes, shares a prophetic gift with myself. Though, until recently it was unreliable.

"Alecia, my third-born child is a gifted fire wielder like her father. She has a feisty personality, but her heart is in a good place. She can be very intuitive at times. Your twin, my fourth born Anastasia, is also a fire wielder. She shares the same empathetic, kind-hearted qualities that I see in you, though she can be easily led astray by Alecia at times. The two fire wielding sisters are as thick as thieves together," The Queen smiled as she thought of her family fondly.

The Queen paused her story and drank the remainder of her cup of tea to let her daughter process what she had said.

Princess Annalyse

Amealiana continued her story. "I am both a gifted sage and strong prophetic; both gifts passed onto me by your grandmother. I sadly did not inherit my father's gifting, and I found it strange that none of my children had either. However, since meeting you today, my sage gifting tells me I have likely been mistaken. My father's gift is very distinct and exceedingly rare. My father is a mind conqueror," Amealiana finished.

Annalyse dropped her cup and it shattered in front of the hearth. Annie didn't even notice she had dropped it until she heard it smash.

'Surely I did not hear her correctly. Mind conquerors only descend from the Royal Quillencian bloodline. King Julian Caston is the only living mind conqueror I have ever heard of.

'I must be mistaken. This cannot be true. If her father is the King, then that makes Amealiana a Princess. No! Not a Princess, she has married,' Annie internally processed.

"You are the King and Queen's only daughter! Amealiana, the sole Princess of the kingdom of Quillencia! But you are married now... oh my goodness gracious, you are the Queen of Alearia!" Annie exclaimed.

All the final pieces of the puzzle fell into place. The Queen just sat there and smiled at her daughter, allowing her the time she needed to process this information.

"But if you are the Queen of Alearia, then that makes my own father the King of Alearia! King Titian Brandistone of the kingdom of Alearia is my father!" Annie stated in disbelief.

"That is right my dear Princess Annalyse," The Queen completed Annie's thought.

"A Princess? I am a Princess! That means I have a last name! An identity! That makes me Princess Annalyse Brandistone of the Kingdom of Alearia," Annie spoke softly, in complete and utter shock.

"There is more my dear Princess Annie," The Queen said.

"Of course, there is...." Annie muttered sarcastically, still in utter disbelief.

The Queen supressed a giggle before continuing.

"When you were born. As well as receiving a prophecy of your premature death, I also beheld another vision over you. One that I did not understand until now.

"That prophecy told me that you would be the saving grace, the peace-bringing balance our kingdom so desperately needs. It is true that you are a gifted sage Annie, I have no doubt your gifting is already as strong as mine, which makes you level headed and wise. But if my intuition is correct, which we both know it likely is, you are not only Princess Annalyse of Alearia, sage and apprentice healer, you likely have another gift, my precious daughter. A gift which your sage wisdom allows you to wield without succumbing to its potential dark side. Annie, you are a mind conqueror."

24

Princess Anastasia

The past several weeks had flown by in the kingdom of Alearia. The magical disease appeared to have been contained, so the royal family was convinced the quarantine measures the King and Queen had in place were working.

Princess Alecia, Princess Anastasia, the King, and Princess Agnes, continued their morning breakfast tradition despite the Queen's absence.

"It is only a matter of time before a cure is discovered," the King announced at this morning's family Breakfast.

The King had also reported receiving a raven message late last night from the Queen Amealiana.

"In the letter," the King informed his children, "the Queen stated that she has recovered a valuable package and is on her way to deliver it to the King and Queen of Quillencia. Queen Amealiana has also reported she will return home promptly afterward and will be scheduled to arrive in the kingdom of Alearia in about a week. The Queen mother sends her well wishes and is looking forward to spending time with us when she arrives home."

"Oh, I am so glad to hear mother is on her way home to us," Anastasia delightedly responded. "I have missed her these past weeks. Alecia and I have been training hard whilst she has been away, I hope she will be impressed by our gift development since she left. It is only a few short months until my sixteenth birthday, and I am starting to feel anxious about the upcoming Heir Crowning Ceremony. Do you have any advice for your potential Heirs' father?"

"As you know, Anastasia, the ceremony trials are different for every new generation of potential heirs. I cannot give away any specifics as I would not want to interfere with the Goddess granted process, but I will say this: whether you are crowned future Queen and Heir, or if you are not chosen," the Kind passed a subtle quick look at Agnes.

"Either way your mother and I will be very proud of you. There are many ways you can help lead our kingdom to glory, Heir or not. As proud members of the House of Brandistone, we must remember our common goal. We must always put the wellbeing of our people and our kingdom above all else. Becoming Heir and future Queen means nothing if you do not have the highest respect for your duty to serve and care for our people," the King concluded wisely.

"Very true father. It is easy to lust after the crown. But our people's needs are what truly matters," Anastasia modestly agreed.

"Well put, Anastasia. What a fine role model you are turning into, praise the Goddess," the King complimented his daughter.

"Father would you excuse us? If it is agreeable with you, Agnes, Alecia and I were planning to start our training a little earlier this morning before the weather gets too warm," Anastasia asked the King sweetly.

The King eyed his daughter suspiciously.

"Have you somehow forgotten Anastasia, that you a fire wielder? You don't get hot," the King replied sceptically. "Is there another possible reason that you are in a hurry to leave breakfast this morning? Might I suggest you try a more plausible excuse next time?" the King said with a smirk on his face.

"My King are you suggesting I would dare lie to you?" Anastasia declared, trying to sound offended whilst wickedly. "I was merely trying to be considerate of Agnes, that is all, but you have ruined my attempt at subtlety and have probably embarrassed my dear sister now," Anastasia replied cheekily.

The King smiled genuinely at his daughter.

"Whatever you have planned, Anastasia, I hope you do not intend on getting up to too much mischief," the King sighed. "Now, the three of you get out of here before I change my mind and curiosity gets the better of me."

"Certainly, father. We will be the Goddess incarnate, I promise," Anastasia smiled all too sweetly.

The three sisters quickly set aside their napkins and exited into the main castle hallway. Agnes and Alecia moved to walk either side of Anastasia as she led the way.

"Fine, Anastasia, I'll bite. Where are we going?" Princess Alecia whispered to her sister as they walked down the hallway.

"Patience my dear sister, you are both going to love my surprise. Now follow me," Anastasia whispered to both her sisters and quickened her pace.

At the end of the hallway, the three sisters descended one of the staircases. Further down, they walked until they reached the bottom cellar of the castle. Anastasia held a finger in front of her mouth to signal for her sisters to be silent.

Anastasia pulled a key from the pocket in her day dress and unlocked the ancient cellar door before walking in, motioning for her sisters to do the same. Through the dark alcoves of the cellar, the sisters followed Anastasia further and further, until they came across a painting of the Goddess at the end of one of the rows of wine barrels.

"You must not breathe a word of what I am going to show you to anyone. Do you both understand me?" Anastasia asked both her sisters, staring each of them in the eyes.

Anastasia's two sisters nodded excitedly in agreement.

"Alright then, follow me," Anastasia said as she removed the painting from its hook on the wall to reveal a small door, barely big enough for a child to fit through.

Anastasia dropped to her knees and crawled through the small concealed archway, beckoning for her sisters to do the same.

"Pull the painting back in front of the doorway after you come in so no-one may see our hiding spot," Anastasia whispered.

Alecia and Agnes looked sceptically at Anastasia but did as they were told. The three Princesses crawled through the small dark tunnel for several minutes before the light at the end of the tunnel started to shine. Following their sister's lead, they crawled out of the tunnel's end and found themselves in a bunker, roughly the same size as a suite. The secret bunker was complete with wash basin, privy, sitting room, a bedroom with the capacity to sleep up to six people and a cupboard full of emergency food supplies.

"What is this place?" Agnes asked in awe.

"More importantly," Alecia rudely interrupted Agnes. "Why are we here Anastasia? Why is she here, more to the point?" She pointed her finger at Agnes. "How long have you known about this place and why have you never shown me before now?" Alecia accused Anastasia.

"Alecia be nice please, just this once," Anastasia requested.

Alecia glared at Anastasia but held her tongue.

"Anyway... I brought you here because I found a book that I wanted to show you both. I was going through the library archives last night, researching ceremony rituals, and I found something I wanted to try. Curious ladies?" Anastasia teased.

Alecia burst out laughing, "you must be joking! You give away your secret hideout just to show us a book!" Alecia teased.

Anastasia stared her down.

"Laugh all you want sister, but I found a magic ritual we can perform that will tell us who has the strongest gift. It won't tell us who will be the future Queen, but we all know the most gifted is usually crowned Heir. Aren't you the least be interested to see who that might be?" Anastasia asked smugly.

Agnes suddenly looked uneasy.

"How exactly does it work and what will it tell us?" Agnes asked nervously.

"Simple, Agnes, I'm glad you asked. The ritual and incantation are all detailed in the book. We start by forming a human triangle, with a candle placed between us. We beseech the Goddess to show us her will, reciting the exact incantation. Then we wait and see what happens," Anastasia said.

"Brilliant, I'm in! Though I have no idea why Agnes is here. It's not like she stands a chance of being crowned," Alecia snickered.

Anastasia ignored her and instead turned to Agnes. "Care to give it a try Agnes?"

"I don't see what good it will achieve. We all know I don't stand a chance, as Alecia so subtly pointed out, but sure, let's do it," Agnes sarcastically replied, staring at Alecia angrily.

"Settle down dear sister, I was only teasing," Alecia replied smugly. The Princess was clearly pleased that her words had made their mark.

"Right, well, it's settled. We need a full moon to attempt the ritual. The next one is tonight, so if we gather in the private family garden at midnight, we can test it out. Agreed?" Anastasia asked.

"Agreed," Agnes and Alecia replied reluctantly in unison.

'Goddess help me, it's going to be a long night with these two at each other's throats...' Anastasia fumed.

"Right, well now that's organized, who's ready to train?" Anastasia asked sweetly, trying to restore some level of civility amongst her siblings.

25

Princess Agnes

Curiosity had got the better of Agnes when she had reluctantly agreed to take part in the incantation with her sisters.

'What if the ritual gives away my secret and they learn about my mind conqueror gifting? Worse still, what if the ritual shows I am not the strongest?' Agnes mused to herself.

Agnes slipped silently through the rose garden in the dead of night like a wisp of shadow, wearing a black long-sleeved day dress.

'If all does not go well tonight, I will need to act quickly.

'The Queen arrives home soon, and I cannot allow her to interfere again,' Agnes pondered.

"Agnes, over here," Princess Anastasia whispered from the shadows of one of the old oak trees bordering the garden.

Agnes walked over to join her sister.

"Where is Alecia?" Agnes asked with disinterest.

"She's by the fountain. We walked down together. I came to find you. Follow me," Anastasia motioned, grasping Agnes's hand and leading the way.

The physical contact surprised Agnes so much that she flinched. Very few people made physical contact with Agnes and the gesture took her by surprise.

Approaching the fountain, Agnes could make out Alecia standing in the shadows, the book, presumably the one with the incantation written on it, open on the soft grass in front of her.

Anastasia handed Agnes a piece of paper. "I transcribed a copy of the incantation for you both. I will recite from the original text."

Anastasia lit a candle, and the smell of lavender oils filled the air as she set it upon a stone in the middle of the space where they were gathered. The bubbling of the fountain would hopefully hide the sound of their chanting voices.

Anastasia pulled a knife out of her pocket and sliced her index finger, before allowing the blood to flow over the candle's flame. Alecia and Agnes took turns following her lead and echoed the same process before taking their position around the candle, forming a human triangle.

Anastasia held the book in her right hand and gently rested her left hand upon Agnes's right shoulder. With her incantation in her right hand, Agnes followed Anastasia's lead and rested her left hand upon Alecia's shoulder. Alecia stared down her eldest sister, as if her touch had burnt her, before following her sisters' actions and closing their triangle by placing her own hand upon Anastasia's right shoulder.

"Stupid stubborn girl! It's not as though I enjoy touching you either," Agnes seethed to herself.

"On three, we will begin the chant. It is important that we all keep reciting the words until the ritual is fulfilled," Anastasia warned, her sisters nodding their heads in understanding.

"One... Two... Three," Anastasia counted.

"Goddess hear us, Goddess please, we summon your powers to guide thee. The strongest gift we seek to know, to serve you as you have bestowed," the three sisters recited repeatedly.

The wind went still, and the candle flickered before roaring into a green flame. It wove towards the sky before coming back down again and forming a Crown of shimmering green flames above Alecia's head.

Agnes and Anastasia gasped in unison, dropping their arms to their sides. The crown of flame disappeared as soon as the human triangle was broken. Princess Alecia just stood there cockily; a smirk painted right across her face.

"Did you expect anything different sisters?" Alecia mocked. "Honestly, this whole exercise was a complete waste of time. I was always going to be Queen. Your gift is growing my dear Anastasia, but you still have a long way to go if you want to catch me. Agnes, you never stood a chance. Now..." Alecia smiled sweetly, acting as though she hadn't just ripped her sisters' hearts to shreds.

"Good night my dear sisters. This Queen needs her beauty sleep," Alecia announced, turning on her heels and walking proudly back towards the castle.

'You just wait sister; your time is coming but not in the way you think. Tonight, I will put a stop to you. I will be Queen, and nothing will get in my way.'

"Can you believe her..." Anastasia sighed as soon as Alecia was out of earshot.

"Her day-to-day arrogance is astounding! I don't know why you are so surprised by her attitude tonight to be honest," Agnes replied.

Anastasia stopped and stared at Agnes, appearing instantly uncomfortable with where she had led the conversation.

"Alecia's not that bad. She's just excited. I'm sure I would have felt the same if the ritual had crowned me. I'm sure she didn't mean to come across so obnoxiously," Anastasia spoke softly to Agnes.

"Perhaps you're right sister, or perhaps you're not. I had hoped it would have been you crowned," Agnes lied.

'Well... I would have wished the fire had chosen her if I didn't want the crown for myself so bad! Oh well... on the bright side, at least I now know who the bigger threat is. Thanks, Anastasia!'

"Thank you, Agnes, that's really nice of you to say. Hey, I have been meaning to talk to you about something. Do you have a minute? I know it's past midnight and you are probably desperate for sleep, but I will be quick," Anastasia requested of Agnes.

Agnes nodded and sat on the edge of the fountain, motioning for her sister to do the same.

'What on earth could she want to talk to me about. Neither of my sisters barely acknowledge my existence,' Agnes reflected.

"I feel awkward saying this... I know I haven't always been the best sister to you," Anastasia began.

"That's an understatement," Agnes muttered under her breath.

"Fair call," Anastasia to her credit admitted. "I have been pretty horrible to you at times. I just wanted to say I am sorry. I am sorry for all the times I ignored you. For all the times I allowed Alecia to tease you about your gift and went along with it so I could feel like I fit in. I'm sorry I chose Alecia over you."

Anastasia shifted irritably on the edge of the fountain, "It's hard to explain, but all my life I have felt like a part of me is missing. I guess since Alecia and I share the same gift I clung to her to help fill that void. I have always been afraid that one day she would turn on me, just like she did on you. I couldn't bear to lose Alecia. But I am sorry that I have sacrificed our sisterly bond in favor of the close bond Alecia and I share. If you would forgive me, Aggie, I would really appreciate if we could start again."

Anastasia took her sister by the hand and this time Agnes did not flinch.

"I would love to get to know you more if you would let me," Anastasia requested. "One last thing... I know I am in no position to make requests of you, but it would really mean a lot to me if you and Alecia would try to get along," Anastasia pleaded.

Taken aback and confused by Anastasia's sudden change of heart, Agnes wasn't sure what to say, but after a moment she replied: "I can't make any promises regarding her royal snootiness, but I will try to keep the peace. I would like to get to know you more too."

Anastasia smiled and leaned over to Agnes to offer her a hug which Agnes returned.

'Well this has definitely been a weird turn of events,' Agnes mused to herself.

"Well, it's getting late. Would you mind if I walked you back to your room?" Anastasia requested.

"That would be nice, thanks," Agnes warmly replied.

In comfortable silence, the two sisters strolled back to the castle and to Anastasia's credit, she escorted Agnes all the way to her bedroom door.

"Good night Aggie, sweet dreams," Anastasia whispered.

"Good night sister," Agnes smiled, before walking into her room and gently closing the door behind her.

'Curse you, Anastasia! Well, that ruins my plans for the night! Being a good sister seriously complicates my plans for Queenly domination. Hopefully tomorrow I'll wake up and put all this sentimental nonsense behind me. Alecia will continue to be her horrible self and I can go back to planning to stab her in the back,' Agnes thought confidently.

'But for tonight, since Anastasia's trying to be a better person, maybe I can too. Just for tonight anyway... Tomorrow is a new day after all!'

26

Princess Annalyse

The Quillencian castle was unlike anything Princess Annalyse had ever seen. Red carpets lined the hallways, and banners of the House of Caston, adorned the walls.

Annie could barely believe how much her life had changed overnight. Annie had felt immense guilt and anxiety for abdicating her duties to the town of Lavender Grove as their only apothecary. But her sage gifting and her heart told her that leaving with the Queen was the right thing to do.

"Believe me, Annie, as Princess you will be able to do so much more for your people. You will help them, and advocate for them, in ways you never thought imaginable," her mother assured her.

"If you are crowned Heir in the upcoming ceremonies on your sixteenth birthday, that will make you the future Queen of Alearia and as Queen, you can change the world," Queen Amealiana had told Annalyse.

Annie knew in her heart that the Queen's words were true and so she agreed to come to the kingdom of Alearia on two conditions. The first being that Queen Amealiana would take her to the castle of Quillencia personally, so that they may beseech the King of Quillencia to consider training her mind conqueror gifting if she indeed possessed it.

Annie's second stipulation had been that her mother arrange for a gifted healer to be transferred to Lavender Grove as soon as possible, to take over her apothecary duties. The Queen had been thrilled with her requests and agreed to her terms at once.

Queen Amealiana was positive her father, King Julian, would be thrilled to train his granddaughter. To finally have someone to share his gifting with would bring him no greater joy, her mother wholeheartedly believed.

"Your Grandmother will also likely take you under her wing and teach you how to hone your sage gifting," Queen Amealiana informed her.

This brought pride and relief to Annie's heart. Walking down the final corridor to the throne room, Princess Annalyse began to feel butterflies in her stomach.

'What if Amealiana is wrong? What if they hate me?' Annie considered for a moment before her Goddess blessed gifting reassured her it would all work out.

Stopping in front of the throne room doors, Queen Amealiana held her daughter's hand and whispered in her ear. "They will love you, Annalyse, just be yourself," Annie's mother advised her.

With a nod of the Queen's head, the castle guards drew open the doors for the two royals. A Herald bowed to the Queen as she passed him a name card, before announcing their arrival:

"Presenting Her Royal Highness, Queen Amealiana Brandistone of the kingdom of Alearia, accompanied by her guest Princess Annalyse Brandistone," the Herald announced.

The King and Queen of Quillencia paled in shock before smiling joyously in awe. Queen Annalyse, who was a gifted prophetic and sage, just like her daughter, rose from her chair and walked down the dais to pull her daughter and granddaughter into a warm embrace.

"Welcome, my dear Amealiana and Annalyse. I am so glad you are both well. I feel like I have waited centuries to meet you, my granddaughter." Queen Annalyse warmly greeted her family.

Relief seeped through Annie's bones. After returning Queen Annalyse's hug, Annie pulled herself away to gently drop into a bow.

"Your Majesties, it is an honor to meet you. Please forgive our unannounced arrival," Annie spoke.

The two Queens giggled to themselves, knowingly looking at each other before her grandmother took Annie by the hand and led her to meet her Grandfather.

"Welcome to the family Annie. We are so pleased to meet you," The King greeted his granddaughter with a warm smile. "You look surprised by our reaction dear Annie. What people often forget, is that whilst your mother Queen Amealiana is a gifted prophetic, she inherited her gifting from my wife. We have been awaiting your arrival since your birth. For your safety, we have never looked for you, or interfered in your life out of respect for our daughter's choice. We know she would not have made the choices she did without a good reason."

The King paused momentarily to look knowingly into his daughter's eyes. An unspoken conversation passing between the two royals.

"That, unfortunately," The King continued, "is all Queen Annalyse has foreseen of you, until you made the choice to travel here yourself. The Queen was overjoyed to foresee your impending visit. We haven't been able to concentrate on anything else these past few days. We were so delighted to hear you were well and on your way to us. We couldn't be happier to welcome you to our home," the King of Quillencia gently concluded.

"Why am I not surprised mother," Queen Amealiana winked at the Quillencian Queen. "Nothing escapes your knowledge," Amealiana warmly complimented her mother.

"Naturally, my daughter. You should never underestimate your mother," Queen Annalyse teased.

"Thank the Goddess!" Annie declared, triggering a fit of laughter amongst the royals.

Relief enveloped Annie as she suddenly realized everything had all worked out perfectly.

"Fairy tale's really do come true. I can't believe I have a family," Annie sincerely spoke, heart bursting at the seams with pure untainted happiness.

Over a banquet of scrumptious food, the Quillencian royal family dined for breakfast the following day with Queen Amealiana and Princess Annalyse. The spread was mouth-watering.

The previous night, the King and Queen of Quillencia had invited Annie and her mother to join them in their private sitting room for canapés and wine. Her mother, Annie cheekily noticed, could be quite witty and sassy after a glass of wine. She had also enjoyed watching her mother and grandmother reminisce over memories, allowing her an insightful glimpse into her family's personal history.

During breakfast, Queen Amealiana disclosed to the King and Queen of Quillencia, the likelihood of Annie's mind conqueror gifting. The King himself, with Annie's permission, was able to guide her through a few mental exercises to confirm her gifting and its strength.

King Julian proudly offered to personally train Annie, stating he believed his granddaughter would likely become the strongest mind conqueror the world would ever see. His declaration of Annie's strength also benefited immensely from her sage gifting, which he discerned was just as strong.

King Julian confirmed Queen Amealiana's theory that both giftings would balance each other perfectly. For that reason, King Julian believed Annie would likely become the strongest gifted individual of her generation. Princess Annalyse was absolutely blown away by his level of faith in her, and humbly thanked him for his offer of training. All her dreams really were coming true. There was only one small problem. 'If *I truly am a mind conqueror as they say I am, how do I learn to wield a gift I never knew I had?'*

"My dear Annie," Queen Amealiana spoke sincerely. "Sadly, I must begin my journey home. I have been gone many weeks. As you are all aware, I still have concerns for Annie's safety. I worry that the prophecy may still play out. Mother and Father, please guard Annie's identity with your life. No one outside of the castle can know who she is. That is until the time comes for her to return for the Crowning Ceremonies."

Amealiana gave Annie an apologetic look.

"Annie, together we will decide when the time is right to introduce you to our family. King and Queen Caston, thank you from the bottom of my heart for caring for Annie." Tears welled in her eyes as she walked over to Annie's chair to take her hand.

"Annie, my dear daughter, I hate that we must be separated so soon. Your Grandparents will take wonderful care of you and when the time comes, they will accompany you to Alearia. Train hard and you will develop your mind conqueror gifting quickly," Queen Amealiana promised her daughter.

"Thank you for everything mother," Annie replied, hugging Amealiana tightly before she left. The Alearian guards were already waiting by the doors to escort their Queen home.

27

Princess Agnes

'It's a new day. I will be a better person. I will try for Anastasia. It's a new day. I will be a better person. I will try for Anastasia,' Agnes chanted repeatedly in her head over breakfast.

"Are you alright Agnes?" Alecia asked mockingly. "You seem rather quiet this morning, did you not sleep well? Anything on your mind?" Alecia teased.

'It's a new day. I will be a better person. I will try for Anastasia.' Agnes chanted one last time in her head before she paused to take a deep breath and turned to face her sister.

"How thoughtful of you to ask Alecia. I slept surprisingly well, thank you. I was merely daydreaming, I am sorry to disappoint you," Agnes chirped, struggling to reign in her sarcasm.

"That's lovely to hear Agnes," Alecia replied sarcastically, clearly disappointed Agnes didn't take the bait and lose her temper.

"In fact," Agnes went on, "I was wondering if you would like to join me for a private training session this morning, and hopefully, we can put all this bad blood behind us," Agnes tried to sound sincere. Internally she screamed, wishing anything but good for her sister.

"That's a wonderful idea Agnes! Shall we go now? I know of a special place we could train, just the two of us..." Alecia replied mischievously.

The King and Anastasia turned to watch the upcoming verbal volley match that was sure to take place.

"Certainly, meet me outside my room in twenty minutes? I need to change into more appropriate training attire first." Agnes added.

"Perfect, see you then," Alecia replied, excusing herself from the dining table and heading up to her own room to change.

After Alecia had left, Anastasia turned her attention to Agnes.

"Agnes, you don't have to do that... At least let me come with you to your training session, just to make sure everything goes well. I could keep an eye on Alecia, try and make sure she behaves herself," Anastasia offered sincerely.

"Thanks for the offer, but Alecia and I need to sort out our differences and we won't be able to do that with you chaperoning us," Agnes replied dryly. "Besides, we are sisters after all, what's the worst that could possibly happen?" Agnes shrugged, smirking at her sister.

"Why do I have a feeling you have something up your sleeve Aggie," Anastasia mused suspiciously.

"I don't know what you are talking about! I swear to the Goddess, I will be on my best behavior today," Agnes declared.

"If you say so...." Anastasia winked. "Well, you better get going or you'll be training in your day dress," Anastasia gently teased.

"Right you are sister. I will see you this afternoon. Wish me luck!" Agnes sarcastically drawled as she left the room, earning a chuckle from her younger sister and the King.

Agnes ran to her dresser, threw open the doors and reached down to remove the hidden compartment where she kept her weapons.

Agnes had mastered the art of wielding daggers through her years of training in weaponry at the castle, and she did not intend to take on her sister without a few secret weapons up her sleeve. To some extent, Agnes felt nervous about the upcoming fight with her sister, but she reminded herself that her body and mind were a weapon. Agnes would not be as easy to defeat as Alecia believed.

Truth be told, Agnes was proud Alecia had taken the bait and been so eager to '*train*' with her. The fact that Alecia elected to train somewhere private played perfectly into her hands.

Focus Agnes, you're running out of time, hurry up and get changed! Alecia will be here any moment,' Agnes coached herself.

Agnes hurriedly pulled on the first pair of loosely fitting training clothes she could find. A pair of black pants with matching loosely hanging top, perfect for concealing weapons.

Agnes strapped a pair of daggers to her waist, her long top concealing any evidence of their placement. Finally, Agnes slipped a small glass vial containing a red potent liquid into the left pocket of her pants. Agnes patted the pocket afterward to make sure it would not be at risk of falling out.

'*A little piece of insurance should our training take a turn for the worse,*' Agnes rationalized to herself.

With deliberate speed, the firstborn pulled on her most comfortable pair of leather training boots, and tucked a small sheathed blade into the inside of her right boot.

Alecia burst through the door without knocking.

"Right, you're ready! Now that no one else is around, let's go have some fun," Alecia declared with an obnoxious smirk.

"Lead the way sister," Agnes dared her, with an equally sinister tone.

"Follow me and keep up," Alecia stated, turning on her heels and strutting out the door.

Through the castle passageways, and over to the trees bordering the far side of the castle property, Alecia led Agnes towards the royal crypt.

"I'm game if you are sister," Alecia challenged, pausing at the heavy metal back door to the crypt.

"Oh Alecia, is this truly the most intimidating spot you could come up with? Honestly, I'm a little disappointed," Agnes sassily remarked. "Lead the way, sister."

Alecia pulled open the heavy crypt door for her sister. Accepting the challenge Agnes waltzed straight in, Alecia following, closing the door behind her and leaving them in pitch black darkness.

"I hope you're not afraid of the dark?" Alecia teased menacingly.

"Not in the slightest," Agnes remarked, all bravado and no bite behind her words.

"Doesn't sound like it..." Alecia teased.

The fire-wielder lit a single flame in her hand and the room illuminated, casting angry shadows across her face.

"How would you like to do this dear sister? This was your idea after all," Alecia taunted, fully aware that right now she held the upper hand. The flickering flame promised Agnes harm.

"Why don't we fight this out the old-fashioned way, unless you don't think you'll be able to beat me without your pretty little party tricks," Agnes tormented.

Alecia scowled and Agnes grinned wickedly as her words found their mark.

"Suggesting I take you on without wielding my fire, only proves that you know you wouldn't stand a chance against me otherwise. If we are going to dual, there will be no rules," Alecia declared.

"That's fine with me, go ahead, don't hold back and I promise I won't either," Agnes beamed with anticipation.

'I know I promised to give Alecia a chance. I told Anastasia I would try and honestly, I have. It's not my fault she has no intention of making peace with me either. Sorry, Anastasia, but Alecia is going to get exactly what she deserves.'

Before Alecia could make the first move, Agnes reached under her shirt, quickly withdrew one of her hidden daggers and flung it straight at Alecia's left shoulder. Her weapon found its mark with ease.

"You son of a harpy! You will pay for this!" Alecia bellowed at her sister before ripping the blade out with her right hand. With a burst of concentrated flame, Alecia soldered the blood vessels in her shoulder and the wound stopped bleeding immediately before closing over.

"You'll have to do better than that sister!" Alecia menacingly spat. "How about a taste of your own medicine," Alicia snickered volleying one fireball at her sister after the next as Agnes tried to flee farther into the crypt, ducking behind different mausoleum pillars or statues for shelter.

"Come out and play Agnes, aren't we having so much fun together?" Alecia narcissistically cackled, enjoying every moment of hunting her sister.

'Game on sister! If this is how you want to play, let's play,' Agnes slyly thought.

Agnes silently opened one of the empty tomb drawers and slid inside; the darkness covering her actions. Hearing Alecia's approaching footsteps, she gently closed the door in front of her and retrieved her remaining dagger from her chest strap.

"Where are you hiding sister. Don't tell me you've given up already," Alecia attempted to sound offended. "All bark and no bite, that's all you are. But you know what? It doesn't matter, because I will be Queen and you won't, and there's nothing you can do about it." Alecia continued to taunt as she stalked around the crypt in search of her sister, passing Agnes's hiding spot and continuing her search.

As Alecia's footsteps began to fade, Agnes silently slipped out of her hiding place and lunged for her sister. Alearian steel brutally met flesh as Agnes stabbed her sister straight into her lower back with her dagger. Alecia cried out in agony, dropping to her knees in pain.

The fire-wielder frantically attempted to pull out the dagger but was unable to get a hold of the hilt. Alecia paled, and for the first time in her life she knew fear.

"Pull it out, Agnes! Pull it out before I bleed to death!" Alecia pleaded.

"Are you scared? I thought we were just playing a game. Are you not having fun anymore?" Agnes mocked Alecia with contempt.

"Now it's my turn to have some fun..." Agnes declared, throwing her mind conqueror gifting into her sister's defenseless mind.

It was as easy as breathing to pinpoint the source of Alecia's gifting. Agnes latched onto the source of her sisters' power and pulled it into herself, stealing all but a handful of Alecia's firepower.

"My gift!" Alecia screamed, "what have you done with it?"

Agnes released a truly devilish cackle. "Not so powerful anymore are you sister? What do you think of my useless gifting now? Of course, I can't have you spilling my little secret can I... So unfortunately, as much as I would love for you to remember this moment for the rest of your life, I'm afraid I'm going to have to wipe your memory as well," Agnes declared.

"Sister please, please take the dagger out, stop the bleeding I beg you, before it's too late! I won't tell anyone what you've done but please get the dagger out!" Alecia begged, tears streaming down her face in pain and anguish.

"Why of course sister, I am nothing but merciful. As soon as I wipe your memory, I will heal you... Or perhaps I'll allow you to heal yourself... if you still can," Agnes pondered.

Agnes lunged her power into her sister's brain again; Alecia losing consciousness from the repeated assault on her mind. Agnes located the memory center of Alecia's mind and erased the last fifteen minutes with but a thought. Agnes then grabbed a hold of the blade embedded in her sisters back, taking great joy in pulling it out, before using the stolen fire wielder gifting to solder up the wound. Quick thinking had Agnes light one of the torches in a wall sconce to flood the room with light.

Alecia, now laying in a foetal position on the floor, slowly regained consciousness.

Seeing Agnes crouched next to her, Alecia asked in a panic: "What happened? One minute I was stalking you through the crypt, the next thing everything went black and I wake up on the floor. What did you do to me?"

"Oh please, I didn't *need* to do anything to you. You slipped and hit your head. As you fell you landed on my dagger, which I kindly pulled out for you, I'll have you know. Then I used the torch to save your sorry self from bleeding out. You owe me! Now that you're awake, shall we finish our duel?" Agnes challenged.

Alecia rose to her feet and stood face-to-face with Agnes.

"Don't worry sister, we will have our rematch, but not today. I'll let you have this win, but I don't believe a word of what you just said. I will get you back for whatever you have done to me. When we rematch, I hope it's in front of a massive crowd at the Crowning Ceremonies. The next time we dual I will humiliate you. Now get out of my way!" Alecia declared as she stormed outside.

"Well that went perfectly," Agnes snickered to herself, before lighting ball of fire in her hands and marvelling at her new ability.

28

Queen Amealiana

The sun was setting on the final day of their trek home to Alearia. As the Queen and her escorts crested over a lush green mountain, they caught their first glimpses of the Alearian castle in the distance.

The Queen urged her horse into one final sprint. The company determined to make it home before darkness fell, making the trip potentially dangerous. The Queen had endured a migraine these past couple of days, and she was looking forward to a long night's sleep in her own bed to help her recover. However, sleep would have to wait a little longer. Amealiana's sage gifting told her something dreadful had occurred whilst she had been away, though she had not foreseen any visions to account for the cause of her anxiety. Amealiana was determined to make it to the evening family meal so she could find out what was going on.

Much to the Queen's frustration, the harder they rode home, the more her head pounded and her vision blurred. The Queen knew she would have no choice but to rest in bed as soon as she arrived home and send for a healer to brew her a pain-relieving tea. Their family reunion would regretfully have to wait until morning.

Princess Annalyse

Annalyse was walking contently to family breakfast after waking from the most restorative sleep she had experienced in a long time. Annie felt at home in the castle of Quillencia, like she had finally found a place where she belonged.

The Princess's new daily routine was packed to the brim by her grandparents, the King and Queen of Quillencia. Annie's day started with family breakfast, followed by sage training with Queen Annalyse and Alearian history lessons.

After lunch, Annalyse trained with the squires to develop her physical fitness, learning basic self-defense and weaponry handling skills. After Annie's combat training, she would bathe. If time allowed before dinner, Annie would stop by the infirmary to assist the healers to prepare their ointments and lotions. After dinner with the royal family, Annie and King Julian would train her mind conqueror gifting until bedtime.

By the end of the evening, Annie felt mentally and physically exhausted, but she was also filled with a sense of relief. Having only herself to worry about, rather than the whole town of Lavender Grove, made her feel as though a weight had been lifted off her shoulders.

The Quillencian rulers wanted to ensure Annie was prepared for the upcoming Crowning Ceremony rituals, though Annie had no idea what the rituals entailed, and her Grandparents had shed no light on it either. Annie's biggest fear was that she wouldn't learn to harness her mind conqueror gifting in time.

'My sisters have had a lifetime to learn their craft and I only have a fraction of the time. How could I ever be chosen as Heir? As a matter of fact, do I even want to compete to be crowned Heir?

'Do I want to be the future Queen of a country I have no connection to other than by name and birthplace? Will the people even accept me as a Princess and potential Heir, let alone their potential future Queen? This is completely insane! I'm a healer! Not even a healer, I'm an apprentice healer. What do I know about leading a country?' Self-doubt clouded Annie's judgment as she completely ignored her sage gifting.

"Good morning, Princess Annalyse," the castle guards greeted her whilst they opened the door to the family's private dining room.

Annie nodded her head in thanks, offering a sweet smile before entering the room and approaching the table where a maid helped her be seated.

A moment later the Queen and King of Quillencia entered from their private entrance, and Annie rose from her seat to curtsy and give her morning greetings.

"Good morning Annie," the Queen spoke whilst being assisted into her own chair. "How are you feeling? I sense you are well rested, but you seem to be internally conflicted. Is there anything you would like to talk about?" the Queen offered.

"You are too kind to me Your Highness, and once again you have read me like a book," Annie smiled. "I'm afraid I am questioning my calling... My whole life I have been an apprentice healer. Now I wonder if I even deserve to attend the Crowning Ceremonies. The people of Alearia do not know me. What right do I have to be considered a potential Heir? I don't know the first thing about ruling a kingdom. I can't even control my mind conqueror gifting, so what right do I have to be potentially crowned future Queen of a whole kingdom?" Annie stressed.

"My darling Annie, you are more powerful than you know," Queen Annalyse reassured her in between sips of tea. "Even if your gifting were not a factor of consideration, you would still make a considerate, empathetic ruler. Caring for the people of Lavender Grove was Lady Lilianna's way of raising you to become the Queen the people need."

"I never looked at it that way," Annie pondered.

"You may not believe in yourself yet," the King added, "but I promise you; if the Queen and I did not believe with our whole hearts that the Goddess wanted you to be considered in the crowning rituals, we would not be preparing you for it. You are just as important as your other siblings Annie. There is a goodness in you that cannot be taught. Your people need you, Annie. It is not for us to question the will of the Goddess."

"You must believe in yourself, Annie. Listen to your sage gifting and let it be your guiding light," Queen Annalyse offered.

"Instead of training with me this morning," the Queen added thoughtfully, "I want you to go to the Goddess's temple and pray. I want you to spend time in that sacred space, reconnecting with your sage gifting. Really listen to what the Goddess and your gifting are telling you. Be comforted by the knowledge you have buried inside you."

"That is incredibly wise advice, Your Majesty. Thank you, Your Highness, I will," Annie agreed.

After a morning spent in the temple reconnecting with her inner sage gifting, Annie felt more in tune with herself than she had in a long time. The Princess's spirit felt renewed, and she was ready to put her doubts behind her, accepting that all she could do was try her best and the rest was up to fate.

If it was the Goddess's will that Annie partake in the crowning rituals, then she needed to trust that the Goddess would not let her go unprepared. With a renewed sense of focus towards her training, Annie embraced all that the day had in store for her.

No matter how many facts Annie failed to recall in her history lessons, she kept trying her hardest, and wrote pages of notes and study cards to help prompt her memory. During Annalyse's combat training, she chose to focus on learning self-defense. By doing this, Annie found she was able to progress her skills more quickly than if she tried to learn different training styles simultaneously.

Annalyse mused that it was probably more helpful to first learn how to prevent someone from potentially maiming or killing her, than learning to harm someone else without knowing how to save herself.

Regardless of the supposed necessary evil of learning to attack as well as defend, harming another living person did not sit well with Annie. After years of training to be a healer and dedicating her life to caring for people, Annalyse was not sure she could intentionally cause harm to someone. It felt wrong on so many levels to her. Almost as if she were betraying her mentor's life work by even attempting to learn how to attack and develop her weapons skills. Annie was sure there must be another way.

'If I am to be crowned Heir, I will not earn the title by betraying everything I stand for. I do not know what lays ahead for me, but if having to hurt one of my sisters is what is required during one of the rituals to become Heir, then I will not do it.

'I must be true to myself. If I want to be the role model our people need, I will not set a precedence that I condone violence in any form. I will learn to defend myself, but I will not cause another harm.' Annie owned her decision to stand by her beliefs. *'If I do not live with integrity, demonstrate kindness and act justly, then I am not fit to rule a kingdom.'*

After their evening meal, King Julian escorted Annie down a dark, stone stairwell passage she had not traversed before. Annie had never been below ground level in the kingdom's castle before, causing the potential Heir to quizzically ponder to herself where the King could be taking her. Annie couldn't figure out why they weren't heading to the library to train as they had during their past sessions.

Descending the spiral granite staircase, passing level after level, further into the depths of the castle they continued. The deeper they ventured, the lower the temperature dropped, and Annie found herself feeling a chill.

King Julian noticed his granddaughter beginning to shiver and silently offered her his cloak. Annie wrapped it around herself gratefully, offering a smile in thanks. The King returned the gesture as they stopped in front of the final door at the bottom of the staircase.

"Dearest Annalyse, being a mind conqueror comes with great responsibilities. Our gifts must only be used for admirable purposes or to achieve an honorable goal that benefits the people," the King cautioned. "We must never use our gifts for selfish purposes or personal gain. It is my belief that your sage gifting will help guide you in when to wisely use your mind conqueror gifting, and when it would be unwise or potentially harmful to do so."

"For many years, mind conquerors were feared by the people and treated as outcasts," King Julian informed her. "Several generations ago, our royal descendants vowed to never do harm with their gifting, and to only use it for noble purposes. If we use our gift, a piece of our soul — our moral code — is taken from us by the Goddess as punishment. Magic always has a price, my Princess. It is vitally important that you remember this."

"Lady Lilianna gave up her life force to save you with her healing gifting, and this maintained the balance between life and death," he explained. "Mind conquerors forfeit a part of their soul, little by little each time they use their gifting, which maintains the balance between the Goddess and her people. We are humans after all, who were never meant to be more powerful than the Goddess, so the cost of our gifting keeps us humble and reminds us that we are only human."

"Reckless use of their mind conqueror giftings is part of the reason our ancestors were driven mad from power," Julian warned. "Their souls were literally destroyed from constantly using their gifts for personal gain. Without a soul, we lose who we are, and all that is left of us is a mere shell of the person we used to be."

"It is important that you fully understand the consequences of your gifting, so you judge whether the reward is worth the price. One day, if I am not careful, I too will go mad from overusing my gifting. It feels like a little piece of my sanity is ripped away from me every time I use it. Which is why I only use my gifting in extreme circumstances. You must remember to do the same, Annie. A power-hungry Queen is not what the people want or need. Our very soul and sanity are the price for breaching other people's privacy and minds. Use of our gift should not be taken lightly. Do you understand what I am telling you, Annie?" Julian spoke to her gently.

"I'm sorry, but this is all too much," Annie said, suddenly feeling lightheaded and nauseous from anxiety. "I knew deep down that just like Lily, there would be a be a cost if I used my gift. But I had no idea how severe it would be. I can't imagine what would motivate someone to trade their very soul for the use of their gift. I would rather die than live a life disconnected from my world and those I love."

"That is wise Annie, and that is why I believe that your sage gifting will keep you grounded. There will come a time when you will need to call upon your gift, but I believe in my heart that your sage gifting will protect your soul and keep your mind intact. Unfortunately, I cannot guarantee that. It is only a theory and as I said, magic always comes with a price, so it is also likely my theory may be wrong," the King sighed sadly.

"I am sorry, Annie, to place this burden on your shoulders. Right now, though, we have the chance to potentially do some good with our gifting. That is why we are here," the King spoke solemnly as he took a bronze key from his pocket and unlocked the ancient door before them.

29

Princess Annalyse

Princess Annalyse stepped into the small, dimly lit antechamber, the King locking the door behind them. The room was sparse; two shelves built in along one wall with freshly laundered linen, hospital gowns and material face masks neatly folded into organized piles. Two wooden chairs sat beside a small wooden table complete with a wash basin, soap and hand towel.

On the opposite wall were large baskets, presumably to place the used linen to be taken away for laundering. On the far wall, opposite the door they entered from, was another locked door. The only indication as to what may be inside was a sign reading: '*Quarantine Area – Restricted Access Only.*'

The King washed his hands in the basin and dried them meticulously. Annie followed his lead and repeated the process. Following the King's lead, Annie removed her cloak and pulled a hospital gown over her clothes. She tied her hair back with a piece of string left on the table and applied a face mask over her nose and mouth. Annie then sat on one of the two chairs to await further instructions. The King knocked on the far door before taking a seat beside her.

"Annie, I need you to keep an open mind and to listen to your sage gifting," the King spoke hesitantly. "Tonight, I hope that we will be able to learn some valuable information that could potentially help many people, so it is important that we succeed in our task. No one except for the healer you are about to meet, a handful of my most trusted guards and the Queen know who is in the next room, and it is vital that it stays that way to prevent a public outcry. You will see what I mean in a moment," King Julian informed Annie who nodded in acceptance of his request.

'*Who in the Goddess's name is in that room?*' Annie wondered. '*I have cared for many clients in quarantine before, but no case has ever warranted such secrecy. In what way does the King possibly think I can help, that a fully-fledged healer could not? And how is my gifting relevant to all of this?*' Annie mused.

A middle-aged healer by the name of Helen entered the antechamber, bowing to the two royals before introducing herself to Annie.

"Your Majesty," Helen addressed the King. "I have discovered little new information about the magic disease since our patient's arrival. He seems fit and well. If he didn't tell me that his gifting had disappeared, I wouldn't have believed him. I can detect his water wielding gifting, which he says none of the healers in Alearia were able to do. However, even though I can feel the aura of his water mage gifting, the patient says he is completely incapable of wielding it as he did previously. It's a complete mystery to me. I am hoping your particularly unique gifting may be able to shed some light on the cause of the disease," Helen concluded.

"Thank you, Helen. I am glad to hear you can detect his gifting as that will make the process much easier indeed. Hopefully, we will have some more answers soon. Is the man awake? Is it a good time to see him?" The King asked.

"Of course, Your Highness, right this way," Helen replied, leading the way into the isolation room.

"Good evening sir," The King greeted a young man in his early twenties, who was sitting on the edge of his hospital cot.

The young man dropped to his knee to bow before the King. "Your Highness, my name is Joseph. You honor me with your presence, but I am afraid I am confused. Why was I taken from the Alearian hospital and brought here to be quarantined?" Joseph asked earnestly.

"It is a pleasure to meet you, Joseph. This is Annie, she is an apprentice healer. To answer your question, - you have been brought here because I have a gifting that may be helpful in potentially diagnosing and treating the cause of your magical illness," The King informed the patient.

"If you would allow me and my young apprentice here, we would like to scan your mind for any signs of what could be inhibiting you from accessing your gift? Would that be agreeable with you?" King Julian asked sincerely, preserving Annie's anonymity.

"Our gifts must only be used for admirable purposes or to achieve an honorable goal if its outcome would be beneficial for the people," Annie recalled her grandfather telling her.

'Finding a cure for an unknown magic disease would undoubtedly be considered a reward worth the cost. Now I realize why he does it. Even if the cost is so detrimental to himself, if we could help these people, I would gladly pay that price as well. But how does the King think he or I can help? Our mind conqueror giftings can't heal a disease... can they?' Annie wondered.

Having come to a decision, Joseph took a deep breath. "Thank you for the kind offer, your Majesty. I depend on my gifting for a living. Without it, I can't feed my family. If there is anything you can do, please try."

The King nodded his head in acknowledgment before pulling a chair over to the gentleman's bedside.

"If you wouldn't mind Joseph, can you please lay down and try to relax as much as possible. I will talk you and the apprentice healer through the process as we go. You should not feel any pain whilst I work, but the more relaxed you are, the calmer your brain activity is, making it easier for me to navigate through your mind," the King stated in a calm tone.

Joseph did as the King asked and lay down, closing his eyes and taking slow, deep breaths to calm himself.

"Thank you, Joseph. Do you mind if I rest my hand on your forehead? It is not necessary, but the physical contact can help to improve my level of control as I navigate through your mind," The King requested of the young water mage.

"Certainly, Your Highness, do whatever you need to do," Joseph replied softly.

King Julian gently rested his left hand upon the young man's brow and closed his own eyes in concentration. Annie pulled up a chair beside her Grandfather so she could watch him work. The King inhaled deeply and exhaled slowly before beginning his ministrations.

"I begin by centring my own mind, focusing on the goal I want to achieve. In this case, I am stretching my mind out towards Joseph's, to form a seamless connection between the two of us, mind-to-mind. Next, I slowly guide my way through his brain, looking for any abnormal signs or signals... So far so good, Joseph," the King reassured the young man whilst explaining the process to Annie.

"Joseph, can you please describe what your gifting feels like to you? How would you picture it inside your mind?" King Julian asked.

"Yes, your Majesty. When I could feel my water mage gifting it felt like an ebb and flow of cool energy inside me. As essential to my soul as air. The moment my gift vanished I felt as if a part of me had been ripped away. I'm not sure if that helps, sorry," Joseph replied.

"Very helpful, thank you," the King praised. "Annie, as I continue to guide my way around his mind, I am looking for any electrical pulses or activity that mimics Joseph's description."

The King sat in silence as he navigated through the gentleman's mind, occasionally pausing his work to seek out further information regarding Joseph's water mage gifting. Minutes turned into hours as the King thoroughly continued his search before withdrawing from the young man's mind and calmly taking a breath.

"Thank you, Joseph, for your patience. I may be able to help you, but for now we both need to rest. Do you mind if Annie and I return again in the morning?" The King asked Joseph.

Joseph sat up, as if sensing the King's uncertainty.

"Should I be worried, Your Majesty?" Joseph asked, concern and worry painted across his face.

"Everything is fine Joseph. I just need time to rest and think. Using my gifting for extended periods of time can be quite taxing, I'm afraid to admit," the King replied unconvincingly.

'*What did he find? Can he help Joseph, or is his condition beyond fixing?*' Annie pondered feeling deep concern for both her grandfather and the young man.

"Goodnight Joseph," the King replied, wobbling as her stood.

Annie took his arm in her own to offer him support before exiting the chamber with Helen. As soon as the door was closed behind them, the King discarded his mask and hospital gown and slumped into one of the chairs along the 'clean' side of the antechamber.

"My King, I am sorry, but I am afraid you will have to wash your hands, as the clean side will now need decontaminating," Helen advised.

"That won't be necessary Helen," the King replied shakily. "The young man is not contagious. I believe I know what is wrong with him, but we mustn't speak of this to anyone until I am sure I can fix him. Move Joseph discretely up to the guest room in the royal wing where he will be more comfortable. Make sure only the most trusted staff know he is there. I will arrange to have a guard stationed outside his room at all times," the King declared.

"As you wish, King Julian. I will arrange his transfer immediately," Helen replied, bowing before both royals before discarding her hospital attire and washing her hands. Then she exited through the main antechamber door to make the arrangements with the castle staff for Joseph's transfer.

Annie discarded her hospital attire and sat down next to her Grandfather, taking his hand in her own, and allowing the King the time needed to process his thoughts. After a few minutes of silence, the King turned his head to Annie, empathy and sorrow in his eyes.

"Annie, I found his gifting. It is intact and complete," the King stated.

"That's terrific news grandfather. Do you believe you can fix him? What does it mean if his gift is intact, but he is unable to utilize it?" Annie asked.

The King's eyes dropped; grave concern painted across his face.

"From my observations, I am afraid to say that someone has likely ripped into his brain and heartlessly severed his connection to his gifting."

Annie inhaled sharply, struggling to absorb what she was hearing.

"What is most deeply disturbing," the King continued, "is that the only a mind conqueror would be capable of this. As I have been in Quillencia serving my own kingdom and you have been in Lavender Grove completely unaware of your gifting, that means that someone else also possesses the gifting and is using it for their own personal gain. What unsettles me the most, is that the only known mind conquerors have descended through my royal bloodline. It devastates me to say this, but whoever is severing these peoples' connections to their gifting, likely comes from our own kin in Alearia," the King said barely louder than a whisper.

Horror filled Annie's heart. '*What sort of family do I belong to, if one of my own kin would want to inflict fear and harm upon their own people?*'

"We can fix this, Annie, if we work together. We will stop whoever is doing this I assure you. Tomorrow morning, once I have regained my strength and composure, I will teach you how to repair this man's connection to his gifting, if you will allow me. You know the cost of using your gift though, so the choice is yours," The King offered.

Annie now fully appreciated the immense sacrifice the King had made all these years as the sole known mind conqueror of all the kingdoms. Annie would not allow her own grandfather to sacrifice the last of his soul to save the Alearian people on his own. She knew what she had to do.

"Please, teach me how to heal my people. We will work with my mother, to stop whoever is doing this. I will not let you heal these people alone grandfather. I am a healer, that has always been my purpose in life and my destiny. Lilianna thought she was preparing me to be a Queen, but she was preparing me for so much more than she ever dreamed. I will help our people. I will be the mind conquering healer that the people need," Annie declared fearlessly.

Pride shone out of the King's eyes as he embraced her.

"I am so proud of you Annie, and I know Lilianna would be too."

30

Queen Amealiana

The birds were chirping happily on the Queen's windowsill. After a demanding journey, the Queen had foregone her usual morning ride in favor of a few extra hours of well-earned sleep. The tea she was given for her migraine the previous night had thankfully resolved the pain, but left a lingering sedating effect, making it hard for Amealiana to feel motivated to embrace the day — especially knowing the likely drama brewing.

"Goddess give me strength," Queen Amealiana muttered to herself as she pulled herself out of bed. The Queen's Lady's Maid was already busy filling the bath in the Queen's bathing chamber. Her favorite scents of lavender and rose wafting into the bedroom.

"Thank the Goddess for you Margarette," The Queen said warmly upon entering her bathing chamber, spotting a hot cup of lavender tea sitting on the table beside the bath.

Margarette turned from the tub to drop into a curtsy before her Queen, smiling warmly. "Welcome home your Majesty. I hope you are feeling better this morning. We have missed you these past weeks," Margarette affectionately greeted her Queen.

"Thank you, Margarette, that is kind of you to say. I have been looking forward to a proper bath. The days of travel have left my body grimy and aching. How glorious it is to have you spoiling me again! If you're not careful I shall take you with me on my next trip. I am getting far too used to your luxurious care," the Queen chuckled to her Lady's Maid.

"The pleasure is all mine, Your Highness," Margarette blushed. "The potential Heirs are all partaking in an early morning training session, so I thought you might like to take the opportunity to relax a little longer this morning. I will return in a while to wash your hair with your favorite oils and treatments."

"Thank you, Margarette, that was very thoughtful," the Queen replied, as she undressed and then stepped into the bathtub.

As the water enveloped her like a welcome embrace on a cold day, Amealiana released a small sigh of contentment. Amealiana took her time sipping her tea, whilst enjoying one of the delicious chocolate pastries Margarette had left for her, savoring every blissful moment of rejuvenating time to herself.

'*Today is going to be an awfully long day, of that I have no doubt. For now, though, all my duties, all my questions, all my responsibilities, can just wait a moment.*'

An hour later, the Queen, assisted by her Lady's Maid, dressed in a formal day dress made of elegant burgundy taffeta. Amealiana's hair was braided and pinned into a coronet upon her head after being luxuriously washed and dried by Margarette. A simple, understated gold tiara was the finishing touch.

"You are a vision, Your Majesty," Margarette smiled.

"Thank you, Margarette, for all of your help," the Queen replied before an urgent knock came at the entrance door to her suite.

"Please let Princess Anastasia in," the Queen advised.

'*There are no surprise visitors when you are prophetic.*'

Margarette excused herself with a small nod to the Queen before opening the door. Just as the Lady's Maid reached for the handle, Princess Anastasia impatiently entered without awaiting permission, rushing over to embrace her mother.

"Anastasia, how lovely to see you, my daughter. I have missed you terribly. Are you well?" the Queen asked warmly.

"Welcome home mother! I just heard you had arrived, otherwise I would have already come to see you, I'm sorry," Anastasia replied.

"It's quite alright my dear. I arrived late last night but I had a dreadful migraine, so I sent for a healer and was asleep not long after. I was hoping to surprise you all at breakfast today, but you have beaten me to it," the Queen warm-heartedly assured her daughter.

Stepping back from their embrace, the Queen took Anastasia's hands in her own and escorted her over to the hearth where they could sit side-by-side to catch-up.

"Now tell me, Anastasia, how are you my darling? What has happened since I left?" The Queen asked.

Anastasia took a deep breath, then succinctly explained openly and honestly the events of the last few weeks. Anastasia emphasized the noticeable recent change to Agnes and Alecia's behavior, but could not account for why it had occurred, only that she was aware they had a recent confrontation of some sort and neither had been the same since.

"The strangest thing happened today in training with Alecia," Anastasia followed on from her story. "Alecia has been avoiding fire wielding practice since her duel with Agnes, which is strange since she normally loves to flaunt her skills. So, this morning during physical training I surprised Alecia by throwing a fireball, which she easily ducked away from, but rather than retaliating and firing back like she normally would, she abused me and stormed off. You always tell me to trust my instincts and I have a terrible feeling that something dreadful has happened to her. What if she has developed the magical disease and she's hiding it from me? She never misses a fire-wielding training session, and she hasn't attended for days," Anastasia emphasized.

Queen Amealiana pulled her daughter into her arms once again and attempted to reassure her.

"Anastasia, you have a kind heart. I know you are especially close with Alecia and so you naturally worry about her more than others. I am sure Alecia will be fine. Their fight was probably just the catalyst for her recent withdrawn nature. Alecia can be hot-tempered and stubborn, so she was probably just annoyed you tried to force her to fight with her fire and that was why she stormed off. I will speak with Alecia though, and I will have a healer assess her to put both our minds at ease." The Queen reassured her daughter.

"I would greatly appreciate that mother, thank you," Anastasia replied warmly.

"Very well. I will speak with Alecia straight after breakfast and I will arrange for Margarette to send for a healer as soon as possible," the Queen assured her daughter. "Would you like to escort me to breakfast darling? I'm sure you must be famished after your early training session."

"It would be my pleasure mother," Anastasia smiled.

The two women rose from their seats, linked arms and made their way down towards the family dining room. The Queen kept a careful, relaxed mask across her face, though internally she was anything but calm.

I had a feeling my moment of peace was going to be short-lived... Surely there is no way that Alecia could have lost her gifting without me knowing. I would have foreseen it. Calm down, everything will be fine. Alecia is alive, praise the Goddess for that, and everything else is purely speculation,' Queen Amealiana coached herself.

After a disappointing family reunion over breakfast, the Queen was certain something was amiss between her eldest and middle daughter. Alecia had sulked and fumed her way through the meal, barely acknowledging her mother's return. Agnes was oddly smug and something about her made the Queen feel uneasy. These were not the same daughters she had left a month or so ago.

Her husband, the King, was incredibly happy to have her return, though that was to be expected. The King and Queen loved each other dearly, no matter how much distance or time separated them. Anastasia spent the meal trying to put on a brave face, making copious attempts at small talk with her sisters which were shut down quickly with every attempt.

'What in the Goddesses name, has happened while I have been away?' The Queen worried.

"Alecia dear, would you mind accompanying me for a stroll around the gardens?" The Queen asked her daughter in the way that all mothers ask their child a question that there is only one correct answer to.

"Certainly, mother," Alecia bristled.

The Queen ignored her daughter's rude demeanor. "Terrific! Let us go now then."

The Queen rose from her chair, Alecia reluctantly doing the same. After politely farewelling the remainder of her family, Amealiana linked her right arm through her daughter's, and escorted her towards the main gardens through the side door leading onto the patio.

Mother and daughter meandered through the rows of beautiful sweet-smelling flowers, taking in the calming scenery. Queen Amealiana eventually lead them over to a bench beneath a hundred-year-old willow tree branch, next to an understated water fountain. The soft sound of water trickling filled the air with a relaxing symphony of sound.

The Queen allowed her daughter a few moments to collect her thoughts before she spoke, considering her words carefully so as not to startle her daughter. "Alecia, I have missed you, I am sorry I have been gone so long. I want you to know that I am here for you, no matter what may be going on in your life or what may be troubling you. I love you, my daughter," Amealiana spoke gently.

A weight seemed to lift from Alecia's shoulders. "I have missed you too mother. I need to talk to you about something but I'm not sure if I should or if you'll even believe me. I barely understand what has happened myself," Alecia replied in disbelief.

"My dear child, you can tell me anything. You are my daughter first and foremost, and a Princess second. I will stand by you no matter what," Amealiana promised her daughter. "Anastasia told me that you and Agnes had a falling out. She said that you have not been the same sine. We are worried about you. I can tell something's bothering you. Please let me help you."

Alecia took a deep breath. "It is easier to show you than explain it, if that is ok with you?"

The Queen nodded encouragingly.

Alecia held her hand out, brow furrowed in concentration, shaking from the effort it took to create a tiny flicker of flame.

"I keep trying, but I can't create anything stronger," Alecia spoke breathlessly.

The exertion of maintaining the single flame, draining all her energy. The Queen sat there in shock as she processed the situation; Alecia, rasping suddenly for breath.

A moment later the flame blinked out and Alecia collapsed onto the ground at the Queen's feet. Amealiana screamed for help as she dropped beside her daughter, drawing her into her arms.

Panic filled her heart.

Guards appeared out of nowhere, running to the Queen's aid.

'Holy Goddess heal my daughter. Restore her powers. Bring her back to me, stronger than ever.'

31

Queen Amealiana

Princess Anastasia and Queen Amealiana sat, by their loved one's bedside, holding silent vigil as Alecia slept deeply in the royal family's infirmary suite. A small team of healers were bustling around the room preparing various tonics and brews for the sleeping Princess.

"Mother, what do you think has happened to her? Did Alecia tell you anything about what was worrying her whilst you were in the garden?" Anastasia asked anxiously.

"I fear your suspicions might not be far from the truth Anastasia," the Queen whispered to her daughter, who gasped in response. The Queen held a single finger to her lips and looked around the room at the healers bustling about.

"Alecia fainted before we were able to delve into the matter. But we cannot discuss this here, I am not sure who we can trust now, so I need you to keep this information strictly between the two of us. Do you understand?" Queen Amealiana whispered. Anastasia reluctantly nodded her head in agreement.

"You must not breathe a word of this to anyone except myself or the King, including Agnes. I am still not sure what is happening here, but I would rather as few people as possible know the specifics of Alecia's condition," the Queen spoke softly.

"As you wish mother. I would never do anything that could potentially bring harm to my sister," Anastasia promised.

The Queen embraced her youngest daughter, whispering into her ear. "No matter what, I promise you, your sister will be healed. I will find out what has happened to her and I will stop it from ever happening again. I will protect you, Anastasia. As soon as Alecia awakens, I will find out the rest of her story and then I will act. We do not know if the magical illness has struck her, or if something or someone else is behind this. I can only act off facts and currently, we have none to work with, only suspicions. I will get to the bottom of this, until then I need you to trust me."

"I do trust you, My Queen," Anastasia whispered back into her mother's ear. Then the two royals pulled away from each other and the Queen summoned the head healer to join them.

"Your Majesty," the healer responded dropping into a low curtsy, "how can I be of service?"

"In light of my daughter's unidentified illness," The Queen declared. "I feel it is in the best interests of the potential Heirs and all the castle's occupants that we go into the final stage of lockdown. No one enters or leaves the castle without the direct permission of myself or the King."

"Princess Agnes is to be confined to her bedroom suite in quarantine, under constant guard for her own protection," Amealiana ordered. "As Anastasia has already had contact with Alecia since she has fallen ill, she may be quarantined here also."

"I apologise, but your team of healers will no longer be permitted to leave the castle grounds," The Queen instructed. "They may send raven messengers to their families to inform them of my decree. If any essential staff have children at home that require their care, they may be summoned to the castle and cared for in the guest wing by our Lady's Maids."

"All non-essential staff may either be sent home to their families or remain in the castle confined to the servant's wing. Please advise the staff that I apologize for any inconvenience this may cause, but the safety of my family and kingdom is my top priority," the Queen ordered.

"I will inform the King of my decisions, whom I'm certain will concur with these decrees. Thank you," the Queen concluded, dismissing the healer with a kind smile.

As the head healer left the room, Alecia began to stir in bed. The other two healers in the room noticed the Queen's redirection of attention and came over to check on their patient. As Alecia woke, slightly dazed and confused, the healers completed a thorough assessment of her. Certain that there was no immediate risk to her daughter's health, The Queen temporarily dismissed the healers from the room, requesting a moments privacy with her daughters before they continued any further medical investigations. The two healers reluctantly agreed, curtsied, and saw themselves out.

Amealiana took Alecia's hand in her own. "My sweetheart, how are you feeling?"

"I'm alright, sorry to worry you," Alecia mumbled, still half-asleep.

"Not to worry, blessing me with so many daughters, I believe, was the Goddess's way of keeping me on my toes," the Queen joked.

Alecia attempted a half smile, before turning to her sister Anastasia. "Stop looking like you're about to cry, Tash. I'm not dead! One moment of frailty and your whole world collapses in on itself. Honestly, sister, I thought I was raising you tougher than this?" Alecia joked, obviously much more alert now.

"Well I'm glad to see whatever is going on hasn't robbed you of your impeccably sarcastic sense of humor sister," Anastasia replied dryly, rolling her eyes.

The Queen smiled broadly at the sight of her daughters' usual banter. "Alecia, I am sorry to have to ask, while I'm sure you are probably feeling miserable right this moment, but I need you to tell me what happened," the Queen stated remorsefully.

"Agnes happened," Alecia responded bluntly.

The Queen and Anastasia stared at her expectantly, waiting for further information. Alecia took a deep breath and slowly retold her story.

"I'm not sure exactly when or how my powers were drained down to a mere speck. I know without a doubt though, Agnes was behind it. A few days ago, we went to do some training together to let off some long overdue frustration between each other. I'm not sure what happened next. One moment I was stalking Agnes around the crypt with a fireball in my hand. The next I was rousing from the strangest dream laying on the floor. Agnes claimed I slipped and hit my head, rendering me unconscious, but I don't remember doing so."

Amealiana slumped back into her chair by Alecia's bedside.

"Something inside me just knew that Agnes was lying," Alecia continued. "After I stormed out of the crypt, I tried to throw a fireball at a nearby rock to let off some steam, but I couldn't even summon a flicker of light. I thought it might have been from my supposed head injury, thinking surely I would be fine the next day, but my gifting never truly came back."

"It drained all my reserves just to summon a hint of my former gifting today. I don't know how it happened but I'm sure Agnes is behind it. There's no other possible explanation," Alecia spoke angrily as she looked back and forth between her family, seeking their reassurance.

Anastasia just stared in disbelief at her sister. The Queen appeared composed, processing everything her daughter had disclosed. Anastasia, unable at first to find the right words to articulate her thoughts, instead crawled into bed beside her sister and hugged her.

"I am so sorry this has happened to you, Alecia. We will find a way to heal you, I promise," Anastasia lovingly assured her.

The Queen took a deep breath. "Alecia I am sorry for what has happened to you and I understand why you suspect Agnes, I truly do. However, Agnes is my daughter as well and without proof, I can't hold her accountable for this. She is innocent until proven guilty, just as anyone in our kingdom would be. We are all bound by the same laws no matter our status."

"My sage gifting," Queen Amealiana continued, "senses the honesty of your account of recent events. However, it is not enough evidence for me to act upon. I promise you though, that I will find out what has happened to you and I will make sure you are healed. You will regain your powers. We will find a way; I have no doubt. You will still be a contender to be crowned Heir. Regarding Agnes, she will remain under close guard, confined to her suite until we can determine the cause of your condition. However, Agnes is not a suspect at this stage. The whole castle will be treated equally and remain under lockdown. The most reasonable explanation for your condition, is that the magical disease has breached the castle and infected you."

Alecia's nostrils flared in frustration, but she did not dare interrupt or argue with Her Majesty.

"Perhaps due to the strength of your gifting and bloodline, you were able to retain the essence of your fire despite infection. However, I promise you that I will investigate all possible causes. Anastasia will stay here with you so you may be of company and support to each other during this challenging time. The three healers will stay in the infirmary and work with you, Alecia, to explore all potential healing remedies and options. We will make sure you are healed my darling," the Queen promised her daughter before pausing and pondering a thought.

"I do have one question for you Alecia... You said before you regained consciousness in the crypt, that you had a strange dream. Do you remember what it was about?" The Queen asked curiously.

Alecia thought back to that day in the crypt, trying to sift through her memory to recall the details the Queen was after.

"I was injured, I think... In my back. There was blood, lots of blood. Agnes was grinning at me like she was enjoying watching me suffer. Her eyes were hungry with power. She said something about stopping me spilling a secret... making me forget something. I can't recall anything else. The harder I try to remember, the more frazzled my memory becomes, almost like my mind doesn't want me to remember what happened..." Alecia recollected.

Queen Amealiana tried to mask her face with confidence but failed miserably.

"I'm sure it was just a dream darling. Nothing to worry about. Now if you will please excuse me, I must be off to talk to The King. I hope you feel better soon sweetheart. Take care, the both of you," the Queen added quickly as she exited the room, heading straight towards the chapel to seek counsel from the Goddess.

In the seclusion of the royal family's private chapel, Amealiana knelt before the altar.

"Goddess help me. Surely Agnes and Annalyse can't both be mind conquerors... can they? How did I not foresee this? Could my own daughter have altered my mind, preventing me from prophesying over her? Is it even possible for a mind conqueror to do such things? This is ridiculous! There is no way she could be a mind conqueror. Agnes only possesses a prophetic gifting... doesn't she?"

"Oh, Goddess help me, I have been so blind! For the first time in my life, I wish I weren't a sage and prophetic. Just once I wish I could remain ignorant. Just this once, so I wouldn't have to admit to the evil taking place in my own home. My own daughter took away her sister's gifting," Amealiana anguished, tears falling from her eyes.

"What sort of a mother does that make me, that my own daughter would commit such an evil crime against her own family? Goddess above, she couldn't possibly be responsible for the magical disease too, could she? Goddess, please guide me. What do I do now?"

32

Princess Annalyse

Annalyse had barely slept the last two nights, anxiety plaguing her and her mind racing. The King was generally struggling to compose himself; his anxiety clearly getting the better of him as well.

Annie suspected that that the use of his gifting on Joseph had taken its toll on him mentally, and the butterfly effect of restoring Joseph's connection with his water wielding gifting had been detrimental to his own mental health. The effects on the King's health was easily seen, though he tried his best to put on a brave front for his people.

Thankfully for Joseph, the King had been able to heal him completely. King Julian had walked Annie through the mind conqueror healing process, so that she could assist with rebuilding Joseph's final connection to his gifting.

Annie felt like her masterclass from the King was exactly what she needed to learn how to wield her gifting. After being guided through the process, Annie now had a feel for how her gifting worked and could now imagine how she would repeat the process again to heal others.

Annie found visualizing her gifting as a wisp of a cloud floating into her target's mind and exploring the many passageways of the brain with fluidity, helped her wield her gifting. Annie found this approach helped her to sort through and identify specific brain signals in a person's mind that needed repair or were missing completely, allowing her to work more effectively and purposefully.

Annie could visualize her own thoughts, taking note of the feel and look of her own mind's electrical activity, allowing her to look for similarities in her target's mind. This methodical process would guide her towards the areas she needed to work on in her patient's mind.

Determined to only use her mind conqueror gifting for good, Annie practiced using it on a man who had a sustained brain injury as a result of a bar brawl. With the man's permission, Annie navigated her wisp of gift around his mind, looking for signs of any impaired electrical activity, and healing the damaged connections. The result was astounding.

The man reported that he could think more clearly, and his short-term memory was more accurate than it had been in years. The middle-aged man thanked the Princess profusely for her help, and Annie, for the first time since leaving Lavender Grove, truly felt like she was fulfilling her life's calling.

By the end of the first full day of active mind conqueror training, Annie was exhausted mentally and physically, but unfortunately, the day was not over. Tonight, Annie needed to re-pack her belongings as tomorrow she would leave for the kingdom of Alearia with King Julian. They would travel by horse with a team of twelve guards escorting them. Their arrival would be unannounced, so as not to raise any suspicion about the purpose of their visit.

It remained uncertain which of their family was betraying the kingdom, so they wanted to maintain the element of surprise. Queen Amealiana would undoubtedly foresee their impending early arrival and understand the urgency for their early visit. Annie hoped that Queen Amealiana had come to the same conclusion regarding the fake magical disease, and put extra security measures in place to protect the kingdom.

Queen Annalyse Caston, would sadly need to stay behind in Quillencia for another two weeks to ensure the day-to-day smooth running of their own kingdom. Annie's grandmother promised she would arrive in time for her birthday and the Crowning Ceremonies.

As Queen Annalyse said her final goodbye to her husband King Julian, she had a knowing look in her eyes, tears trickled down her cheeks.

"I love you my dear Julian, we will meet again soon. No distance or amount of time apart could separate our joined souls. May the Goddess always guide you. Know that I will always treasure you in my heart. I am so proud of you, my selfless husband. I love you my darling, goodbye."

"I love you too my darling. I will always be with you. No distance or amount of time apart, could separate our joined souls," King Julian echoed in reply to his beloved wife.

The next four days of travel would be hard, but for the good of the Alearian people, they would travel as quickly and efficiently as possible, stopping for breaks only when necessary. The sooner they arrived in the kingdom of Alearia, the sooner Annie could start using her gifting to reconnect people with their own. The knowledge that one of Annie's own kin was behind the disastrous magical disease sickened the Princess to her very core.

33

Princess Agnes

Agnes grew more restless. She had filled her time reading and doing basic exercises in her room to help maintain her physical and mental fitness. However, after four days of confinement to her suite, the Princess's patience was running extremely low.

Princess Agnes was so bored that she had even resorted to making a list of ideas of how she planned to sabotage her future wedding, which was scheduled for a few months after the Crowning Ceremonies. Luckily though, everyone was so preoccupied with the upcoming events that little attention had been drawn towards the planning of her supposed wedding. Agnes wasn't worried though. Soon she would be crowned Heir, and her first order of business would be to cancel the wretched arranged marriage.

'I do not need a King by my side to rule our kingdom. I will rule on my own and no one will stand in my way,' Agnes smugly thought to herself.

A knock on the door drew Agnes from her thoughts, her attention instantly redirected towards the visitor, eager for any break from the monotony of her suite. Agnes's Lady's Maid answered the door and bowed deeply as the Queen of Alearia entered the room, wearing her formal attire and crown. Agnes dropped into a curtsy, realizing that it was the Queen wearing her crown, that had come to address her, not her mother.

"Your Majesty," Agnes spoke. "How lovely it is to see you. To what do I owe the pleasure of your visit? Is there any news regarding the magical disease?"

"Good afternoon Agnes, I am afraid your questions will have to wait. For now, I need you to come with me. Some important guests have just arrived, and I am summoning our whole family to meet with them," the Queen replied vaguely, keeping her motive close to her chest.

Agnes attempted to penetrate the Queen's mind but was met with a firm shield preventing her from intruding.

'What is this? Why can I not get through? Does she suspect me? Who would be so important that the whole family would be summonsed from quarantine to meet with them? We are in lockdown, for that matter. How have visitors even been admitted into the castle?'

"Follow me please," Queen Amealiana requested as a team of six guards entered the room to escort them to their meeting.

Down the hallways they traversed; the Queen, her daughter Agnes and their six-guard escort. Past the entrance to the throne room, down a spiralling granite staircase, deeper and deeper, into the heart of the castle they ventured. The staircase was dimly lit by low burning torches every few feet, perched in sconces along the passageway wall. The temperature dropped as they made their way further below ground.

'The Queen must suspect something amiss to be accompanied by an armed escort in her own home. What if I am walking into a trap? If that is the case, I will not go down easily. I will defend myself.

'There's my hidden dagger tied around my right thigh. I have my physical training to fall back on and the arsenal they will least expect, my mind conqueror gifting and my dear sister's fire wielding gift. I'm practically invincible.

'Now that I think about it, what was I even worried about? I am not defenseless anymore. I am a weapon and I will not go down without a fight.'

Agnes held her head high as they approached the entrance to the dungeons, the most secure facility in the castle.

Queen Amealiana

Queen Amealiana hammered on the ancient door knocker to the dungeon entrance, announcing her arrival; a signal and warning to the dungeon's inhabitants, to prepare themselves.

'Deep breaths Amealiana. This must happen for the good of the kingdom, for the greater good of my family. We must get to the bottom of all this senseless havoc. The perpetrator of all this must be discovered, proven and held accountable. I can do this. I must do this,' Amealiana assured herself as the dungeon warden came to open the door.

The warden secured the entrance door behind them after The Queen and her entourage had all entered the antechamber. There was no going back now, the plan was set in motion.

The dungeon warden approached the front of their group to address The Queen, "If you would kindly follow me, Your Majesty, your remaining companions are in the interrogation room. Right this way," the warden instructed.

The Queen followed the warden, protected by two of the King's guards. Agnes walked directly behind and the remaining four guards kept an eye on her through the dingy dungeon maze they traversed.

Queen Amealiana, had given her personal guards extended leave to spend with their families after their long journey, so Tomlin and Lawrence were not by the Queen's side as usual. Their absence in this particular situation, made the Queen uneasy.

The door to the interrogation room was made of half a foot-thick iron with three locks on both sides of the door in case of emergencies. The dungeon warden unlocked each of the elaborate locks, each with a different key, before opening the door and gesturing for the group to enter before him. As soon as the group was inside, the warden closed the door behind them, re-locking the door from the outside, and effectively trapping the royal family and their guards inside.

A small peephole in the door could be opened to observe activity in the room from the outside. When the Queen gave the signal through the peephole, the warden would reopen the door to allow them back outside.

The interrogation room was full to the brim, clearly not designed to hold this many people, but it would have to do. In the center of the room, the usual table with two chairs facing opposite each other had been replaced by a circle of seven chairs.

Queen Amealiana took her seat beside her husband, Princesses Alecia and Anastasia sitting on the alternate side of King Titian of Alearia. Seated in two of the remaining three chairs were Annie and King Julian of Quillencia.

Queen Amealiana had met with Annie and her father as soon as they had arrived in Alearia earlier that day. They had shared their knowledge and both the King of Quillencia and Queen of Alearia, regrettably both concurred that Agnes was the most likely culprit behind the mystery magical illness.

Queen Amealiana was still coming to terms with the fact that her daughter was a likely traitor to the kingdom; her motive remained unknown. Though Queen Amealiana was pleased to hear that both King Julian and Princess Annalyse were both capable of healing those affected by the underhanded mind conqueror. However, as Queen Amealiana had said in the past to her other daughters, Agnes was to be considered innocent until proven guilty, despite what her sage gifting told her. It was the law of the kingdom and everyone was treated equally under the law, even royalty. That was where Annie came into the plan for this meeting.

Annie was to be introduced as the King of Quillencia's personal assistant today. Ensuring Annie's identity remained a secret a little longer. Annie was at the meeting purely to work her gifting on each of the family members, initially focusing on Agnes. Searching for proof of the family's covert mind conqueror.

As soon as she had the proof needed to confirm the Queen's suspicions, Annie would signal the King of Quillencia and then either Queen Amealiana or King Julian would enlighten the guards and the rest of her family.

Agnes begrudgingly took her place in the remaining seat available in the circle, though attempted to mask her frustration at the situation with an overconfident front.

"Thank you for coming everyone, I am sorry for the short notice and the location, but all will become clear shortly. The Quillencian King and I have both discussed the best way to approach this discussion, and we felt that here was our only option," The Queen began.

King Titian looked unconvinced by the Queen's assurances, having not been included in the planning, but motioned for her to continue.

"What we must discuss today is of extreme importance for our Kingdom and family. King Titian, Princess Agnes, Princess Anastasia, and Princess Alecia, please warmly welcome my father, the King of Quillencia and his personal assistant, Annie. They have traveled here from Quillencia a little earlier than planned, as they have some important news to share with us. King Julian, thank you again for coming all this way. Would you please inform us all of your recent discoveries?" Queen Amealiana requested of her father.

King Julian smiled warmly towards his daughter and greeted each of his kin one at a time.

"Thank you, King and Queen Brandistone, for welcoming myself and my assistant. Annie, as the Queen has already introduced, is my personal assistant but also an apprentice healer and has been working with me in Quillencia to treat one of the victims of the Alearian magical disease," King Julian explained.

"What is the meaning of this Amealiana?" King Titian abrasively asked.

Attempting to restore peace to the conversation, King Julian continued. "Amealiana felt that my gifting might have been beneficial in treating the victims of the mysterious disease and it turns out her instincts, as always, were correct. The young gentleman that we treated, by the name of Joseph, has regained full connection with his water mage gifting, praise the Goddess. I am certain that the treatment can be replicated for the remaining victims, starting with yourself Princess Alecia, if you would allow me to try," the Quillencian King advised, stalling time for Annie to search Agnes's mind.

Anastasia and Alecia were elated by the good news. Alecia welled in Alecia's eyes at the prospect of her gift returning to her. "I would greatly appreciate any help you could give me, thank you, King Julian," Alecia sincerely replied.

King Julian nodded his head in acceptance of his granddaughter's thanks. Then he redirected his gaze to Annie for confirmation on whether she had found proof of the traitor with her gifting. Annie nodded sadly towards King Julian and then again towards her mother in confirmation. King Julian and Queen Amealiana's eyes met for a brief instant, horror-struck by the realization of what they had officially proven.

"Carry on please King Julian," the Queen reluctantly advised.

King Julian took a deep breath and uncomfortably looked each of his kin in the eye before at last making final eye contact with Princess Agnes.

"I am afraid to confirm King and Queen Brandistone, that Agnes it seems, is also a mind conqueror. Furthermore, we have proof that she has been making these people deliberately unwell, including her own sister Princess Alecia. Agnes perpetrated this whole fake illness as a cover-up, though her motive is unclear. It is my belief that Agnes has been severing the people's connections to their giftings all along," King Julian summarized.

There were gasps from the King of Alearia, Anastasia and Alecia. Princess Agnes stared at King Julian in anger as he ruined her rouse. Alecia went to dive across the group to attack her sister for harming her, but Agnes was too quick.

Princess Agnes

Agnes knew her luck had run out and she was not willing to go down without a fight. Agnes reached beneath her skirt with lightning quick reflexes and retrieved her dagger before diving across the group, stepping behind her grandfather and holding the dagger firmly to his throat.

"Now you've done it! One wrong move from anyone and the King dies," Agnes declared.

The whole room stilled, the guards' hands resting on their weapons, ready to attack at the King or Queen of Alearia's command.

"I would have gotten away with it if it wasn't for you and your meddling," Agnes accused her grandfather. "But do you want to know something? I'll let you all in on a little secret. I didn't sever your gifting Alecia, I stole it," Agnes declared throwing a wall of fire around the room, turning each of the guards into cinders in a heartbeat. The world seemed to stop in shock.

"Let me go free, or you will all face the same fate," Agnes declared fiercely.

The King of Quillencia inhaled sharply, choosing his words wisely before speaking; every slight movement of his neck drawing a trickle of blood from the knife pressed sharply against his throat.

"Agnes, you don't have to do this. I know you would never mean to harm anyone. I'm sorry for accusing you so harshly. You must believe me, Agnes, you have fallen susceptible to the dark side of our gifting. It's not your fault that you had to learn to wield your gift blindly without any training or being made aware of the consequences," King Julian empathised with her.

"You see Agnes," The Quillencian King continued, "every time we use our mind conqueror gifting. a little part of our soul and sanity is ripped from us as well. I am sure you felt consumed by the need for power and you likely couldn't stop yourself from using your gift. 'Just one more time,' you would have told yourself, but it will never end. The more you use your gifting, the madder you will become, and there will be no coming back from what you will become if you do not resist your gifting's hold on you now," he warned.

"All can be forgiven; all your work can be reversed. No one else must suffer. I would even sacrifice myself to take away your gifting, to give you another chance at living a full life if you would allow me. But I cannot erase what you just did to those guards." King Julian spoke only loud enough that Agnes could fully understand his offer.

"It's too late for your help," Agnes spoke loudly and aggressively, no sign of remorse in her voice. "King Titian will never let me live for what I have done to his precious fire wielding daughter," Agnes spat.

"We still care for you Agnes despite all you have done. But we cannot ignore the fact that you are guilty of crimes against our people," King Titian reasoned. "The Queen and I are responsible for keeping our people safe. You will be held accountable for your actions. Please don't make this any worse on yourself. Just put down the knife; your grandfather has done nothing wrong," the King of Alearia said with as much sincerity as he could muster; trying to mask the disgust he felt towards his daughter.

Agnes cackled madly.

"You expect me to believe this rubbish? You haven't cared for me for a single day of your life, so don't pretend to care now," Agnes mocked.

"*Agnes the Ungifted,* is all I will ever be to you; even as a mind conqueror you despise me. Maybe it should be you standing between me and my knife rather than grandfather. Care to take his place?" Agnes laughed madly, threatening her father.

The Queen stepped in boldly in front of her husband towards Agnes.

"For Goddess' sake Agnes," The Queen pleaded, "let my father go! He is a good man. I love you, my daughter. Nothing is unforgivable, even this. Please just let him go, and you may go free. I swear that we will not stop you," the Queen stated firmly, briefly staring down the King over her shoulder who quite obviously maintained a different opinion on the matter.

"Will you really let me go, mother?" Agnes asked, daring to hope in a rare moment of humanity that someone still cared for her.

"Of course, my darling, just please let my father go," Queen Amealiana repeated, tears welling in her eyes.

Queen Amealiana

Agnes suddenly dropped to the floor unconscious; barely breathing, pulse weak, but she was not dead.

The Queen looked towards Annie, realizing she must have been responsible for this turn of events.

"Thank you, Annie, my darling, for saving his life," the Queen whispered to Annie's ear as she threw her arms around her, tears of joy flowing freely.

King Julian fell to his knees in relief, tears pouring silently from his eyes as he put a hand to his throat. King Julian could still feel the soft trickle of blood that was still oozing from his wound.

The King of Alearia, Princesses Anastasia, and Alecia, stared in shock at the scene before them, utterly gob-smacked.

34

Queen Amealiana

Time seemed to stop. The air stilled, as if the world was frozen in motion. The tension was high as all waited to see what would happen next. The room felt uncomfortably warm, even though Agnes's flames had long become nothing more than cinders and ash.

"Can someone please tell me what the hell is going on?!" King Titian Brandistone bellowed, breaking the empty silence. "My daughter is apparently a Goddess damned mind conqueror, and somehow stolen or severed magic, or I don't even know what, to the people of MY kingdom! Now of all things, she's apparently stolen Alecia's gift! How is that even possible! Amealiana – what is going on here? Why are you hugging an assistant, apprentice healer or whoever she is, whilst my daughter is laying on the floor unconscious? Answer me damn it! No more secrets or half-truths. Tell me everything!" The King roared at his wife.

Queen Amealiana calmly broke her embrace from Annie, giving her a reassuring smile before taking her daughter's hand and turning around so they were both facing the King.

"King Titian, my dear husband. I would like to introduce you to Princess Annalyse Brandistone, our daughter, and Anastasia's long-lost twin," Amealiana spoke softly but assuredly.

The room went deadly silent again. Anastasia's mouth dropped to the floor. The King of Alearia simmered with rage as he processed what the Queen was saying.

"Of all the treasonous things Amealiana, how is this even possible! Are you telling me all these years I have had another daughter and not even known she existed? You are not an exception to our laws, wife! If you don't explain yourself, I will have no choice but to charge you with treason for withholding this from me," King Titian declared.

The Queens' face dropped momentarily as she regained her composure and told her story.

"Almost sixteen years ago," Amealiana began, squeezing Annie's hand reassuringly, "I was waiting for the impending birth of Annalyse and Anastasia. Lady Lilianna supported me through the throes of childbirth. I wanted to keep our twins birth a secret and make some grand gesture after they were born, declaring our beautiful twins to you and the world."

"Devastatingly," Amealiana continued, "after Annalyse was born, I had a vision that she would not live long enough to enjoy life. It was prophesised that she would be betrayed and murdered in our own home. I could not allow that to happen. I would not allow harm to befall upon my beloved daughter, so I begged Lilianna to take Annalyse away that night and raise her in secret. I entrusted Lilianna with our daughter's life, knowing that she would always put Annalyse first."

King Titian slumped back into his chair; his face ashen.

"Recently I felt the bond between Annalyse and I fraying," Amealiana recalled. "I felt her life fading away into the After World and I mourned her impending loss. A miracle occurred that night, and I awoke to our bond restrengthening. Lady Lilianna sacrificed her life by using her remaining healing gifting to save our daughter, and she perished from our world into the next."

Annie rested her head against Amealiana's shoulder, wrapping her arm around her mother's back in support and reassurance.

"We owe our unending gratitude for Lily's endless love and protection of our daughter until her very last breath," Amealiana spoke solemnly. "One day, when the Goddess calls my name to the After World, I will re-join my friend and spend eternity repaying her for that debt. After I felt Annie's life being renewed, I knew I had to find her and bring her back to us. After losing our son, I could not bear the thought of losing another one of my children. It is a loss no mother should have to suffer. Annie is the precious gift I went to retrieve from Quillencia."

"Thank you," Annie spoke softly, squeezing her mother a little tighter.

Amealiana resumed her seat beside her husband and looked lovingly into his eyes.

"Annie is our daughter, our family, our own flesh and blood. Annie is the reason we all survived just now. Annie is a sage and mind conqueror, the perfect balance between power and control. She is the reason Agnes is unconscious but not dead. Annie saved her and us, even when most people would have ended Agnes's life without a second thought, for the threat she made against us all. Annie is merciful and kind. I am so proud to be her mother," Queen Amealiana sincerely declared before turning to look at the piles of ash that now filled the room.

With great despair, Amealiana concluded: "I am so sorry my blind trust in Agnes — my overconfidence — led to those brave soldiers premature, pointless ends. I thought I had chosen the safest path for this meeting, but I was so very wrong. Agnes will face the consequences of all her terrible crimes."

"That we can agree upon Amealiana," King Titian stated in disbelief.

The Alearian King rose from his seat to address is family.

"Annie, I am sorry for my rudeness earlier. It appears we all have a lot to process. Alecia and Anastasia, I am sure this has been as thorough a shock to you both as it has been for me. Please go back to Alecia's chambers; the two of you can comfort each other tonight, and tomorrow we will all meet to discuss where we stand," the King softly addressed his daughters.

Then he walked over to the peephole in the door and gave the signal for the door to be opened. Agnes still lay unconscious on the floor near the King of Quillencia.

"Father, what is wrong?" Queen Amealiana asked anxiously, kneeling before the King of Quillencia.

King Julian's breath rasped, and his eyes suddenly glazed over as if he were in a deep trance. He appeared as though he had aged ten years in the space of the last ten minutes; his face deathly pale. The King's eyes cleared for a moment while he gazed into his daughter's eyes as he softly spoke.

"I love you my daughter, but I cannot allow her to live a fate worse than death. I could never live with myself," King Julian explained. "Annie can heal the others, I know she can, but the power has consumed Agnes; she has gone mad and there is no coming back from what she has become. But I can help her in a small way, and I can protect our people from her. If I steal her mind conqueror gifting, Agnes won't be able to harm anyone anymore, and the darkness in her heart will not grow any further. Annie may be able to restore Alecia's gifting back to her if I allow Agnes to keep it for now. I will not be able to withstand the lure of the mind conqueror power any longer though once Agnes's gifting is combined with my own. All magic has a cost. So please understand why I must do this," King Julian begged his daughter.

Queen Amealiana stilled before her father, tears welling in her eyes. "Please father, do not do this, there has to be another way. I love you and I need your guidance," Amealiana pleaded.

King Julian kept a brave front as he continued, "please tell my wife and son, that I love them with all my heart. I hope they can forgive me for leaving them."

The Quillencian King's eyes once again closed over, with one hand resting on his granddaughter Agnes, and the other hand holding her dagger. The King screamed in pain as he ripped every last shred of Agnes's powerful mind conqueror gifting from her and drew it into his own mind. With a maddening cackle, the mind conqueror gifting overwhelmed his soul.

King Julian held the dagger with both of his hands and in his last moment of clarity before the power completely overcame him, he fatally injured himself, his soul passing from this world into the next.

The Queen screamed; a gut-wrenching sound tearing itself from her most inner being. The whole room around her ceased to exist in that moment, as she realized the incredible sacrifice her father had just made for his people.

Agnes, who had succumbed to the dark side of her gifting, thanks to her grandfather's own heroic sacrifice, no longer possessed the mind conqueror gifting she had used previously to destroy peoples' lives.

Devastated by the loss of her father, Amealiana threw herself over the Quillencian King's body, embracing him with all her might. Washing away his blood with the endless flow of her tears.

King Titian, Princesses Alecia, Anastasia, and Annalyse, all knelt around the Queen and her father. Bowing their heads and holding each other's hands, they formed a human chain protecting the Queen Mother and the deceased King of Quillencia.

In respect and reverence, they softly prayed for his soul and the souls of the six guards, to be at endless peace with the Goddess in the After World.

35

Princess Anastasia

The first light of dawn was just starting to show. The sky was a light grey hue, and soon the sun would begin to rise over the surrounding mountains. The first snow of the season had begun to fall overnight. It felt like fall had only lasted a few brief weeks, but that was not uncommon for the mountainous kingdom of Alearia.

The change in weather was a sign that the Crowning Ceremonies were approaching. The winter solstice and the twins' sixteenth birthday were only a short while away.

Anastasia stood on her balcony watching the Queen Mother leave for her morning ride. Off to clear her head, Anastasia was sure, and to have some much-needed time to herself to work through the immense grief that weighed heavily upon her.

Anastasia had not slept a wink all night. The events of the past day had shaken her to her core. Anastasia could barely come to terms with the fact that her eldest sister maliciously murdered their guards right before her eyes, and then threatened to do the same to her own family.

The young royal felt as though she had recently become closer with her eldest sister, so she could not fathom why she would behave like this. To make matters worse, their own grandfather had sacrificed his own life to save Agnes's remaining soul and protect the people by eliminating her devastating mind conqueror gifting.

'Did Agnes deserve grandfather's kindness? Did she deserve Annie's compassion?' Anastasia mused. *'My poor grandmother and mother will never heal from this loss. It will break their hearts. How is my mother meant to carry on with her day-to-day duties like nothing has happened, when she has lost not only her son, but her best friend and now her father all in one year? So much senseless loss. Could Agnes have been the one who killed Alexander as well? He was her brother. Her own flesh and blood. Surely she could not have done that?'* Anastasia worried, stricken with unimaginable anxiety.

The Princess stood shaking on the balcony, watching the sun begin to rise; barely able to control her breathing.

'How can the world continue to go on without grandfather or Alexander in it?'

Anastasia legs were no longer strong enough to support her as she collapsed to the ground; anxiety suffocating her, each breath a dry rasp. The world was spun as Anastasia's vision became clouded by constantly flowing tears.

The world closed in around her as she struggled to remain tethered to reality. The anxiety and grief overwhelming her.

Huddled on the balcony floor, Anastasia felt as though her heart would shatter and all the oxygen in the world could not save her.

Anastasia's Lady's Maid stepped out onto the balcony to bring the Princess some tea but dropped the cup in shock at the sight of the Princess laying in a foetal position hyperventilating.

The Lady's maid screamed for the guards' help; a million tiny pieces of porcelain teacup now scattered across the floor. She rushed over to Anastasia and drew her into her lap.

Stroking the Princess's hair gently, the Lady's Maid attempted to reassure and calm the terrified Princess. A few minutes later, a healer from the infirmary arrived at the Princess's suite to administer treatment. Anastasia was given a sedating tea and transferred to the infirmary immediately for monitoring.

Queen Amealiana

The Queen's head pounded; she had barely slept in the last week. Her body ached and her soul felt shattered. Amealiana had barely enough energy to stay upright on her horse. However, riding amongst the mountainous terrain, the sight of fresh snowflakes falling gently, brought her some semblance of peace.

The first snowfalls of the season brought with it the promise of a new beginning, a soon to be Heir, and a fresh start for her kingdom. When everything in life seemed like it was falling apart, at least Queen Amealiana could count on her morning rides with her horse Ebony to help lift her spirits.

Today marked the first official day of mourning after King Julian's passing yesterday. The black mourning banners had been hung around the kingdom to signify the mourning period. Their presence was a constant reminder to the Queen of all she had lost over the last year.

Amealiana's mental health was suffering significantly from the impact of her father's death. As Her Majesty rode through the forest on the edge of the castle grounds, dressed in all black, Amealiana tried to process her thoughts and feelings surrounding her eldest daughter.

So much had transpired in the past twenty-four hours. If Agnes were to be trialled under the law as a normal citizen would, she would surely be sentenced to death. Queen Amealiana was ruminating anxiously over so many conflicting thoughts and questions with no clear answers. Even her Goddess bestowed sage wisdom was unable to offer clear guidance on what path to take next.

'I pray that father was right. I pray that Annie can restore Alecia's fire wielding gifting to her. If Annie can do this, then my father's sacrifice will not be in vain.

'King Julian could have easily killed Agnes instead of prolonging her life and giving Alecia a chance to regain her gifting. Perhaps if he chose to do so instead, he would be with us now and she would not.

'Is Alecia's gifting worth the cost of his life?

'Father said he didn't want Agnes 'to live a fate worse than death'. Did King Julian mean that Agnes hasn't yet fully succumbed to the dark side of the mind conqueror gifting?

'King Julian explained that there was an immense cost that came with the use of the mind conqueror gifting. A gift and a curse, just as I consider my prophetic gifting. For King Julian and Agnes to be able to manipulate the minds of others, their sanity was indeed the demanded price. The Goddess's way of maintaining the balance of power.

'Agnes used her gifting for selfish, immoral purposes and paid the cost with her own sanity. We do not yet know what Annie's cost will be given she is also a sage, but there will be a cost, there always is.

'Agnes was too powerful and dangerous to risk leaving alive with her mind conqueror gifting. I understand that. Agnes could have destroyed us all the moment she regained consciousness if King Julian didn't steal her gifting.

'What should we do Father? Please guide me Goddess.

'Agnes has committed murder. Children have been left fatherless as a result of her actions. Others have had the connections to their gifting severed; for some this meant losing their livelihoods, their way of supporting their families.

'The people have suffered from reduced access to apothecary services. Ward beds used up pointlessly by the magical illness victims. Healers time and energy wasted trying to treat a condition that it appears only a mind conqueror is capable of fixing.

'The butterfly effect of Agnes's selfish actions is astronomical.

'You told me, King Julian, that Agnes was mad from power and that she would never again be who she once was. Is there still any trace of goodness left in her heart? I am so confused.

'I can't be impartial due to the love I still feel for my eldest daughter. It clouds my judgment. My heart and mind are so conflicted. Our circumstances help mold us into the people we are. Even royalty are not immune to envy or jealousy.

'During the founding years of Agnes's life, she watched on from the sidelines whilst her siblings thrived in their giftings. Agnes has spent most of her life being taunted for her lack of gifting. I'm sure that would have been extremely hard for her to cope with.

'What Agnes did though was inexcusable. From the very first time Agnes severed someone's ability to access their gifting, she made a conscious decision to use her gifting for malicious purposes.

'Agnes is my daughter, yet she threatened to end our whole family in the interrogation room. She murdered six guards right in front of us. What sort of a person has she become to kill others and threaten to kill her own family? Thank the Goddess that at least now her mind conqueror gifting has been eliminated thanks to my father's sacrifice.

'After all this time processing through my thoughts, I am still no closer to knowing what to do.' Releasing a heavy sigh, The Queen turned her horse back towards the castle and began to make her way to the stables. *'It's going to be an awfully long day,'* Amealiana sadly thought to herself.

As Ebony trotted into the stable, the stable hands all bowed in respect for their Queen. One of the young gentlemen came to the Queen's aid to assist her down from her beloved horse.

"Thank you, young man," the Queen softly spoke, lacking the energy to mask her feelings with her usual regal persona.

"My pleasure, Your Majesty. If I may be so bold, I wanted to say how sorry we all are to hear of King Julian's passing," the stable hand replied, releasing her hand as she landed gracefully on the ground.

The Queen nodded her head in thanks for his kind words. Wanting to delay her inevitable return to reality just a little longer, Queen Amealiana brushed Ebony's mane and fed her a handful of grain as a treat.

After thanking the stable hand for tending to her horse, Queen Amealiana took a deep breath to calm herself, and began walking up the cobblestone steps towards the family's private castle entrance.

36

Princess Annalyse

Annalyse strolled contently through the castle gardens, in awe of the white winter wonder land. It was the first time Annie had ever seen snow, and the sight of it falling softly from the sky was mesmerizing.

Annie had piled on layer after layer of coats and scarves, unsure of what to wear in the snow. As soon as she had awoken to the sight of the fresh blanket of powder on the windowsill, she couldn't get dressed and outside quick enough.

For the first time, the Princess noted the black mourning banners hanging outside in stark contrast to the picturesque scenery and her heart sank at the thought of her grandfather's passing.

The brief joyful moment spent enjoying the serenity of the snow-covered gardens was overshadowed once more by her grief.

As per Quillencian tradition, King Julian's body would be cleansed in the burning ceremony tomorrow morning at sunrise; on the second day after his passing. His remaining soul would be free then to pass from this world into the next. Annie hoped that her grandmother would arrive in time for the farewell ceremony. She had no doubt that her grandmother, Queen Annalyse, had foreseen her husband's tragic passing.

It would explain why she was so emotional when she was farewelling her husband, A blessing and a curse; that's how both Queen Amealiana and Queen Annalyse described their prophetic giftings. What torture and internal turmoil their giftings must bring them.

For my grandmother to foresee her own husband's passing and know that his sacrifice was his own decision to make, must have been so emotionally traumatic,' Annie thought solemnly to herself.

The Princess hoped that wherever Queen Annalyse was on her journey to Alearia, that her sage gifting brought her peace and understanding.

It feels so cruel to have only recently connected with my grandfather before unfairly having him taken away from me. Why does everyone I get close to pass away? Is it worth the risk to allow myself to form any sort of close connection with my family? What if the next person I get close to passes on to the After World.

Please, Goddess, let there be no more death,' Annie beseeched the Goddess.

"Excuse me, Princess Annalyse," a guard unexpectedly interrupted Annie from her thoughts.

Annie turned around startled to see a guard bowing behind her, standing on the freshly cleared cobblestone garden path.

"Yes, Sir. How might I help you? Are you unwell, do you need a healer?" Annie asked.

The guard stood up straight quizzically. "Pardon me, Lady, you are Princess Annalyse, are you not?" The guard asked again.

"Yes, I am. How can I help you?" Annalyse asked equally confused.

The guard smiled warmly, "I am sorry to interrupt your walk, Princess. It is I who is here to help you. The King advised that I am to be your personal escort around the castle grounds as the castle is still officially in lockdown. My name is Sean, Princess," the guard introduced himself, bowing his head again in respect.

A little stunned at the apparent need for a glorified babysitter, Annie replied graciously: "Thank you, Sean, that is exceedingly kind but unnecessary I assure you. I am perfectly capable of exploring the grounds on my own thank you."

"I am sorry Princess, but I must follow my orders," Sean regretfully replied.

"Very well then..." Annie replied uneasily. "Would you possibly grant me two little consolations then please?" Annie requested.

"Yes, Your Highness. Anything I can do for you would be an honor," the guard replied.

Annie smiled warmly, "Please call me Annie. Not Princess, just Annie. I am an apprentice healer; I do not feel like a princess who needs a guard. I do need a friend though. Would you be my friend Sean, and call me Annie?"

The guard's eyes bulged; a look of astonishment crossed his face at her request.

"My Lady, that would not be proper, but if it would please you, when we are alone, I will address you informally. I would very much like to be your friend as well Annie," The guard replied warmly.

"Very well Sean, we have met a compromise. Now friend, what is next on the schedule you have no doubt been given as well as my guard duty?" Annie joked warmly.

"Princess, I mean, Annie. Sorry, my Lady. Your presence has been requested to meet with the royal family in the infirmary," Sean finished.

Annie's heart began to race. It would be the first time she would see her family since the interrogation. The previous day's events had not exactly been the civil family introduction she had been hoping for.

After inhaling and exhaling deeply, Annie replied: "Very well, lead the way please Sean."

"Certainly, Annie," Sean bowed his head shallowly, before leading Annie back towards the castle.

Annie entered the Royal family's infirmary suite, while Sean remained outside for the meeting. Chairs had been brought in, to surround the single bed in the center of the room where Princess Anastasia lay.

The King and Queen were sitting on one side of the bed, Alecia on the other, and a spare seat waited for Annie next to her sister. Princess Agnes was noticeably excluded from the gathering.

"Good morning Queen Amealiana and King Titian," Annie greeted her parents with a bow upon entering the room.

Princess Alecia stared at her distastefully as she resumed her seat in the empty chair beside her. Annie, who had plenty of experience with people just like her in Lavender Grove, ignored her sister's sneer, depriving her of the pleasure she would gain from making her appear uncomfortable.

"Good morning Annalyse, and thank you for coming so promptly," the King spoke kindly but authoritatively. "I have called this meeting here due to Anastasia's ill health. I have had enough of watching my family suffer. The Crowning Ceremony will be upon us shortly and a time that should be joyful for our Kingdom has instead been marred by death and ill health. We must restore peace and prosperity to Alearia. In order to do that, we must make some difficult decisions for the betterment of our family and Kingdom."

"I couldn't agree more my love," Queen Amealiana added, taking his hand affectionately in her own. "This past year has been difficult for us all. We have all lost people dear to us. Titian, we have lost our son. No parent should ever have to go through that pain. We have all lost people we care about, and we are all facing our own struggles. Alecia, I can't imagine how you must be feeling without your gifting. Annie, your life has literally been turned around recently, what a whirlwind of emotions you must be going through. How do we move forward from this?" The Queen asked her husband earnestly as tears welled in her eyes.

The family turned their attention from the Queen to the King expectantly. Anastasia even managed to blearily open her eyes, to look up towards her father in hope.

The King turned toward Annie. "Annalyse, is it true that you are a mind conqueror capable of healing our people?" The King asked simply.

Annie was a little startled by the turn in conversation but strangely felt elated by the link the King had made between her gifting and healing.

"King Titian, it is true," Annie began to explain. "I am an apprentice healer, but I am also a sage and mind conqueror. King Julian, bless his soul, was teaching me how to wield my gifting before he passed away. Thankfully, he was able teach me how to heal the connections in people's minds between their giftings."

That was where the good news ended and so Annie found herself squirming in her chair and looking at her feet as she continued.

"Agnes succumbed to the dark side of her gifting because she used it recklessly. I am confident that my sage gifting will protect me from being drawn to the dark side of my power, but all magic has a cost. I cannot heal people's minds without facing the consequences. I don't know what my cost will be, but to help those in need, I will gladly pay whatever the price is. It is what any healer would do," Annie declared bravely.

The King sat more upright in his chair, his face contemplative as he considered her words carefully.

"Thank you, Annalyse, that is very brave of you and the people will thank you. Of course, we must not rush into this; people can live without their giftings, but you cannot live without your mind. We must weigh the cost and benefit diplomatically. Annie, please forgive me, given what you have just revealed, I am sorry to ask you, but is there any way you can reunite Alecia with her stolen gifting? Or will Agnes retain it from now on?" He asked hesitantly.

Annie pondered his question for a moment before replying.

"Forgive me, Your Majesty, but I don't know if it is possible, though King Julian seemed to believe it was. Healing people's connections with their gifting is like healing magic, therefore it is easier for me to understand its process and adapt my mind conqueror gifting to suit that purpose. As Agnes is no longer able to return what she has stolen, I would have to steal the fire bringer gifting from her, which I do not know how to do, and then theoretically transfer it from myself back to Alecia. Just healing one person's connection to their gifting will be exhausting. I will require overnight rest between mind conqueror sessions in order to heal each of the townspeople. It could take me a while to determine how to abstract Alecia's gifting from Agnes, and if she is unwilling to part with it, it will be even harder as her mental barriers will be in place. All I can do is try best," Princess Annalyse promised.

"Thank you," Alecia whispered sincerely.

Annie looked at her sister in surprise and then with empathy. "That's okay, Alecia. You are my family and you need my help, just like everyone else who has been separated from their gifts. I promise I will try my best to help you. I hope that I can, I really do." Annie turned to look at each of her family one at a time.

"Up until recently, I was an apprentice healer living in a little village. I have never truly been accepted by anyone else other than my mentor Lily, and I miss her. After I met you Queen Amealiana,

I felt like I finally belonged. Discovering my mind conqueror gifting was a blessing and a surprise. I learned so much from King Julian in such a short time. Now that he has passed, I am the only living mind conqueror alive and with that comes great responsibility. I will carry on my grandfather's work. I will heal you, Alecia. I will find a way. Cost or not, I will also heal all the Kingdom's people — it is my duty and calling. I will not let our people, or you, Alecia, down," Annie vowed to her sister, her family, and her Kingdom.

Annie would help her people no matter the cost.

Alecia offered her sister a small smile in appreciation.

"Annalyse, you level of maturity is beyond your years. You remind me of your mother," he spoke warmly.

Annie felt her heart flutter a little at the compliment.

"I am glad I have finally had the pleasure of meeting you," The King continued. "Let us first start with helping Alecia, and then afterward you can help the Kingdom, one person at a time. However, if your health suffers from using your gifting, you must stop. The cost to you is not worth the reward to others. Thank you, Annalyse," King Titian concluded.

Turning to look at each of his family in the eye, he took a deep breath, preparing himself for what was next to come.

"After Alecia is healed, Agnes must face the consequences of her actions. She will not get away with the crimes she has committed against our family and our Kingdom. Considering Agnes's discovery, the Kingdom will no longer be under lockdown. To avoid uproar amongst the people, I will make a public announcement that the cause of the magical disease has been discovered and the threat eliminated. It pains me to say this, but I feel it is a likely assumption that Agnes had a part to play in the death of Prince Alexander," King Titian declared.

The whole room seemed to stop in shock. It had not occurred to Annie that the Prince's death could be linked to Agnes.

Annie felt her heart race, along with her anxiety. Being a mind-conqueror made her just as big of a threat to her kingdom as Agnes. She worried that she would lose control and harm someone. With little training, she worried that she was making promises regarding healing her sister and the other's that she couldn't keep.

The King interrupted Annie's thoughts. "We will need proof of this, of course, we cannot accuse her of murder and treason of her own kin without proof. I will need you, Annalyse to find the proof I need so I may act," The King ordered his daughter.

Annie sat there in shock, trembling as she became overwhelmed by the potentially horrific consequences of her gift. Speech suddenly felt impossible and she found herself nodding in reluctant agreement.

"My King, I must object!" The Queen declared. "Agnes would never harm her own brother; she loved him and mourned his loss just as we did."

Annie found herself processing everything that was going on around her. Suddenly the room felt too claustrophobic as Annie's sage wisdom awakened a realization in her. Taking a deep calming breath, Annie uneasily interrupted: "I agree with the King. I think Agnes killed Alexander."

All eyes turned towards Annalyse. The room felt electric. Annie took another deep breath, feeling the weight of her every word.

"It has never occurred to me that my mind conqueror gifting could be used for such evil purposes as death. Devastatingly, my sage gifting assures me it is possible and that thought terrifies me. When I was sifting through Agnes's brain, there was an uneasy aura around her mind. I could see her brain was wired similarly to my own, but under toning her every thought was a coating of essence that I cannot describe other than evil. Agnes's mind was consumed by her power, she could have been capable of anything, just as sadly, I could be as well," Annie softly spoke, trailing off in disbelief.

Alecia, to Annie's surprise, reached over to Annie and took her by the hand. "You are not like her Annalyse. You wouldn't be offering to sacrifice your own wellbeing to help myself or anyone else if your mind had been tainted by evil intentions. My sister Agnes and I have never got on, to put it mildly."

Anastasia choked on a small laugh at that comment, to which Alecia sarcastically rolled her eyes, however, she continued.

"Inside the crypt," Alecia hesitantly voiced, "I had a dream that Agnes was taunting me. Only, she wasn't my sister anymore. She was possessed by something. It must have been her mind conqueror gifting taking over, destroying her humanity. I barely know you and I am not a sage, but my instincts are usually right about most people. As much as I try to dislike you for being an impostor to our family, I can't. You are good. I can see that," Alecia said warmly, squeezing Annie's hand gently in reassurance.

Taken aback and humbled by Alecia's sudden change of heart, Annie returned a smile. "Thank you."

The King rose from his chair decisively.

"Annalyse, would you feel comfortable analyzing Agnes's brain again to find proof of her treason?" The King asked.

Queen Amealiana spoke gently, reaching for her husbands' hand.

"I beg your pardon husband, but considering the large task ahead of Annie in healing Alecia and the town, might it be appropriate for you and I to interrogate Agnes ourselves? My sage gifting will tell me if she is lying or telling the truth. Then when we know for sure and we can decide upon the appropriate action to take afterwards," the Queen suggested calmly.

"Very well. The Queen and I will go now to see Agnes. Alecia and Annalyse, you are both welcome to stay with Anastasia. I can see the color is starting to return to her cheeks and I am sure she would appreciate the company," the King stated, taking the Queen's hand as the two of them exited through the infirmary door.

37

Princess Agnes

The dungeon quarantine room was cold, damp and eerily quiet. After Agnes had awoken in the interrogation room the previous day, the healers had deemed the Princess physically fit enough to be transferred into seclusion. There Agnes had remained, within the cramped, windowless, single cot filled quarantine room in the palace dungeons. Also packed into the cramped confines was a wash basin, a lit lantern secured in a cage to the wall and a bucket to use as a privy.

Due to Agnes's royal status, she was afforded the privacy and minimal comforts that the quarantine room offered, compared with a barred, open plan, straw bed cell.

Typically, all people in the kingdom of Alearia were considered innocent until proven guilty. However, Agnes's violent incineration of six guards in the presence of the King and Queen instantly deemed the potential Heir guilty of murder and treason. Now Agnes had no choice but to await her fate.

'Surely they wouldn't order their own daughter to be executed? If I were anyone else though, I would be on my way to the stocks by now or a stage to be hung. My body left out for the crows to peck at, deemed unfit for burial.

'How my life has changed in the last year. I was always jealous of my siblings. I have always had my eye on the crown, but I was never as power hungry as I am now, until I discovered my mind conqueror gifting.

'Alexander's passing was an accident, but mistakes happen. Yesterday, I did what I needed to do to look after myself. I was backed into a corner with no way out. I didn't realize how much my gift and I had assimilated into one powerful, fearless being. Who needs self-control?

'I rather enjoyed holding Alecia's life in the palm of my hand in the crypt. I should have ended her life as soon as I stole her gifting, while I still had the chance. That spoiled brat had it coming, and I still possess her fire wielding gift. That sister of mine will be driven mad without her precious fire wielding gifting to lean upon.

'I guess that's why I am still alive. They must believe they can restore Alecia's gifting to her... Well, that gives me a card to play, doesn't it?!

'I will never be Queen now though, just a nameless nobody living in a dungeon on borrowed time. All my planning, all my scheming, was for nothing. Ruined by my own grandfather who ironically then decided to sacrifice himself to take away my mind conqueror gifting. If he kept his filthy mouth shut, we could have both been alive, free and powerful. We could have ruled both kingdoms as mind conquerors.

'I'm not even the slightest bit remorseful for killing those bloody guards or stealing Alecia's gifting. I never thought I was capable of intentional murder, but I did it without a second thought and I don't even regret it. I would do it again in a heartbeat now that I realize how easy it is. A simple matter of a thought, and all barriers before me can be erased. Grandfather wasted his soul to try and save Alecia's precious gifting and my life. There is nothing left of me worth saving. If only the bloody water mage guard would remove these water restraints from my hands so I could use my fire wielding powers and break out of this place,' Agnes angrily thought.

A knock came at the quarantine room door.

'A strange notion, to knock on a prisoner's door, pretending they have any option of refusing their entry,' Agnes pondered from her cot, not even bothering to acknowledge the door knock or sit up. With a click of the outside locks and a turn of the handle, the heavy iron door groaned as it was pushed open for the King and Queen to enter accompanied by four water mage guards.

"Ha!" Agnes mocked, "I can see you have learned your lesson from last time, though do not fear, until I figure out how to break out of these water gloves, I can't wield my powers. But I'll figure it out soon, don't worry," Agnes mocked. "Or are you here to carry out my sentence? Is this how you will do it? Drown me from the inside out? Come on father, you can be more inventive than that. Tell me, when do you plan to kill off your own flesh and blood? Probably as soon as possible I'll wager. Make a spectacle of my death in front of the kingdom!" Agnes cackled from her bed, not even looking in her parents' direction as she spoke.

The room was barely big enough for the furniture, let alone the seven people now crowded inside.

"Silence Agnes, I have had quite enough of your rubbish. Guards - bring her to the interrogation room," the King ordered.

With a final sneer towards his daughter, the King turned and led the Queen abruptly from the room.

In unison, the water mages flung their giftings out towards Agnes and wrapped her in a sphere of ever-moving water. Rolling the sphere of water encasing her down the hallway, the guards transported the Princess into the interrogation room.

Upon the interrogation chair, the mages forced their prisoner, her arms chained behind the back of the seat. The guards then morphed the sphere into a thick impenetrable wall of water surrounding her.

The King and Queen sat poised in thrones that had been transported from the room upstairs. Before them was a desk, and Agnes sat opposite, surrounded by a cylindrical wall of water. The water mages moved to either side of the protective water barrier to maintain its structural integrity.

The elderly Matriarch, the Queen of Quillencia walked gracefully into the room, and ignored the Princess entirely as though she were a speck of dirt beneath her shoe. Agnes was sure she had come to see justice served. An additional chair was brought into the room and Queen Annalyse Caston sat to the right of her daughter; Queen Amealiana Brandistone.

"What an unpleasant surprise this is," Agnes sneered. "Come to relish in my sentencing have you, grandmother? Of course, you know that your darling husband gave up his life for me. What a waste that was since we both know what happens to murderers here," Agnes taunted the Queen of Quillencia.

"I bet he thought taking away my mind conqueror gifting would save my soul and make me good. But… I am who I am, and no self-sacrificing rubbish is going to change that. Though I suspect he truly saved me because he wanted Alecia's gifting restored to her. It's always all about precious Alecia, the predicted future Queen," Agnes smirked.

The royals simmered in their seats, fuming at the horrible excuse for kin that sat before them.

"Of course, he was right to take away my gifting," Agnes mused. "If he didn't, as soon as I would have regained consciousness, I would have wreaked havoc on all of your minds. I would have killed you all off, one after the other, until naturally I was the only one left of our bloodline and then I would be Queen."

"Why did you do all this Agnes?" Queen Amealiana asked, brow furrowed, a mixture of concern and disbelief etched across her face. "What did you think you would gain from any of it? Why now do you only wish death upon us? Do you not realize how much I still love you, despite all you have done?" Amealiana pleaded.

"Oh Mother, don't you see, it was always about the crown. *'Ungifted'* or not, I was always determined to be Queen, and nothing was going to get in my way. So, when I realized what I truly was, I wasn't going to waste the opportunity. It was just a matter of eliminating my competition, one sibling or family member at a time," Agnes smirked, no trace of remorse or humanity in her face.

"It's true then," Queen Amealiana gasped. "You killed my son!"

"Alexander's death was an accident, I admit. He was my first experiment. I only meant to sever his gifting, but I got a little carried away and couldn't help myself. Holding a life in the balance of your hands is so devilishly seductive. Who could resist? His death made me one step closer to becoming Queen," Agnes mocked.

The King rose from his chair, fists clenched and bellowed, "Agnes, you will pay for this treason! There is no way you will ever compete for the crown! Alexander was my only son! You are beyond redemption, beyond love, and beyond my mercy. Executing you now would be a gift, and you do not deserve such kindness yet. You will be executed one day, but until then you will rot in the darkest, dingiest cell until Alecia's gifting is restored to her. That will be the last opportunity you have to redeem any part of your soul. Mark my words though, if your sister does not get her gifting back, you will wish I had granted you the mercy of sending you to the After World today."

Queen Amealiana and Queen Annalyse sat in shock, staring at Agnes who cockily smirked in return, realizing that the King had just confirmed the remaining card she still had left to play.

"You need me alive to restore Alecia's gifting. What incentive could I possibly have to give it back if it only means an earlier death? The game is not over yet King. You think you have won, but it is I who holds the cards now," Agnes declared.

Queen Amealiana

Queen Amealiana stared at her daughter in disbelief. The coldness in Agnes's eyes sent a chill down to her very core. This was not her daughter. Whoever sat in front of her was beyond help and reason.

"Where did I go wrong as a mother, for you to turn into this empty, cold-hearted shell?" Queen Amealiana spoke mournfully. "I do not forgive you for Alexander's death. All your life I have stood by your side. I loved you. I didn't think you were capable of evil, but I was wrong. I will not let my father's death be in vain. I thought that King Julian saw some part of you worth saving, but he just didn't want the madness to completely overtake you. Because becoming a complete power-hungry monster, killing your own family and leaving yourself completely isolated, would be '*a fate worse than death.*' I see that now. My sage gifting confirms it. He didn't really sacrifice himself to save you, no, not really, he sacrificed himself for Alecia and to protect our family and people from you by eliminating the immediate threat you had become. I have lost too many loved ones already, and I will not lose the rest of my family because of you," Queen Amealiana Brandistone spoke softly but forebodingly, tears flowing from her eyes.

Queen Annalyse Caston of Quillencia stared into her granddaughter's eyes, before taking a deep breath.

"Agnes..." Queen Annalyse spoke sorrowfully, "in the last day I have lost the love of my life, and my kingdom has lost their King. I have been married to a mind conqueror for many years and in that time, there have been struggles. I am sorry you had no one to guide you through your gifting. Magic always has a price and I am sorry that you have paid for it dearly with the loss of your humanity. My heart is broken. I don't know how to move on from losing my husband, but with my family's support, I know I will get through it. For the good of my kingdom, I must heal. It is what my husband would have wanted. King Julian loved his kingdom like he loves his family. He was an honorable, generous man, right until his last breath. Please honor my husband's sacrifice and do the right thing. Allow Alecia's gifting to be restored to her. For my own wellbeing, so that I can begin my journey of healing, I choose to forgive you for all you have done, but I never want to see you again. May the Goddess look mercifully upon your soul when the time comes for you to meet your end. Goodbye," Queen Annalyse Caston concluded.

The Quillencian Royal stood silently, head held high, took a deep breath and gracefully walked out of the room without looking back. Queen Amealiana took her lead, gave her husband a parting embrace and exited the room silently.

'Goddess have mercy on Agnes's soul.'

38

Princess Annalyse

The sun was rising over the snow-covered peaks of Alearia; the horizon bathed in rich purples and oranges. A funeral pyre stood in the royal family's private gardens. Only the immediate Alearian royal family, Queen Annalyse of Quillencia, her son Prince Joshua, and their party of guards, were permitted to attend the burning ceremony. Agnes remained locked up in the castle dungeon under water mage guard.

The Alearian royals had forgone their traditional black gowns, in respect for the Quillencian tradition of wearing colorful attire to reflect the joy of their loved one's life, foregoing mourning veils altogether. In the privacy of such a small group and without the pageantry of a formal ceremony in front of the kingdom's people, the Royals were free to openly grieve. A rare occurrence, Annie was sure, for the Alearians to allow themselves the freedom to experience.

King Titian, Prince Joshua of Quillencia, and two of the Quillencian guards carried King Julian in an ornately carved, open wooden casket to the top of the pyre. Queen Annalyse kneeled beside her husband on the pyre alter and privately said her goodbyes before kissing him reverently one last time upon his lips. Queen Amealiana joined her and said her own farewells. Finally, the Heir of Quillencia, Prince Joshua, stood solemnly next their father, tears welling in his eyes.

Queen Annalyse leaned over her husband's body and gently removed the crown from his head, The Quillencian Prince dropped to his knees as the Queen gently laid her husband's crown upon her son's brow.

"You will make the kingdom of Quillencia proud as our future King, my son. Your father was truly proud of the man you have become. You will make a wise and just ruler," Queen Annalyse spoke fondly.

"Thank you, your Majesty. I will always strive to be the great leader my father was," the Quillencian Heir replied, before bowing his head to his mother and descending the pyre.

Queen Amealiana went to re-join her family at the base of the pyre. Princess Annalyse stood beside her mother and took her hand gently in support. Tears fell softly down their cheeks. Princess

Anastasia and Alecia held each other's hands in solidarity, as they grieved in their own ways.

King Titian stood on the other side of his wife and held her other hand, standing strong; being the rock his wife needed him to be in that moment. A strong leader, a husband, a father and a King, to guide their family and kingdoms through their grief.

As Princess Annalyse watched her grandmother say her final goodbyes to the love of her life. Annie wondered how the Queen remained so strong in the face of such despair and devastation.

Annie left her mother's side and climbed the pyre steps to take her grandmother's hand as she farewelled her grandfather.

"Thank you, grandfather, for all you have done for me in the short time we have had together. I wish we had longer together. but the love we shared will remain in my heart for a lifetime. Please give Lily a hug for me in the After World. I know you will care for each other. Please watch over me and guide me through my gifting. Help me to be the wise mind conqueror you were. I love you, King Julian. I always will," Annie spoke sincerely.

Annie turned to look into her grandmother's eyes, still holding her hand, and spoke from her heart. "Grandfather loved you with all his heart. I am so sorry for your loss. King Julian is in the After World now, and his soul is free forevermore. He would want us to go on, live our lives to the fullest and carry on his work, which is just what I intend to do to honor Lily and grandfather's memories."

Queen Annalyse gave a small smile and nod of thanks to her granddaughter before Annie left the pyre to re-join her mother.

Queen Annalyse turned towards her family to deliver the King's eulogy. "Thank you all for being here to support me. Thank you for your loyalty to my husband, my King. Our Quillencian King was an exceptional man. He dedicated his life faithfully to serving his kingdom and family. King Julian prided himself on never leaving anyone behind. It was his strong values and love for his people that formed the foundations of our mighty kingdom. No-one was ever without a meal or shelter during his reign. An outstanding legacy for any ruler to leave behind and a legacy that my son and I will carry on in his memory. Generosity, loyalty, strength, kindness, and compassion were the pillars on which he built his Kingdom. We will always remember you my husband, my King, my love," her final words spoken quietly but proudly.

Queen Annalyse turned to give her husband one last kiss on his forehead before leaving the pyre altar. High Priestess Elizabeth led the family and guards in prayers to the Goddess for blessing of the King's soul. They prayed for the cleansing of all his past sins so that their beloved King would be free; blessed with eternal peace.

With a nod of affirmation from the Quillencian Queen to King Titian and Princess Anastasia, the two royals took their places at opposite ends of the pyre and released their cleansing fire upon the altar.

King Julian's remaining body and soul dispersed into the endless peace of the After World. His soul now free, forevermore.

39

Princess Anastasia

The time for mourning was over, and the Brandistone red and gold house colors were once again fluttering around the castle; the mourning black banners packed away. With the winter solstice and Crowning Ceremonies fast approaching, the Quillencian Queen had elected to stay on in Castle Brandistone for the festivities. Her son, the Quillencian Heir; Prince Joshua, had left following the burning ceremony to return home, adopting the title of Acting King Regent, to lead their kingdom in the Queen's absence.

Over family breakfast, the King had requested, given the impending Crowning Ceremonies, that Annalyse attempt to reunite Alecia with her gifting as soon as she felt able. Princess Anastasia pitied her long-lost twin. She couldn't help but feel that rather than embracing Annie as a member of their family, they were instead using her for their own personal gain. A mind conqueror puppet to wield as they needed.

Anastasia had not felt brave enough to approach Annie before today. However, given the heartache she had suffered in the past year, Tash felt that the time had come for her to reach out to her new sister and welcome a little happiness back into her heart. Just after breakfast, Anastasia dressed in her training clothes and approached her twin's bedroom, knocking gently on her suite door.

A moment later Annalyse opened the door herself, much to Anastasia's surprise, who was used to relying on her Lady's Maid for such things. Anastasia noted Annie had also changed into new clothes after breakfast, and was wearing a comfortable loose-fitting dress, holding open a book that she must have been reading before she had interrupted her.

"Good morning Anastasia," Princess Annalyse, welcomed her warmly. "Is there anything I can do for you? Please excuse my attire, I was just trying to make myself more comfortable and relax before attempting to help Alecia this afternoon."

Anastasia found herself smiling at her sister's calm and casual nature.

"Good morning Annalyse, or do you prefer to be called Annie? I am sorry for the intrusion. May I come in? I thought it might be nice to get to know each other a little. That is, if you don't mind?" Anastasia asked shyly.

"Of course! Come in, and please call me Annie! I have been hoping we would have a chance to catch up. Excuse the mess," Annie said, holding open the door for Anastasia to come in, and directing her towards the two wing-backed velvet chairs by the toasty hearth.

All around the room were piles upon piles of books, from romance fiction to reference texts on magical history, Anastasia observed.

'Annalyse clearly has a love for reading, I wonder why she doesn't just read in the library...' Anastasia thought to herself as she sat in the seat closet to the burning fireplace.

"Would you like some tea and sweets?" Annalyse offered her sister.

"Thank you, that would be lovely. Would you like me to ask your Lady's Maid to prepare some?" Anastasia offered.

Annalyse smiled sweetly at her sister. "There's no need; I went down to the kitchen overnight and baked some cookies. I have been having trouble sleeping, you see, and the routine of baking helps to relax me. Fortunately, I have just made a fresh pot of chamomile tea we can share," Annie indicated to the pot on the side table.

Annie ambled over to the small wooden cabinet in the sitting room and collected a second cup and saucer, as well as two side plates and the jar of freshly baked apple and cinnamon cookies, before setting them gently upon a hand-sewn tablecloth on the table.

"The tablecloth was hand made by my mentor, Lilianna. She was like a mother to me and raised me in the little town of Lavender Grove in Quillencia," Annalyse offered, whilst taking her seat opposite Anastasia.

"In our little white cottage by the river where I grew up, Lily and I would sit side by side in chairs like these in front of the hearth at night. It was our little reward after a full day of apothecary work. I would usually read a book, and Lily would either read or knit beside me. I miss those nights with her," Annalyse shared, a silent tear falling from her eye. "Sorry for being all sentimental. You probably don't want to hear any of that. Tell me about you?" Annalyse quickly changed the subject.

Anastasia was warmed by Annalyse's honesty and sincerity.

"I would actually like to hear more about where you grew up, Annie, if you don't mind. You see, all my life, I have felt like something was missing, and I never realized how true that was. All this time I have had a twin and I feel like I know very little about you. Please tell me as much of your story as you feel comfortable," Anastasia asked sincerely, leaning forward and resting her elbows on her knees, and planting her chin on folded hands, eagerly ready to listen.

Annalyse smiled in return and folded her legs beneath her on the chair, pulling a blanket over her lap and taking a sip of her tea before sharing.

"As I said, I was raised in Lavender Grove by my mentor Lily. Lady Lilianna was training me as an apprentice apothecary healer. Lavender Grove, where I grew up, is a small rural village along the outskirts of Quillencia, and our town was surrounded by forest and a small river flowed behind our house into a bigger river channel. Lily and I, in our rare moments of free time, would walk along the river, admiring the wildflowers and picnicking by its edge. Last year for my birthday, Lily and I went for a picnic at sunset and went ice-skating. It was our favorite thing to do together in winter, despite the cold weather," Annie recalled fondly.

After taking a small nibble of one of her cookies, Annie continued her story. The smell of the freshly baked cookies filled the air with a delicious aroma.

"We had our own herb and vegetable garden behind our cottage, which we nurtured with the upmost care. Its herbs were vital for our potions, lotions and healing ointments," Annie informed her sister. "I would often spend hours assisting Lily with brewing and preparing such things. You never know when you might need something. Accidents and emergencies happen all the time and we had to always be ready to help at a moment's notice.

"I used to love helping Lily welcome the new babies into the world. You see, we helped everyone regardless of social status or wealth, through birth, illness, and death. Lily taught me that to be generous, kind and compassionate were the most important virtues.

"I didn't fit in amongst the people our age in town. They used to taunt me behind my back. I felt alone at times, but I always had Lily, whom I could depend upon. Lily was the most selfless person I have ever known," Annie paused her story becoming teary from the grief her memories were dredging to the surface.

Anastasia reached out a hand gently towards her sister, to softly squeeze her hand reassuringly. Annie smiled in appreciation, wiping her eyes with the sleeve of her dress.

"A few months ago," Annie continued timidly, "I was heading into the forest for some quiet time, but I ran into some trouble. I tried my best to get away, but a group of men cornered me in a cave and my only option was to either be caught or jump in the river. I drowned that day, so I have been told. The next thing I remember was waking up in my bedroom at the cottage. Lily had used the last of her healing life-force to bring me back to life and in turn, sacrificed her own life. I am forever in her debt," Annie trailed off, tears now steadily flowing from her eyes which she tried desperately to hide with no success.

"I am sorry for your loss Annie. I can't imagine how difficult her passing must be for you. I am sorry there is nothing I can do to take away your pain," Anastasia gently spoke.

Anastasia allowed Annie the time she needed to recollect herself, while she sipped on her tea and focused on the fire of the hearth, giving Annie a sense of privacy to grieve.

"Thank you, Anastasia," Annie replied after a few silent moments.

Taking a deep breath and masking a fake smile upon her face, Annie attempted to change the subject. "Please tell me about you. What was it like growing up with a castle full of siblings? I can't believe I have had a twin sister all this time."

"It's quite mind-blowing, isn't it? I'm still coming to terms with the idea of having a twin myself... Anyway, I was raised here my whole life as I am sure you have guessed. I have sadly never left the city. Mother was always very protective of us, growing up. I didn't understand why when I was younger but knowing everything that has come to pass in the last year, I realize she was right to be worried. Growing up, I always felt like I was missing a part of me... I just never knew it was you. Alecia helped to fill that hole. We have been inseparable for as long as I can remember. Well, at least we were until our brother's passing. Then everything changed. Alecia became more headstrong and competitive. She has always had a stronger gifting than me, though I have been slowly catching up the harder I train, but I have never been competitive in the way she is. I would like to be Queen, but if I don't, it's not the end of the world to me. I can still help our kingdom as a Princess. I care for our people," Anastasia explained warmly.

"I wish I had practical skills like you do for healing people though," Anastasia confessed. "Maybe you could teach me one day? If it wouldn't be an inconvenience that is. I want to make my mark on the world and help to bring about positive change. I want to be a role model who inspires our people. I want to be a mother one day too. I want to be a good sister to you, Alecia and Agnes. I have heard from father that Agnes will be sentenced to death after Alecia is reunited with her gifting. *'For the greater good of our people'*, he said... I know Agnes has fallen so far, but she is our sister. I want to help her in any way I can. No one deserves to be alone in their final days of life," Anastasia spoke truthfully from the heart.

"I completely agree," Annie spoke openly and honestly. "Thank you for sharing your story with me. You can be whoever you want to be; your only limit is your imagination. You are wise Anastasia, and if I didn't know better, I would think you were sage gifted, though perhaps you are in some way. Your heart is pure. I can tell you only want the best for your family and your people. Anastasia, you said you hoped you could learn the art of apothecary healing. Will you come with me this afternoon? Will you help me today, as I attempt to restore Alecia's gifting to her?" Annie asked humbly.

"I am not sure what help I could possibly be, but I will support you in any way I can, Annie. I would also like to be there for Agnes, whether she still cares for us or not," Anastasia promised, leaning over the table to hold Annie's hand in her own.

"Do you mind if I come and visit you more often?" Anastasia meekly requested. "I would very much like for us to become true twin sisters, not just in blood but in bond. To help each other, support each other and walk through life together. If you want to, that is?" Anastasia asked hopefully, her heart pounding a million miles an hour. Anxiety coursed through her whole being as she wholeheartedly hoped her sister felt the same way.

"I would love that Tash," Annie said with a broad grin.

"Really?! I am so happy you feel the same way!" Anastasia beamed with joy.

The two sisters leaned across the table and embraced in the first hug they had shared since birth. Two sisters reunited and destined to be lifelong friends.

40

Princess Annalyse

In the private family garden, in the fading light of the afternoon, Princesses Annalyse and Anastasia sat side by side on a bench by the water fountain; both wrapped in warm winter coats and fur-lined knee-high boots. The water fountain had been turned off for the winter and only a shimmering pool of ice remained. The snow-covered garden looked like something out of a fairy tale, with the picturesque Alearian castle in the background.

Annie had felt that a less clinical and condemning environment might aid the process of returning Alecia's gifting. In order to maintain a calm and peaceful atmosphere, Annie had requested that Alecia and the other royals remain inside, to avoid enraging Agnes any further. Annie hoped that if she talked peacefully with Agnes, and with Anastasia's support, Agnes might see reason and be more willing to let down her mental barriers, making her task easier.

Anastasia was radiating anxiety, her body slightly trembling. Annie whispered a reassuring word of encouragement in her sister's ear and after a few deep breaths, she was much calmer, praise the Goddess.

The wind was starting to pick up, flowing through the gardens, making the already cold afternoon almost unbearable. It was one of the downfalls of living in the alpine kingdom, Annie had discovered, though the clean crisp air of the mountains also felt strangely exhilarating.

In the distance, Annie could hear the group of guards escorting Agnes, approaching through the hedge maze. Anastasia stiffened but Annie just gave her hand a reassuring squeeze, and her twin composed herself. An art all Alearian royals were taught at a young age, Annie was sure.

A short while later, Annie and her sister beheld Agnes walking towards them, guarded by no less than ten water mages. Water restraints binding Agnes's hands prevented her from releasing her stolen powers.

'*So much for subtle, calm and understated,*' Annie thought to herself as she eyed her rogue sister's entourage of guards.

Annie and Anastasia rose from their seats to greet their sister. Anastasia, as Annie had requested, took the lead.

"Good afternoon Agnes. I am sorry we are not meeting under better circumstances. I would like to formally introduce you to our sister, my twin, Princess Annalyse, though she prefers Annie," Anastasia reported to Agnes.

Annie offered Agnes a warm smile. "Pleased to meet you, Agnes." Annie turned to face the guard in charge. "Sir, I will require a chair for my sister Agnes, if you would be so kind. I would also like all but two of your most gifted water mages to stand down and move to the perimeter of the gardens. We will be perfectly safe, I assure you. Agnes won't hurt us," Princess Annalyse requested with Queenly authority.

The guards obeyed reluctantly, leaving only the head guard and his second in command behind. The two guards adopted positions on either side of Agnes; arms at the ready, prepared to drown the traitorous Princess with the full might of their giftings, should she pose a threat.

Agnes chocked on laughter, "*'Agnes, won't hurt us... Stand down...'* Ha! What an overconfident little witch you are Annalyse. Welcome to the family!" Agnes mocked. "I can see you have made yourself at home."

Turning her attention towards Anastasia, Agnes inquired sarcastically: "Do tell, Anastasia, where did this so-called long-lost sister come from? Wait a minute, don't tell me, I don't actually care in the slightest!" Agnes cackled, before returning her attention back to Annalyse.

"Are you a fire-wielding witch too or are you as un-gifted as I once was?" Agnes mocked.

Annie remained calm, not letting Agnes get to her in the slightest. Anastasia followed suit, leaving Agnes to awkwardly stand while awaiting the arrival of a chair.

"Agnes please, just hear us out. Please stop fighting us, as it will achieve nothing," Anastasia wisely spoke.

"Oh, certainly dear sister. But why have you both arrogantly summoned me out into the freezing cold? Plan on burning me alive? Oh wait... no, that won't work on me anymore, not while I control Alecia's gifting. Though it's not actually Alecia's' gifting anymore, it's all mine," Agnes sneered.

I was hoping I could reason with her. Do this the easy way. If Agnes doesn't see reason soon, I will have no choice but to take control of the situation,' Annie mused to herself.

Annie silently called upon the Goddess to guide the conversation.

"Agnes, I know you don't know me, but I would appreciate the chance to get to know you. I am sage gifted. I was training to be an apothecary up until recently when my mentor sadly passed away and I took on her full duties in her absence. Queen Amealiana has kindly arranged for a replacement healer to serve my village in my absence. I may be able to help both you and Alecia. I would like to try if you would be willing to allow me," Annie requested.

"How in the Goddesses' name are you going to help me?! As soon as Alecia gets her precious gifting back, if she ever gets it back, the King will dispose of me. He said so himself! Though, the chances of Alecia getting her gifting back are highly unlikely since there are no longer any living mind conquerors to complete the task. So, I guess I will make myself as comfortable in the dungeons as I like, because the way I see it, I'm not going anywhere for now," Agnes said with a smirk.

"Now is probably the time to tell you, that I am a mind conqueror. Though I have sworn to only use my gifting for honorable purposes. I believe I may be able to help you and Alecia," Annie offered.

"Ha! Another mind conqueror! King Julian thought he was the only blessed one, but little did he know there were three of us. Of course, my gifting is gone now, stolen by the King himself. Sacrificial bastard! But I digress, back to you Annalyse. Honourable purposes? What rubbish! There is no such thing as a mind conqueror who doesn't use their own gifting to benefit themselves. How is stealing one gifting from one sister and giving it to another considered honorable," Agnes mocked.

"You are right. It is not fair of me to do that. Just as it was not fair of you to steal Alecia's gifting in the first place. It was never your power to begin with. But if you do cooperate, then Anastasia and I could tell the King and Queen how you willingly allowed me to return Alecia's gifting to her. Perhaps then, the King and Queen will take pity on you and allow you to live, though I can make no promises," Annalyse offered sadly.

Anastasia spoke sincerely from the heart, "please Agnes, you are my sister and despite all you have done, I don't want you to die. Let Annie give Alecia back her gifting. It is your only hope for any leniency from father."

"What do you think Agnes? Of course, I did say I would try to help you as well, so if I see a way to repair your mind, I will also attempt to do so. Do we have a deal?" Annie asked.

"Not a chance. I will not give up Alecia's gifting freely! Father will end me either way, so I don't need either of your sympathy or your so-called help. If I am going down, then so is Alecia's gifting," Agnes spat.

'For goodness sake, why won't she allow me to help her! It makes absolutely no sense. I guess we are going to have to do things the hard way...'

King Titian paced furiously around the infirmary room while a frazzled Queen Amealiana and Queen Annalyse sat proudly by Annie's bedside. Anastasia sat on the other side of Annie's bed. Alecia was off training her fire wielding gifting cockily once again in the training arena, her powers restored to her in full.

Annalyse's head pounded and her body ached; the world felt as it were spinning around her. Completely exhausted, Annie felt as if she had one foot in the After World and she wished that the King would leave the room and grant her some time to rest.

The news had not gone down well with the King about Agnes's refusal to cooperate. Agnes had needed to be restrained by the water mages in an orb of water, whilst Annie held her arm through the orb to maintain physical contact with Agnes and forcibly remove Alecia's gifting from her. The physical effort and use of her mind conqueror gifting to retrieve the fire-wielding gifting from Agnes and then return it to Alecia, had been incredibly draining on Annie.

The healers were deeply concerned about the life force Annie had exerted in using her gifting for such a complex task; unsure of the long-term physical consequences on the Princess from the excessive use of her power. Thankfully, her mental health remained intact.

"You almost killed yourself trying to restore Alecia's gifting to her! Why couldn't Agnes just cooperate for once in her life? She will pay soon for all she has done. She has disgraced herself yet again today when she was given an opportunity for redemption. Agnes is more monster than human!" The King roared.

Annie still to lift herself up in the bed to address the King but didn't have the energy.

"I am sorry my King," Annie croaked, laying down. "I did what I felt I needed to do for the betterment of our family. I did what you asked of me and reunited Alecia with her gifting. I also tried to heal Agnes's mind while I was in there, but she didn't want my help. Her subconscious fought me every step of the way. I can't bring her back to you, I am so deeply sorry. I thought I could help Agnes, but I either can't, or she just doesn't want me to."

The King snorted in reply, his fury at his eldest daughter clouding his judgment.

Queen Amealiana took Annie's hand and softly reassured her. "Just rest my darling. The King just needs time to process all that has occurred. We are so proud of what you have achieved today. Trying to help your sister, was extremely thoughtful of you. Thank you for trying. King Julian was right, your sage wisdom balances out your mind conqueror gifting beautifully. For now, you must rest and regain your strength."

"I couldn't agree more," Queen Annalyse Caston interjected. "Your grandfather would have been incredibly proud of you today, just as I am. You did all you could. You tried to reach out to Agnes, but she wouldn't see reason. You can't help someone who doesn't want to be helped."

Annie felt her heart swell with pride. All she had ever wanted was a know her birth family and to have their love and support.

The King stopped his pacing and looked at the four women in front of him inscrutably. "Queen Annalyse, I am sorry for your loss, I really am. But that girl killed my son, and her selfishness led to my newest daughter being hospitalized. You could have died today Annie! Agnes stole my daughter's gifting and took Alexander's life. All for her own selfish means. She didn't deserve your compassion today. Her actions today prove without a doubt that she has lost her humanity. After the Crowning Ceremony is over, Agnes will be executed for her crimes."

41

Queen Amealiana

The lead up to the twins' birthdays and the Crowning Ceremony flew by. An announcement had been made by King Titian the previous day, informing the people of Alearia of Agnes's past crimes and indiscretions. Her death sentence was formally announced, leaving the Queen with conflicting emotions and renewed feelings of grief.

Of the remaining potential Heirs, Alecia and Anastasia, trained harder than they had ever trained before, whilst Annie continued to recover her strength in the royal infirmary suite.

After Annie had fully recovered, Anastasia took it upon herself to give Annie daily combat lessons, reminding her twin that it would be beneficial to know how to defend herself in times of conflict. Alecia and Anastasia resumed meeting for their daily fire wielding training sessions, and their competitive natures made them push their giftings further than they had before. Their personal progress in training was astounding.

Queen Annalyse of Quillencia had taken it upon herself to train Annie daily in nurturing her sage gifting and listening to her Goddess-given inner voice. The youngest potential Heir practiced basic mind conqueror healing skills on voluntary patients brought into the castle from the hospital that could benefit from her unique gifting.

True to the King's word, Agnes remained in the castle's dingiest, vermin-infested, dungeon cell imaginable, awaiting her fate. Any mercy King Titian retained for his eldest daughter was eliminated after Annie's excessive life-force consumption to restore Alecia with her gifting. Anastasia had attempted to visit her eldest sister in the dungeons on several occasions, but Agnes had ignored her mercy and sent her away, preferring to remain isolated for her remaining days.

'What a sad existence she lives, awaiting the walk to her inevitable death. Agnes had such potential as a skilled fighter and academic, but she let all that go to waste in her quest for power. I can only hope now, that when the time comes, the Goddess forgives my first born for her sins and deems her worthy of the endless peace of the After World. Despite all Agnes has done, I still love her, and I always will. No-one deserves to spend eternity in limbo or worse... Goddess have mercy on her soul,' the Queen prayed.

The weather had intensified; the raging snowstorms occurring more frequently around the mountainous kingdom of Alearia. The winter solstice would be upon them tomorrow. Every room in the Alearian castle was full of dignitaries from each of the ruling kingdoms. Only Queen Annalyse and her most trusted guards and Lady's Maids remained from the Quillencian Kingdom.

King Julian, Prince Alexander and Lady Lilianna's absence weighed heavily on Queen Amealiana's heart. Everyone had come to witness the Crowning Ceremony rituals and partake in the birthday ball.

The formal announcement of Princess Annalyse's heritage and title of potential Heir would be the main announcement at the royal ball, which was sure to bring about mixed responses from the Alearian kingdom and visiting dignitaries. However, the King and Queen of Alearia hoped the news of Annie's return would help to bring some joy and happiness back into the kingdom, given the recent announcement made regarding Agnes's crimes and sentencing.

Up until now, Annie had only been permitted to stay inside the castle grounds. Only the palace guards and staff were privy to Annalyse's identity, both as a security measure to protect Annalyse but also to avoid any further uproar or scandal before the Crowning Ceremonies began.

Queen Amealiana had decided to treat herself to some personal time this morning by exploring the mountains on her beloved horse Ebony. It was a much-needed chance to refresh her soul and reflect on the previous year. The picturesque snowy mountainside was one of Queen Amealiana's most treasured views in the world. Winter was when the kingdom of Alearia truly shined in all its glory.

Feeling a sense of renewed peace in her heart, Queen Amealiana had been able to refocus on the tasks ahead and the final preparations needed to host all their guests, whilst simultaneously running the kingdom and arranging the final preparations for the Crowning Ceremony trials themselves.

Amealiana had little spare time to acquaint herself with her long-lost daughter or comfort her family through their grief. Every moment of her day was planned, and Queen Amealiana hated herself for it. She would have loved nothing more than to spend some precious time with her family, but she had no choice but to accept that until the royal ball, her motherly nurturing would need to be temporarily put on hold for her Queenly duties. The feeling that she was neglecting her own children for the sake of ruling her Kingdom was one of the hardest challenges of being Queen for Amealiana.

I wonder, if my children truly understood the sacrifices one must make to be Queen, if they would even want to compete for the crown. There is no greater honor than to be crowned Queen but there is an astounding sense of fulfillment and joy that comes from being a mother.

It is a daily struggle between juggling a family and a kingdom. All mothers are amazing and those that are fortunate enough to be able to spend endless quality time with their children are the most blessed by the Goddess. For all those women who want nothing more than to be a mother, but for whatever reason have not been blessed with children, I feel great sadness and empathy for them. My children mean the world to me.

If I had a choice between spending my time with my children and serving my kingdom, I would always choose my children. But such musings are fools' dreams. I must learn to live with the cards that fate and the Goddess have dealt me. The rest is all dreams and make-believe,' Amealiana sadly reflected to herself.

'How different my life would be if I were anyone else.'

Princess Agnes

'The darkness draws me near. It calls to me like a mother to her child. Annalyse thought she could fix me but there is no coming back from what I have become. I have learned to appreciate the darkness. I find peace in it. Living in the darkness helps you to appreciate the light that most people take for granted.

'My mind conqueror gifting and fire-wielding days may be over, but I still have a few tricks up my sleeve. My body is a honed weapon both physically and mentally. I will not give up. When I find a way out of here, I will unleash fury! Revenge will be mine for all those years I was treated as less than worthy.'

Princess Anastasia

Before the hearth, Anastasia sat in a velvet wing-backed chair, holding a cup of soothing chamomile tea. It was the eve of her sixteenth birthday and Anastasia felt a mixture of excitement and anxiety. The coming days would determine her future role in the kingdom, and the thought of potentially being crowned Heir was both exhilarating and overwhelming.

After Alexander's passing, Anastasia had suffered intense grief and anxiety. Those fleeting treasured moments she used to enjoy flirting with Joel the stable boy, were long behind her. Anastasia no longer felt capable of maintaining any sort of non-essential relationship and whatever superficial crush she had previously felt for the stable boy had long gone.

'*What a difference a year makes,*' Anastasia reflected to herself. '*This time last year I was a naive Princess with a crush. So optimistic and dreaming of the amazing things to come in life. Little did I know how much loss I would face, and how taxing the constant drama and grief would be upon my mental health.*

'*I feel like a shell of the girl I used to be. Sometimes I can push my feelings aside and allow myself moments of peace and joy, but those moments are few and far between.*

'*Spending time getting to know Annie has helped to bring hope back in my life. My twin doesn't make me feel guilty for wanting to be my own person, and for wanting to help people. Annie doesn't push me to be anyone I am not. Instead, she challenges me to be the best version of myself that I can be. Spending time with Annie is the only time I feel like I am free to express myself, whether I am suffering from anxiety or embracing the small hopes that life still has to offer.*

'Annie came into my life at just the right time and I am so happy with how close we have become over the past couple of weeks. Annie has taught me how to mix a few of her healing lotions. It is immensely satisfying knowing that something I have prepared will help people in a practical way.'

"Excuse me Princess Anastasia," Charlotte, her Lady's Maid softly spoke, drawing her out of her musings. The Princess turned in her chair to see her Lady's Maid dropped in a shallow curtsy.

"Hello Charlotte, is my bath prepared?" Anastasia asked warmly.

"Yes, Princess, and your favorite oils have been added to the water. Is there anything else I can do for you?" Charlotte asked.

"I would like to be alone tonight. Please lay out my bedclothes and I will tend to myself after my bath," Anastasia requested.

"Certainly, my Princess. I hope you have a relaxing bath and restful sleep. Tomorrow will be a big day. Good night Princess," Charlotte curtsied and excused herself to attend to her task.

Anastasia walked into the bathroom and placed a hand over the bath, heating the water to her ideal temperature. The lighting was soft; only a couple of scented candles burned. The room smelled glorious and Anastasia enjoyed a long soak in the bathtub, allowing the hot water to ease the tension from her tired muscles.

'Praise the Goddess for life's simple pleasures such as this."

42

Day One of the Crowning Ceremony

Princess Anastasia

The sun was rising in all its glory on the morning of the winter solstice. The birds were chirping sweetly on the palace balcony, the sky was crystal clear, a fresh blanket of snow glistening on the grounds. It was as though the day was Goddess blessed.

For the first time in a long time, Princess Anastasia was sleeping soundly past day break in her luxurious bed. The chamomile tea and bath soak prior to bed last night had enabled the Princess to release her pent-up anxiety and tension, allowing her a more restful sleep.

A loud knock at the door woke the Princess up with a start.

"Good morning Tash! Happy birthday!" Annie bellowed, excitedly rushing into the room and jumping onto the bed next to Anastasia; a strange wrapped package in her hands. "Wake up sleepy head — it's our birthday!"

Anastasia sat up, rubbing her eyes to fully wake herself, and beamed a smile back to her twin.

"Happy birthday Annie! Oh, my goodness, I just realized this is the first time we've been together to celebrate a birthday! Happy sixteenth birthday Annie!" Anastasia squealed with excitement, now suddenly alert and filled with joy and anticipation.

Annie launched herself at her twin, embracing Anastasia in a warm hug.

"This is the first birthday I will share with my birth family! Birthdays were always special days with Lilianna, which I will miss dearly, but she would want me to be happy today. So, I will enjoy today in honor of her memory," Annie smiled.

"That sounds like a wonderful way to remember Lily," Anastasia replied sincerely, squeezing her sister's back in another warm hug. Annie's return smile was infectious.

"I have a present for you," Annie exclaimed, thrusting the hemp cloth-wrapped bundle into Anastasia's lap. "It's not much since I don't have any money myself and I'm not allowed out of the castle grounds to go shopping, So I made you a gift from the heart."

"Thank you so much, Annie! That is so sweet of you," Anastasia replied, excitedly unwrapping her gift.

Inside the cloth bundle were two glass jars and a small bottle with a dropper in it for measuring.

Annie picked up the small bottle containing a swampy green liquid. "This is a special tonic I brewed especially for you, to enhance your fire wielding powers. If you feel as if your gifting is becoming strained from overexertion, just take a few drops of this under your tongue and it will temporarily restore your gifting to full strength. You can only use it once a day though or the levels of some of the ingredients may become toxic in your blood if the tonic is over consumed inappropriately," Annie warned gently.

Anastasia's jaw dropped in awe, "you made this, for me?"

"Of course," Annie replied pleasantly, "it's my way of saying thank you for being so kind to me since I have arrived. I hope it will be of great help to you during the Crowning rituals."

"Thank you, Annie, no one has ever made something so thoughtful for me before. It truly means a lot to me," Anastasia thanked her twin.

"You are very welcome," Annie smiled. "The smaller jar with the clear ointment contains a long-lasting lip balm so that your lips won't keep drying out from the heat of your fire wielding during training. The larger jar filled with tea leaves and herbs, is a unique combination designed to improve your sleep and temporarily relieve your anxiety. Drink one cup of this tea before bed and whenever you are feeling especially anxious during the day, and this tea should help calm you. I can make more of these for you as you need them."

Anastasia embraced Annie in another long warm hug, whispering her thanks in her twin's ear. Annie squeezed her sister into a tighter hug in response.

"It just so happens," Anastasia excitedly spoke as she jumped up out of bed and ran over to her closet, "I ordered some new training clothes recently. Loose fitting cotton tunics and brown leather pants. I would like you to have them instead. I have noticed you have been making do with your old clothes during our training sessions. You're one of us now Annie, so you should look the part too," Anastasia proclaimed, handing the two new tunics and pants to her twin.

"Thank you, Anastasia, that is very kind of you. I will wear them with pride," Annie replied warmly.

"Splendid! Now, let's pick out something gorgeous to wear from my wardrobe, or we'll both be late for family breakfast," Anastasia giggled.

Just then a knock at the door came and Charlotte, Anastasia's Lady's Maid entered the room, dropping into a curtsy and wishing the two Princesses the happiest of birthdays. Charlotte assisted Annie and Anastasia to quickly change into gowns from Anastasia's wardrobe. Annie chose Anastasia's velvet emerald green full-length winter day dress, whilst Anastasia opted for her favorite lavender silk day dress, cinched in at the waist with a full skirt, and complete with a petticoat for extra volume. The Lady's Maid then quickly arranged their hair in matching braids pinned up like coronets, and they were ready to leave for family breakfast.

Princess Annalyse

The twin Princesses linked arms, happily walking side by side down the twists and turns of the castle hallways, to join their family for their traditional family breakfast. The two guards stationed on either side of the dining room doors formerly greeted the two Princesses, before bowing in synchronism and opening the doors for the ladies. The doorman inside the formal dining room announced their arrival.

King Titian, Queen Amealiana, Queen Annalyse and Princess Alecia, all stood to greet Princesses Anastasia and Annalyse, in honor of their sixteenth birthday.

"Good morning sweethearts, happy birthday!" Queen Amealiana sang merrily.

"Good morning Princess Anastasia and Princess Annie. Happy birthday," the King formerly greeted his daughters.

"Good morning your Majesty's," Annie and Anastasia sang in unison with a giggle. "Good morning Alecia," they sang again.

Princess Alecia couldn't help but smile at their infectious joy this morning.

"Happy birthday!" Alecia smiled, leaving her place at the table to give Anastasia a hug; the Queen Mother electing to do the same, to embrace each of her daughters.

"I am so happy to finally share a birthday with both of you! This day is made even more special since it is your sixteenth birthday as well. It makes my heart sing to have us reunited for this special occasion," Queen Amealiana warmly declared, before bestowing Annie and Anastasia each with a beautiful necklace from her own jewellery collection, which the Princesses were both immensely grateful for.

Queen Annalyse of Quillencia warmly wished each of her twin granddaughters a happy and healthy birthday, and blessed year ahead. "Your Grandfather would be so proud of you Annie," the Quillencian Queen whispered into Annie's ear. Annie whispered her thanks in return, for the Queen's kind words.

The Royals took their seats back at the dining table; King Titian at the head of the table, flanked by each of the two prophetic Queens in their places of honor. Princess Alecia seated herself on the other side of her mother, with Anastasia opting to sit next to her fellow fire wielding sister, leaving an empty seat beside the Quillencian Matriarch which Annie happily filled.

The table was dressed beautifully, with an opulent banquet of sweet and savory dishes; all the twins' favorite pastries and delectable treats were included. Annie looked over the spread in awe and excitement. She had never seen such a feast served for breakfast, and the exquisite smells make her mouth salivate. Annie inhaled the wonderful smells deeply.

"Thank you for such an amazing breakfast your Majesty's. I feel truly blessed," Annie sincerely thanked her parents.

"The pleasure is all ours Annalyse," the King warmly reassured her before adding, "besides, you will need all your strength for today's ball and the coming rituals ahead. So, make sure you eat well."

Annie gave a small smile of thanks to the King. "Thank you for your consideration, Your Majesty" Annie replied hesitantly.

'*What sort of rituals could I possibly need energy for? My giftings are of the mind. What sort of activities could they expect me to partake in? I am no fighter like my sisters, and I have no elemental gifting to demonstrate,*' Annie apprehensively mused to herself.

The King rose from his chair, drawing Annie from her musings.

"Before we begin indulging in our breakfast feast," the King continued, "I would like to announce that the first Crowning Ceremony ritual is scheduled for tomorrow morning at sunrise. I suggest you all get a good night's sleep and don't celebrate too late into the night at the royal ball. Tomorrow is sure to be a testing day for each of my potential Heirs. Let us see if you are truly worthy of the title of Heir and Future Queen," the King declared obscurely in a menacing tone.

The family seemed to collectively intake a breath at the tone of the King's voice.

'*What arduous tasks he has planned, only the Goddess knows,*' Annie thought to herself anxiously. '*Whatever it is, I'm not sure I am ready for it.*'

43

Princess Anastasia

High up in the Alearian castle, excited giggles could be heard from the hallways of the royal family's private wing. Queen Amealiana had invited Queen Annalyse, and her daughters, to her suite to prepare for the celebratory birthday ball and the beginning of the Crowning Ceremony festivities.

The Crowning Ceremonies were an understated name for the week-long rituals and events. The official beginning of the ceremony festivities was marked by the winter solstice sixteenth birthday ball celebration of the youngest potential Heirs. At the end of the week's events and rituals, one of the potential Heirs would be crowned Heir and future Queen of the kingdom of Alearia.

Merrily, the women dressed in their elaborate ball gowns and jewellery. The Lady's Maids had prepared a salon in the Queen's suite so that the five royal women could all be attended to in the one suite. It was the first time Princess Annalyse would be introduced to the kingdom, and it was clear that the idea of wearing such an elaborate ball gown and tiara was out of poor Annie's comfort zone. Sensing her twin's unease, Anastasia made sure the servants kept the wine flowing to ease everyone's nerves. Though the wine could not stop Anastasia from thinking about her eldest sister in the dim dark dungeon.

Princess Agnes would not be permitted to attend the ball or watch the Crowning Ceremony events and remained in her dungeon cell awaiting her fate. Anastasia planned to re-attempt to visit her sister again this week if Agnes would allow it. Anastasia felt sorry for her, she was her sister after all, though Anastasia knew there was little she could offer her other than her company.

Agnes was no longer deemed a security risk with her mind conqueror gifting and fire-wielding gifting taken from her. Given her impending execution, King Titian had shown some leniency towards his eldest daughter and allowed her to be transferred back to the basic quarantine cell which at least offered the comfort of a bed. As Agnes was no longer closely guarded inside her cell, the door to her cell was always locked, with a guard posted outside. Agnes's privacy was at least returned to her. A small consolation at best.

Anastasia had managed to sneakily deliver a few books to Agnes to read during her final days, smuggled down with her meals or hidden amongst deliveries of clean clothes or fresh linen.

Princess Anastasia was drawn from her thoughts back into the moment.

"Mother, you look absolutely stunning," Princess Anastasia gushed at Queen Amealiana.

"Thank you, my dear. I must say you look incredible in that gold dress. I see you were going for a subtle look; understated elegance," the Queen teased her daughter, all in good fun.

Anastasia feigned shock at her mother's sarcasm, "I'm afraid I don't know what you mean mother dearest. Is my perfectly fitted gown not appropriate? I think it compliments all my assets perfectly. It is my night to shine tonight after all," the Princess replied with a devilishly cheeky grin.

Alecia and Annie fell into fits of laughter at their sister's sass.

"My dear sister, your dress makes me look like a delicate flower… practically holy!" Princess Annie teased playfully.

Annie's long blond tresses hung in loose flowing curls. She was dressed modestly in a full length, blush pink, voluminous ball gown with pink satin cloak overlaying her frock. Both Queens couldn't help but giggle at Annie's rare moment of boldness.

"Quite right Annalyse," Alecia smirked, redirecting her attention back to Anastasia, "for once the potential suitors might pay more attention to you than me."

Anastasia spluttered out a laugh.

Princess Alecia's black organza bodice framed her figure perfectly; tiny rubies embroidered around the low, daring neckline. The gown then bloomed out into a full skirt of chiffon and organza from her hips down, with a small train elegantly trailing behind. Her lips were painted a daring bright red to match the rubies adorning her dress.

"Tell me, Anastasia, have you been down to the stables recently? I hope the stable boy, Joel, has been taking special care of you and your horse," Alecia continued to taunt.

Anastasia sent her a stare that could have flattened mountains.

"Darling sister, I'm afraid the wine has gone to your head," Anastasia replied passive aggressively.

Queen Amealiana smiled amusingly at the girls' not so subtle bickering, taking another sip of her wine, as she enjoyed the show.

Queen Annalyse coughed awkwardly, raising her glass of wine to break up the tension between Alecia and Anastasia. "Ladies, I would like to make a toast." The Princesses and their mother redirected their attention to the Quillencian Matriarch.

"I would like to say how proud I am of all of you," Queen Annalyse confided. "No matter what happens in the coming days, know that the King, Queen and I, will always be there for you. Regardless of the outcome, we love you all equally. A toast to the potential Heirs. In the pursuit of power, only one may be crowned Heir. May the Goddess bless you throughout the Crowning Ceremony rituals. For family and kingdom, may we always strive for greatness, kindness, and compassion."

"For family and kingdom," the three Princesses and Queen Amealiana echoed.

Queen Amealiana

The grand ballroom was elaborately decorated for the winter solstice birthday celebration ball. Beneath the fifty-foot-high cathedral style ceiling, water mages had suspended millions of snowflakes above the dancing guests, creating an indoor winter wonderland. Each snowflake dazzled like a star as the light from the candelabras reflected off each flake. The indoor scene echoed the glorious snow-covered mountains that could be seen outside the floor to ceiling windows in the fading light of sunset. The sky was filled with exquisite shades of burnt orange, fuchsia and soft sky blue.

The room was buzzing with energy as several hundred visiting royals, dignitaries and specially selected townspeople, danced merrily to the renowned assembly of musicians and singers showcasing their talent at the event. Upon the stage, five thrones were set upon the dais. The King and Queen of Alearia sat in the center of the dais, overseeing the celebrations.

King Titian rose from his throne to approach the front of the stage, and the room instantly quietened; a silent signal for the guests to take their allocated seats. Once everyone was seated, the King spread his arms before the crowd.

"Welcome, Queen Annalyse, honored guests, dignitaries, and my people," The King began. "Queen Amealiana and I are grateful that you could all be here with us to celebrate such a milestone in our kingdom's history. Today marks the sixteenth birthday of the youngest potential Heir and blessed be the Goddess that it falls so fittingly on the blessed winter solstice; one of our most cherished days of the year. Unfortunately, tonight we are notably missing two potential royal Heirs. Prince Alexander was tragically taken from us exactly a year ago, Goddess bless his soul. Please join me in a toast, in remembrance of Prince Alexander. He was an honorable leader, a brilliant shape-shifter, and would have made an incredible ruler. To Prince Alexander, whom we will always remember and will always be a King in our hearts," the King declared, lifting his glass of wine and taking a sip.

"To Prince Alexander," the people toasted.

A tear trickled down Queen Amealiana's cheek as she remembered her son.

'May the Goddess protect you, my child. May you, King Julian and Lady Lilianna, enjoy the endless peace and happiness of the After World,' the Queen silently prayed.

"The other remaining notably absent person; Agnes," the King continued, "has been stripped of her royal titles. As a traitor to our Kingdom, and the person responsible for the dreaded magical disease and murders, she remains confined in the dungeon, awaiting the consequence of her actions. But today is a happy occasion. A celebration. We must not dwell on the past but look gloriously towards the promising future of our kingdom. Later tonight, I will outline the first Crowning Ceremony task, so that the Princesses may have the night to prepare for tomorrow's ritual. As tradition demands, up until today, the potential Heirs know nothing about the times, locations or tasks involved in the ritual ceremonies. Tonight, will be the first time they are provided with information related to the Crowning Ceremonies. For family and kingdom, may our potential Heirs always strive for greatness, kindness, and compassion."

"For family and kingdom," the crowd echoed in one voice.

"I will now introduce my wife, the Queen Mother, Queen Amealiana; whom will introduce our potential Heirs," the King concluded.

The crowd rose from their seats in respect for the King and Queen and bowed in their places. King Titian turned towards his wife who was now standing beside him, and leaned over to embrace her, whispering a mischievous *"good luck,"* in her ear before taking his seat.

The Queen gave her husband a concealed poke in his side for his cheeky comment before she turned back to the now re-seated crowd.

"Good evening, Queen Annalyse, distinguished guests, and my people. How wonderful it is to see you all here tonight," Queen Amealiana spoke warmly. "Thank you for joining us on this prestigious occasion. Please stand to welcome our mighty kingdom's first potential heir. It is my pleasure to introduce Princess Alecia, the fire wielder," the Queen announced.

The great hall guests rose to bow and clap, as Princess Alecia entered through the main entrance doors, looking a vision. The mighty fire-wielder cast a brilliant aurora of various colored flames dancing around the ceiling amongst the suspended snowflakes, demonstrating her glorious power as she walked through the hall and took her place beside King Titian.

'I'm sure it's not just her amazing gifting the potential suitors are admiring tonight,' Amealiana cheekily thought to herself. *'My daughter has never been one for subtlety.'*

"Now it is my esteemed pleasure to introduce our next potential heir, Princess Anastasia. Join me in wishing her the happiest of birthdays and good wishes for the crowning rituals ahead," Queen Amealiana declared as the crowd again rose to bow and clap in respect for the youngest potential heir.

Not to be outdone by her sister, as Princess Anastasia made her entrance, she sent the candelabras into a roar of flame, that then dissipated back into its usual calming light. The crowd's applause roared in appreciation for the show they were receiving.

'One thing I am certain of, is whoever is crowned Heir will not be dull. The future of our Kingdom is looking very 'bright'. Show-off!' The Queen amusingly thought to herself, releasing a little chuckle.

Princess Anastasia took her seat on the other side of her mother's throne. Queen Amealiana took a deep centering breath to prepare herself for the surprise she was about to bestow upon her Kingdom and guests.

"I myself would like to acknowledge my son tonight. Prince Alexander, you are dearly missed. May you continue to enjoy the endless peace of the After World. Now, sadly it may appear as though we are down to only two remaining potential Heirs; however, I do have an exciting announcement to share with you all. Queen Annalyse, would you please join me on the dais please?" The Queen requested of her mother, who nodded her head in recognition and made her way onto the stage to support her daughter through the coming announcement.

"As you all know, Queen Annalyse and I are both gifted prophetics and sages," Amealiana continued, "therefore we have glimpses into the future that sometimes do not always promise good news. But our sage wisdom allows us the guidance to act accordingly without bias. Sixteen years ago, I welcomed not only Princess Anastasia but also her twin Princess Annalyse, into the world."

The crowd drew in a collective breath as everyone's attention was centered on the Queen's startling news.

"After each potential Heir's birth, I foresaw a brief glimpse into their futures and their giftings," Amealiana informed the crowd. "Unfortunately, I did not take note of Princess Annalyse's gifting at the time, as the vision I foresaw for her future was bleak. Someone wished harm upon my child and I could not allow that vision to occur. All these years my daughter, Princess Annalyse, was raised in Quillencia as an apprentice apothecary, and I would like to take a moment to acknowledge her immense talent in the profession," Amealiana spoke proudly.

"Princess Annalyse is a compassionate, empathetic, wise young sage," Amealiana revealed with her head held high. "Recently, before the tragic passing of King Julian of Quillencia, and before returning home to our beautiful kingdom of Alearia, the Princess was able to train her rare second gifting under the guidance of her grandfather, King Julian. Now that the threat against her life no longer remains, she has returned home to our wonderful kingdom of Alearia to take her rightful place as our third potential Heir. It is my greatest honor and pleasure, to introduce our final potential Heir, who is also celebrating her sixteenth birthday today. Please welcome Prince Annalyse, gifted sage and mind conqueror."

The crowd quickly stood to their feet in triumphant applause to welcome their newest potential Heir. News of a mind conqueror in the Kingdom gave the people a sense of pride and awe. Her identity could not be questioned, thanks to her rare giftings and the visual support onstage of the Quillencian Matriarch Queen Annalyse. The people were more than happy to instantly embrace Princess Annalyse as one of their own.

The youngest potential Heir entered the room a little apprehensively, but held her head high, and waved to the crowd as she nervously made her way up the dais to take her place beside her twin. The applause from the guests lasted until the Princess was seated. This change in events gave the people a renewed sense of excitement about the coming Crowning Ceremony rituals ahead.

'Honestly, I do not know what we were so worried about. The people already love her just as I do,' Queen Amealiana mused with a satisfied smile.

Queen Annalyse embraced her daughter, Amealiana, in encouragement, then turned to embrace each of her granddaughters before returning to her allocated seat at the head table, with the other visiting royalty from nearby kingdoms. Queen Amealiana resumed her place back upon her throne, beaming a smile of relief towards her husband, who returned her smile in recognition.

'Praise the Goddess, we might actually get through a royal event without something terrible happening,' the Queen thought gratefully to herself.

King Titian took his place, center stage of the dais, to resume his address to the guests.

"Thank you, my Queen, and welcome to each of our potential Heirs. May the Goddess bless you and keep you safe over the coming crowning rituals ahead," the King declared ominously. "Now, before we get on with the celebrations tonight, it is time to share the first task for the crowning ritual with you all. The first task is about power. A ruler must be powerful to protect their people. They must be strong and dependable. Tomorrow at sunrise, in the training arena, each of our potential Heirs will be required to give a demonstration of how their gifting will help to protect their people in the future," the King announced.

Princess Alecia and Princess Anastasia grinned at each other as if the crown were already as good as theirs. This task would be as simple as breathing for the two fire-wielding sisters, but not for Annie. The youngest potential Heir had no defensive elemental magic. The Queen wondered how Annie would she demonstrate her strength if she was determined to only use her gifting for honorable purposes?

44

Day Two of the Crowning Ceremony

Princess Anastasia

The sky was clear; the temperature just below freezing. A thick blanket of snow covered the training arena. Additional stands for seating, protected by an overhanging temporary roof surrounding the arena, had been erected to accommodate the thousands of people who would come to watch the Crowning Ceremony rituals. All visiting royals and dignitaries from surrounding kingdoms would be seated in the King and Queen's personal observation deck, while the people of Alearia and any other visitors would be seated in the main stands.

After each ceremony, a place would be awarded to each potential Heir based on their performance and crowd approval. However, at the end of the week, the overall winner would be determined by High Priestess Elizabeth, representing the Goddess herself, in conjunction with the kingdom's ruling King and Queen.

The priestesses claimed that each ritual involved in the ceremony must allow the Goddess to assess the potential Heir's worth. It is said that throughout history, the Goddess has only chosen to physically present herself once at a final Crowning Ceremony ritual to determine the Heir, when she deemed the Heir chosen by the High Priestess, King, and Queen, unsuitable. Therefore, the tradition of holding the Crowning Ceremony rituals had been upheld for as long as records dated back, to determine the rightful Heir of the kingdom of Alearia.

The previous night's birthday ball celebrations had carried on long into the early hours of the morning. Anastasia was indeed cursing herself for only getting a few short hours of sleep, as her head pounded from overindulging on wine and sleep deprivation. Her body screamed at her to go back to bed and rest for the day.

Alas, the first light of the morning was just starting to peak above the horizon, and Anastasia's Lady's Maid was hurriedly assisting her to get dressed into the Alearian Kingdom's royal military attire that she planned to wear for each of the tasks during the Crowning Ceremony. The young Princess gulped down a jug of water and shoved a piece of bread into her mouth before sprinting down to the castle hallways, through the castle grounds and into the back entrance of the training arena where a waiting room was set up for the potential Heirs.

Princesses Alecia and Annalyse were already waiting in the room, each seemingly lost in their own thoughts. In the waiting room, each of the potential Heirs would be required to wait their turn to demonstrate their gifts to the kingdom's rulers, the High Priestess Elizabeth, and their people. Water mages stood guard all around the arena barriers, for both protection of the potential Heirs as well as the people. The priestesses had deemed the guard presence too imposing, however, given the unpredictable nature of the last year, the King stayed firm on the requirement of their presence as a necessary security measure.

A trumpet sounded from the middle of the arena where a small platform had been erected for the potential Heir to stand upon if they wished, given the arena was blanketed by snow. The herald and palace appointed commentator for the Crowning Ceremony, Sir Corneal, put down his trumpet as the sun crested on the horizon, and bellowed his message to the crowd. His voice amplified around the arena by his elemental wind whisperer gifting.

"Your Majesties, esteemed visiting royalty, dignitaries, and of course, the mighty people of Alearia, it is my greatest honor to welcome you to the first Crowning Ceremony ritual," the commentator announced. "My name is Sir Corneal, and I have the privilege of being your commentator through this week's proceedings," said the tall, thin, mature aged gentleman dressed in the kingdom's royal colors.

"As the King himself announced last night," Corneal continued, "the first Goddess deigned ritual is a demonstration of power. In order of their birth, each potential Heir will have the opportunity to demonstrate their ability and power to protect the Kingdom. Each potential Heir will then be placed in rank order of first to third on the leader board. The scoreboard will be updated throughout the week's proceedings. The leader board is not a binding contract as to whom is crowned Heir. However, for our visiting guests and those that are not as familiar with our Alearian history; it should be noted that only once in our history has the scoreboard winner not been crowned heir. That singular instance was at the discretion of the glorious wise Goddess herself, who revealed herself to deliver her verdict. That year was a pivotal year in Alearian history, as it was the year that civil unrest broke out amongst our kingdom's people and our neighboring kingdom of Quillencia. The Goddess' appointed ruler was able to work with the Quillencian rulers to restore peace to both mighty kingdoms, and turned Alearia into the peaceful, prosperous kingdom we know and cherish today. Who will be crowned our next Heir and future Queen, only the Goddess knows. For family and kingdom, may we always strive for greatness, kindness, and compassion," Sir Cornell declared.

"For family and kingdom," the gathered spectators spoke as one people.

"Before I introduce our first potential heir, I will outline the rules for this round," Sir Cornell continued. "Under no circumstances may any spectator interfere with the demonstrations. The only exception to this rule is our water mage guards who have been ordered to act in the case of an emergency. If you stay for the demonstrations, you do so at your own risk. The potential Heirs are expected to showcase their power today and for that, anything is possible. There are no rules for today's ritual. With that said, could you all please stand to honor our first potential heir, fire-wielder, Princess Alecia." Resounding applause sounded from the audience as Princess Alecia entered the arena.

"Good luck Alecia!" Anastasia yelled from the waiting room.

Queen Amealiana

Alecia took her position on the wooden platform and waved graciously towards the crowd as they again took their seats. Sir Cornell cast his gifting around the arena to amplify the potential Heir's voice, as he would continue to do for each of the potential Heirs throughout the week-long ceremony.

"Thank you, everyone, for your support," Princess Alecia spoke. "This morning I will prove to you all that I am just as powerful as ever and I will fight to earn the title of crowned Heir!" Alecia declared to the crowd, who murmured amongst each other in anticipation.

"Guards, please bring in the ice!" Princess Alecia ordered.

The heavy double door entrance on the far side of the arena was pulled open by a team of guards. Into the arena trotted a procession of ten horses, pulling a large delivery wagon with the walls and roof removed to reveal an enormous block of ice. To the spectators, it appeared as though something was suspended inside of the ice, however, the block was too thick to identify what it was. The horses stopped at the foot of the stage in front of Princess Alecia and the coachmen unhitched the horses from the cart and led them back out of the arena.

The main entrance door once again closed, leaving only Alecia, the block of ice and the water mages standing guard in the arena.

"For my demonstration, I will prove to you all how my power will benefit our Kingdom. I will do this by saving a life," Alecia announced confidently.

The crowd stilled as they sat in confusion, unsure as to how the Princess planned to save a life using a block of ice.

'What on earth, is she doing? Surely there isn't a person in there? Alecia is wild at heart, but she isn't reckless,' the Queen thought to herself.

Princess Alecia raised her hands dramatically above her head and released a mighty flame into the sky, signalling the start of her demonstration. Lowering her hands and aiming them towards the slab of ice, Alecia released her mighty power, enveloping the wagon and ice in flames. The magnitude of her flame quickly disintegrated the wagon and the block of ice dropped with a loud thud upon the carpet of snow on the arena floor. Alecia reigned in her flame until it was a mere curtain over the ice, slowly, and precisely removing layer by layer of ice.

"There's a person in there!" One horrified spectator yelled from the stands, causing the crowd to uproar.

The Queen watched on in horror, unsure of how to manage the situation. *'Do I interfere? This is not right; she should not be doing this. What a terrible example she is setting for our people!'* Queen Amealiana thought frantically to herself. *'Goddess please let whomever that poor person is live.'*

"Silence!" Princess Alecia declared, extinguishing her flame.

The crowd stilled, not a sound could be heard in the whole arena for a moment.

Alecia took a deep breath and addressed the crowd firmly. "No one can interfere, remember. I am not causing her harm, I am saving her life! This young woman volunteered of her own free will to assist me with this demonstration. Now watch closely as I bring this woman back to us," Alecia stated with a grin across her face. "Isn't that what you all came for, a show?"

Alecia returned her attention to the block of ice encasing a woman who was indeed suspended inside. Little by little, the ice melted away layer by layer as Alecia meticulously melted the ice without causing her captive harm.

As the final encasement of ice around the young woman's body melted away, the woman's identity was revealed. Agnes's former Lady's Maid gasped to catch her breath as she was revived from her cryogenic stasis and landed arms deep in a pool of water, shivering from the cold. A stark look of confusion and fear crossed her face as she trembled in the puddle of water. The crowd stood to their feet and a great roar of cheering filled the air at the magical display they had just witnessed.

'A girl perceived to be literally frozen to death brought back to life with a potential Heir's mighty fire wielding gifting. What sort of power have we unleashed on our kingdom, allowing Alecia to develop such a strong gifting? Clearly, the power has begun to go to her head.

'Have we made a mistake in putting so much trust in Alecia? Surely this display was just a one-off poor judgment on my daughter's behalf. Did she see no other way she could have better showcased her skills without selfishly risking someone's life?'

The crowd was overwhelmed with excitement at the history-making demonstration of power they had just witnessed. Everyone, that is, except for the royal family and High Priestess, who saw it for what it truly was; a demonstration of reckless power with little regard for human life.

Princess Annalyse

Princess Annalyse burst through the waiting room door and sprinted into the arena, running for the Lady's Maid, and calling for assistance from the healers as she ran.

'What sort of a person would do such a horrible thing to another human being. I will not let this poor woman be scarred for life because of my sister's arrogance. What possessed her to attempt something so reckless to demonstrate her power?' Annie thought to herself.

After calmly approaching the freezing maid, Annie knelt beside the frightened woman in the foot-deep pool of water.

"Madam, I am sorry for all you have been through today. I understand you willingly agreed to do this. Is that the case?" Annie asked uncertainly.

The poor maid shallowly nodded her head in confirmation that she had, in fact, had agreed to volunteer for the display much to Annie's disbelief.

Annie took a deep breath and continued, "very well. It was your choice to make. It is your life and I accept your choice. However, if it would be alright with you, I would like to wipe your memory of today's events, so you never have to re-live these feelings of hopelessness and fear ever again," Annie kindly offered her.

The whole crowd sat on the edge of their seats at the scene unfolding before them between the royal healing mind conqueror, and the Lady's Maid, watching on in suspense. The wind whisperer captured every spoken word between Annie and the maid for the audience to hear.

The Lady's Maid nodded her head subtly, unable to find the words to express herself. Annie gently pulled the young woman into a standing position. Then the Princess removed her own cloak and draped it around the girl's shivering shoulders and escorted her up the stairs of the stage, where she could sit on a dry surface.

Alecia, who remained standing upon the platform as well, cast a warm breeze in the Lady's Maid's direction, using her fire wielding gifting to heat the surrounding air, and drying the poor woman's drenched clothes and increasing her core temperature. The Lady's Maid looked towards Alecia in recognition and bowed her head in thanks.

"I sincerely apologize for frightening you. I thought you were fully aware of what you were volunteering for. I would have never gone through with it if I knew it would cause you harm. I am sorry for my reckless misjudgement," Alecia bravely apologized to the Lady's Maid for the whole audience to hear.

Annie released a relieved breath. '*Thank the Goddess, Alecia acknowledges her mistake. This was obviously just a very grave, temporary misjudgement on her part,*' Annie thought to herself as she sat down on the stage.

"I am an apothecary and sage first, and a mind conqueror second," Annie declared to the Lady's Maid and the crowd. "I promise you, the people of Alearia, that I will never hurt you or use my gifting for anything other than honorable purposes. My mind conqueror gifting can be used to heal. As my demonstration today, would it be agreeable with you, our dear Lady's Maid, if I removed your memories of today's events, so you can go about your life in peace instead of fear?" Annie asked the woman before her.

"Please Princess Annalyse, I would greatly appreciate your help. I'm not sure I could enjoy ice or snow again, if I forevermore associated it with the cold trapped feeling of being suspended in the ice," the Lady's Maid spoke openly and honestly.

Princess Annalyse nodded her head in understanding whilst still holding the young woman's hands in her own. Annie closed her eyes so she could concentrate and asked the young woman to do the same.

"Open your mind to me. Let down any barriers you have in place and recall your memories of today," Annie requested.

The girl's eyes glazed over as her subconscious mental defenses dropped simultaneously. Annie navigated through the woman's brain as though she was following a road map; following the thoughts that floated like a breeze throughout the Lady's Maid's mind. She sifted through memories as she would look through pages of a book, until Annalyse found the memory she wished to retrieve.

Annie grasped the memory with her own mind's power and pulled it from the girl's mind as if pulling a single strand of hay from a haystack. On Annie's journey out of the girl's mind and back into her own, Annie discarded the devastating memory of the girl's freezing and revival into the atmosphere.

Taking a deep breath, and feeling quite weak, Annie opened her eyes and asked the girl to do the same. The girl looked around, startled, as if she had just woken from a trance.

"Princess Annalyse," she said in shock and bewilderment. "What are you doing here? What am I doing here? How did I get here?"

The crowd jumped to their feet and applauded louder than anyone had thought possible. Annie just smiled at the maid and whispered to her, "you're okay. Everything is fine. Let's go back to the castle for a nice cup of hot tea."

The girl looked a little stunned. "I am sorry my Princess, my memory is a little hazy. Never mind. What sort of tea can I make for you Princess Annalyse?" The Lady's Maid asked the potential Heir as the two walked side-by-side down the stage, out of the arena together and back towards the castle.

'Crowning ritual tradition be damned, I'm going to have a pot of tea, followed by a long bath when I get back to my suite,' Annie thought blissfully to herself.

45

Queen Amealiana

Queen Amealiana paced deep in thought around the official deliberation room. High Priestess Elizabeth, an old crone of whom years and wisdom surpassed all others, was watching on contemplatively from her wooden rocking chair by the hearth. The King was doing his best to appear calm and dignified as he stood at the room's viewing window, staring out at the empty arena stage.

"Forgive me Your Majesties if I am speaking out of turn, but as we are currently considered equal in the judging of the potential Heirs in the eyes of our kingdom and the Goddess, I would like to request that we focus on the task at hand," the High Priestess stated plainly. "Queen Amealiana, King Titian, I understand that Agnes has been stripped of her title for her crimes, which I am strongly in support of. Thus, we are left with three remaining potential Heirs, and our duty is to deliberate their placings. Might I suggest we start critiquing their demonstrations to not hold up the audience any longer? I am aware that it has been a confusing and interesting display, but we must look at today's events diplomatically. Do you agree?"

Queen Amealiana paused her pacing to face the crone and smiled. The Queen felt as though she had aged a century in the past twelve months. The resounding feelings of endless grief, sacrifice, and the pressure of holding together an unstable family and kingdom, were wearing on the Queen and she felt that the High Priestess's sense of focus was a much-needed breath of fresh air.

Focusing on her breathing to calm herself down, the Queen moved to take a seat on the opposite side of the table to the High Priestess.

"You are right, High Priestess Elizabeth, let us focus and begin our deliberations," Queen Amealiana agreed. "Your input is highly valued and welcome; as the third judge of the Crowning rituals. But before we begin, I would like to fully brief you on the events of the past year. I feel full and open disclosure is needed to allow you to form a fully educated opinion of our potential Heirs and offer a fair judgment."

Withholding no small details, the Queen unfolded the whole truth of the past twelve months to the High Priestess, who took it all in her stride. The High Priestess, who had lived a life more pressured than most, had gained an immense amount of wisdom following her years of experience serving the people of Alearia in a manner of different ways. The High Priestess mulled over all that had been disclosed to her as the King took a seat beside the Queen.

"It appears as though the Goddess has a plan for this Kingdom which has not yet unfolded," High Priestess Elizabeth offered. "The players on the board are in position; it is simply a matter of manoeuvring the pieces correctly to ensure the game is won by the right player. Forgive me for saying so, but I feel with Princess Annalyse, though she is a sage and her judgment sound, we know little about her and therefore she is an unknown quantity. Princess Anastasia has always been consistent and would rule the people fairly though she is more a servant than a leader. Her demonstration today was ordinary. Anastasia holds back her power as if she is afraid of reaching her full potential. Princess Alecia surprised me the most today. Whilst her methods were unorthodox; she earnt the peoples' support. The crowd loved her display, even if it was reckless," the High Priestess spoke bluntly.

King Titian stood from chair and warned, "High Priestess, your opinion is valued for the Crowning Ceremony deliberations, but might I suggest we stick to evaluating today's performance rather than over-analysing the personal traits of each potential Heir. As for your comment regarding Princess Annalyse *'as an unknown quantity,'* I assure you that Annie is loyal to this kingdom. Since her arrival, the Princess has gone above and beyond to help her family and kingdom, and I disagree with your interpretation of Princess Anastasia's performance today. She gave a skilled demonstration of her fire wielding gifting. It showed great finesse and control, even if it was not as dramatic a display as her sisters. Alecia's performance was unorthodox, as you say, but she made her point and the Lady's Maid consented to volunteer for the demonstration, so our hands are tied where she is concerned," King Titian stated firmly.

The Queen looked from her husband and back to the High Priestess, processing both of their opinions and points of view. With a resigned sigh, the Queen offered her thoughts.

"I feel that Alecia was reckless, and though it pains me to say this, '*recklessness*' is not a good quality in a leader. Annie's demonstration showed her love for the people, and her ability to manipulate minds is astounding. We have seen what she has achieved in the past with her mind conqueror gifting, but it appears as though there is no limit to what she can do," Amealiana offered.

"Agreed Your Majesties," the High Priestess remarked. "Let us score the potential Heirs based on their performances and see where each Princess places on the leader board."

Princess Anastasia

Standing on the platform in the center of the arena, Anastasia felt hopeful but uneasy about the first judging ceremony. Beside her, Princess Alecia stood looking overconfident.

'Where is Annalyse? Honestly, if she wants to make a good impression with the people, she needs to show up for judging ceremonies as well as our tasks. The people may mistake her

absence for arrogance, which is not a good quality in a potential Heir.'

Finally, the commentator, Sir Corneal, joined the fire-wielding sisters centre-stage. His voice carried around the arena, thanks to his wind whisperer gifting.

"Your Majesties, Lords, Ladies, and people of Alearia. Thank you for your patience while the judging deliberations were held. All deliberations are taken very seriously, as in the pursuit of power only one shall be crowned Heir and future ruler of our mighty kingdom. Without further ado, I would like to introduce High Priestess Elizabeth, who will award the placings for this round. For family and Kingdom," Sir Corneal concluded his introduction.

"For family and kingdom," the people echoed.

The High Priestess utilized her cane to walk across the compacted dirt arena; the previously fallen snow disintegrated into mist during Princess Anastasia's fire wielding demonstration. The old crone slowly climbed the stairs to the stage before taking her place in front of two out of three of the potential Heirs. Princess Annalyse was still noticeably absent, and evidently was not planning to attend this judging ceremony.

"Welcome everyone," the High Priestess spoke. "Thank you for joining us today for the first of Crowning Ceremony trial. It is the Goddess's will that this ceremony is completed and that at the end of the week's trials, an appropriate Heir will be chosen based on their attributes as a leader, as well as their performance. King Titian, Queen Amealiana and I, have had the honor of acting as representatives of the Goddess, in awarding today's placements on the leader board. It was a challenging decision and a ruling we did not make frivolously. As you all know, public opinion plays a large role in the deliberation process of awarding the first ritual challenge places. It is only fitting that the kingdom's people have a say in their future ruler. After this challenge, all ceremony placements will be awarded by their royal majesties and myself. First place today is awarded to the person who showed the most potential to wield their power to protect the Alearian people. We felt that the person who most accurately met the brief, with the greatest support from the people, should be awarded this status. The current leader of the Crowning Ceremonies is Princess Anastasia, for her creative and powerful fire wielding display," the High Priestess announced.

'What?! Did the high priestess just name me winner of the first ritual?! Surely there is some mistake… I didn't get nearly as much support from the crowd as Alecia or Annalyse… This doesn't feel right. Alecia must be furious with me, I can see it in her tense posture and stone-cold stare,' Anastasia fretted to herself.

'Please join me in congratulating Princess Anastasia on currently leading the Crowning Ceremony rituals competition," the High Priestess requested.

Soft polite clapping could be heard around the arena, but the crowd was confused, muttering their disbelief amongst themselves. Anastasia blushed with embarrassment.

'This is not right. This is not what the people desire at all. They feel like their opinion has been completely disregarded,' Anastasia thought to herself.

High Priestess Elizabeth continued on: "next I would like to congratulate Princess Alecia, on being awarded second place in today's trial. She showed great skill and powerful craftsmanship of her fire wielding gifting. Please congratulate Princess Alecia," the High Priestess stated, clapping to honor the Princess.

Alecia smugly grinned from ear to ear at the mention of her name, though the tension rolling off her was palpable, as the crowd could tell she was not impressed that she was not in first place. The crowd roared their support, clearly preferring Alecia over Anastasia.

"Rigged!" A young man from the crowd yelled. "We want Annalyse and Alecia in the lead! This isn't what the people want. It's a rigged competition!"

The guards approached the man and he was arrested for disrupting the peace. As much as crowd opinion was valued, they were still living under a Monarchy, and any disrespect would not be tolerated. The High Priestess carried on announcing Princess Annalyse as coming third. The High Priestess ruled that Princess Annalyse's demonstration, whilst clearly showed the capability of her gifting, did not adequately portray how she would protect the Kingdom with her power.

The crowd was outright furious by this point, yelling how they felt cheated, that the result was rigged and not in-line with the peoples' wishes. Many people started to throw items over the arena barriers at the High Priestess, in protest of the rulings.

The crowd grew rowdier and the guards worked hard to contain the riot that was breaking out in the arena stands. The royal family, High Priestess, visiting royalty and dignitaries were evacuated immediately from the arena and back to the safety of the castle.

46

Day Four of the Crowning Ceremony

Princess Annalyse

The past thirty-six hours had flown by like a whirlwind. The snow had fallen lightly on Day 3 of the crowning rituals, making movement and access around the castle more comfortable and efficient. The castle had gone into temporary lockdown for several hours after Princess Anastasia was awarded first place in the initial trial. A small group of people in the crowd had revolted against the decision, throwing objects in protest at the High Priestess and attempting to scale the balcony with propped up benches, to the royal family's private platform where the King and Queen were seated.

Twenty people aged between fourteen- and forty-years-old were arrested for disturbing the peace and interfering with the Crowning Ceremony process. New security screening measures were being put in place for the next trial, to ensure the safety of the High Priestess and royal family.

The Crowning Ceremony ritual scheduled for the third day had been cancelled to allow time to input new security protocols for the remaining two rituals. However, an impressive dinner party held in the grand ballroom with all the castle's hosted royals and visiting dignitaries, was an overwhelming success on the night of day three of the Crowning Ceremonies. At the dinner, Queen Amealiana announced that the trial for day four would be to deliver a short speech to the Alearian people, explaining how they as a potential Heir would show kindness and compassion for their people if they were crowned Heir and future ruler of Alearia.

Princess Annalyse stayed up late into the night of the third day, debating how she could best communicate her deep care and compassion for her people.

The sun was shining and the castle looked once again like a winter wonderland surrounded by a couple of feet of glistening, fresh snow. The cooks and palace staff were all working long hours to keep up with the extra demand of serving the additional hundred royal guests and visiting dignitaries. The castle was an endless hive of activity; the only escape from the hustle and bustle was for people to retire to their allocated guest suite, or enjoy one of the many peaceful palace library alcoves.

Princesses Annalyse, Anastasia, and Alecia, prepared for the day's Crowning Ceremony ritual in Princess Anastasia's suite. It was a complete change of pace from the previous trial when they wore the kingdom's official military attire. This time each of the potential Heirs were encouraged to dress their best to portray themselves as the regal potential Heirs they were.

Each of the Princesses were dressed in their finest, most elegant, modest gowns, with matching cloaks and of course a tiara of glimmering gemstones. The Lady's Maids had outdone themselves, having applied the Princesses make-up perfectly and styling each of the potential Heir's hair in individual elaborate designs.

Today's crowning ritual would take place in the grand ballroom, where each of the potential Heirs would have their chance to stand upon the dais and present their speeches to the audience. After a small lunch of sandwiches whilst being primped and pampered, the three Princesses made their way to the grand ballroom arm-in-arm, a rare moment of sibling bonding.

The grand ballroom was filled with rows of awaiting royals, visiting guests and vetted townspeople, who'd come to watch the second Crowning Ceremony ritual. For most present, it would be the first time the kingdom's people would hear more than a few words from the potential Heirs, and the excitement in the room was buzzing. The rioters arrested at the first trial remained in the palace dungeons as a safety precaution, but would be released after the Crowning Ceremonies had concluded.

Upon the dais of the ballroom on the left-hand side of the stage, sat Queen Amealiana, King Titian and High Priestess Elizabeth, with a spare chair reserved presumably for Sir Corneal, the commentator. The Matriarchs and High Priestess eagerly awaited the Princesses' speeches, and to judge their performance during the second Crowning Ceremony ritual.

The middle of the stage remained clear for the Princesses to deliver their speeches, and on the right-hand side of the stage, thrones were placed for each of the potential Heirs to await their turn to deliver their proposals to the people. Sir Corneal introduced each of the potential Heirs individually as they entered the grand ballroom. The several hundred guests rose from their seats to bow in respect and applaud the potential Heirs as they each made their grand entrance. Each of the Princesses gracefully walked down the red carpet in order of their birth, waving politely to the guests they passed before sitting in their thrones upon the dais.

'Don't fall over Annie, watch those high heels,' Annie coached herself as she tried not to stumble on her way down the red carpet. *'What I wouldn't give for my comfortable apothecary attire right now,'* Annie mused, feeling out of place in her suffocating gown and stunning but uncomfortable shoes.

Sir Corneal was wearing a perfectly tailored black suit for the occasion, with an overlaying cloak in traditional rich red with gold trim.

"Welcome your Majesties, visiting guests and dignitaries, to day four of the Crowning Ceremonies. There are only two remaining trials, including the event we are about to witness. It is my pleasure to introduce his Royal Majesty King Titian, to give the opening address before today's three royal proposals from our potential Heirs commence. Please bow in respect for King Titian," Sir Corneal announced, moving back from the center of the dais and taking his place in the spare chair beside the three judges' thrones.

King Titian was dressed regally as always in his house colors. Thankfully, the King appeared more relaxed than the previous day when Annalyse saw him overseeing the new security measures being put in place to ensure no further safety risks from the crowd at future events.

"My Queen Amealiana," King Titian began, "Princesses Alecia, Anastasia and Annalyse, High Priestess Elizabeth, visiting royals, dignitaries, and my people, welcome to today's Crowning Ceremony event. Today will showcase each of our potential Heirs' personalities and leadership qualities. Our role as rulers is to serve our people. Today you will see how each potential Heir plans to serve you if they are crowned Heir at the end of the Crowning Ceremony week. Exact scores are not revealed to the public for any of these events, in respect for the potential Heirs. This is a competition, yes, but we are also a family," the King paused to offer daughters a nod of respect.

"Family and kingdom are both highly valued and respected, which is why only placings are announced," The King continued. "At the end of today's speeches, Queen Amealiana, High Priestess Elizabeth and I will deliberate privately before delivering our decision on the current leader board placings. Now, please welcome in order of birth, Princess Alecia to deliver the first address to the people. For family and kingdom," the King concluded.

The guests stood and bowed, "for family and kingdom," they echoed.

King Titian resumed his place upon his throne as Princess Alecia portrayed herself as a picture of calm and tranquillity, taking her position at the center of the dais.

"King and Queen of Alearia, High Priestess, and esteemed guests, thank you for coming today to join us for the second Crowning Ceremony ritual. I have always been taught that knowledge is power," Alecia began. "That is certainly true, but giftings are also power. Where would we be today without gifted healers and apothecaries to heal us, or our skilled water mages to put out fires? Where would we be without our trained fire wielding soldiers on standby to protect us from harm; to defend our mighty Kingdom should war devastatingly come to our doorstep?"

Alecia paused momentarily to allow her people time to reflect upon her questions.

"I have trained all my life to wield my gifting to protect our people," Alecia continued. "I have been trained to help our people in both a practical and diplomatic sense. Without the training I received, I would not be as strongly gifted as I am today. Education of the mind is important but defending my people with my Goddess-given gifting is my calling. Fire can be used not only to harm but to heal. On the battlefield, a fire wielder can staunch a bleeding wound and save a life. In the farms, fire wielders can cleanse the land to make way for new crops to grow. Water mages can prevent a forest fire from destroying a home and they can water drought-affected fields and save crops. Healers can save lives, assist babies to be brought safely into the world, heal illness and prevent the spread of disease. Without our peoples' gifts being fully nurtured, we cannot reach our full potential as a people," Alecia declared.

"If I am chosen as your future Queen of Alearia," Alecia promised, "I plan to help our people to nurture their gifts whilst also ensuring the smooth running of our mighty kingdom. Our Kingdom needs our farmers and our bakers, to eat. Our country relies on its workforce to be fully functional. People rely on their earnings to support their families. It is not practical for everyone to leave their jobs to train full time in their giftings. Therefore, we must strike a balance between our day-to-day responsibilities and cultivating our Goddess-given giftings. I propose that all people of Alearia, regardless of social standing, be offered two free training sessions per week in their giftings, so they may reach their full potential. I personally will set aside time in my schedule each week to volunteer to teach the kingdom's fire wielding gifted children. As a people, we will strive to reach our full potential and raise up the next generation of talented gift wielders. For family and kingdom, thank you," Princess Alecia concluded, taking her seat back in her throne.

The crowd rose to their feet and cheered loudly in praise for Princess Alecia's proposal. Sir Corneal, Princess Anastasia and Queen Amealiana also rose to their feet, applauding Princess Alecia's revolutionary plan for the kingdom.

Sir Corneal then resumed his position at the front of the stage. "Thank you, Princess Alecia, for your inspiring proposal. If all the proposals are as outstanding as this, we, the people, can rest assured that the kingdom's future looks truly bright. Next, can you please rise to welcome our final two potential Heirs and twin sisters. Firstly, Princess Anastasia will address us, followed by Princess Annalyse. Please make Princess Anastasia, our current leader of the Crowning Ceremonies, feel welcome," Sir Corneal announced, taking his seat and nodding in respect for Princess Anastasia as she took his place at the center of the stage.

The peoples' clapping dulled as Princess Anastasia inhaled deeply before commencing her address.

"Thank you for your warm welcome, my people. Good afternoon your Majesties, High Priestess and all our wonderful guests here today," Anastasia spoke sincerely. "It is an honor to stand before you and give my first formal address to the people of Alearia. All I can offer you is my service and my loyalty. Queen Amealiana has raised me to always put others first. This past year I have struggled with grief and anxiety after the loss of my brother Prince Alexander. It is not very regal of me to admit to such things, but these struggles have helped form me into the person I am today; someone the people of Alearia can truly relate to."

Anastasia looked around the room, making eye contact with the people as she spoke. "I am sure I am not alone in my daily struggles and being Royal does not make me immune to grief or hardship. The responsibility of leading a kingdom is not something I take lightly. I will always strive to do my best to care for our people, and constantly put my peoples' needs before my own as any worthy leader would do. I intend to learn apothecary skills from my sister, Princess Annalyse, who has kindly offered to train me so that I may serve my people in a practical hands-on way."

"As Princess Alecia smartly pointed out," Anastasia continued, "fire wielders can use their powers for many different reasons, and

I would like to learn to adapt my skills to help more people. I would like to be a practical pro-active leader. Whether I am crowned Heir or not, I will always strive to support my people. I would also like to help our people by setting up a support program, for people like myself who struggle with grief, anxiety or other mental health concerns, where they can come to access free holistic care and support. Thank you for your time, for family and kingdom," Princess Anastasia concluded.

"For family and kingdom," the people echoed clapping their hands in support of the potential Heir.

Princess Anastasia began to walk back to her throne and Princess Annalyse met her halfway to embrace her.

"That was very brave sister, I am so proud of you," Annie whispered to her twin before releasing her from her embrace and taking her position at the front of the stage.

'Breathe Annie, you can do this,' Annie gave herself a pep talk as butterflies flew around her stomach.

"Good afternoon everyone," Annie began her proposal. "I am not accustomed to delivering speeches or addressing such a large audience. Whilst my siblings were raised in the ways of royalty, diplomacy, and leadership, I was raised as an apprentice healer. For as long as I can remember I have served the townspeople of Lavender Grove in a practical hands-on way, under the guidance of an immensely kind and compassionate healer. Lily raised me to always put others first. The values Lady Lilianna installed in me, though I didn't realize it at the time, were to prepare me to lead my Kingdom in a new direction. To lead an *'other'* focused kingdom. A kingdom where people care for each other as they would their own family. The kingdom of Alearia will be known as a place where everyone is treated equally. Where the poorest people have the same access to care and support as the wealthiest of nobles. I know that today's ritual is meant to be about communicating how we intend to care for our people, but for me, caring has always been about actions rather than words. If you would all indulge me, I would like to give a demonstration on one of the ways I intend to help my people," Princess Annalyse declared.

All around the room people murmured amongst each other; a buzz of excitement and anticipation filling the ballroom. King Titian, Queen Amealiana and High Priestess Elizabeth did their best to hide their surprise by Annie's unanticipated demonstration.

"Guards, can you please escort young Charlie into the ballroom," Princess Annalyse requested.

The crowd turned to the main ballroom entrance to see a scared young boy around ten years old escorted into the room by a royal guard and led up onto the dais to stand beside the Princess.

"Welcome Charlie," Princess Annalyse said warmly. The young boy was shaking, concern written across his face.

"Don't be afraid," Annie reassured him. "I am here to help you. Do you remember what we talked about this morning?" Charlie nodded keenly. "Very good. Do you mind if I share with the people what you told me this morning?" Annalyse asked.

Charlie nodded shyly in response.

"As you are all aware," Annie addressed the room, "the magical disease threat has now been eliminated through my sister Agnes's arrest. As we are now certain that the condition was created by Agnes and not contagious, all the people affected have been released from quarantine. This morning I asked the royal guards if they could locate the youngest person affected by the supposed magical disease and have them brought to the castle to meet with me."

Annie gestured towards the boy standing beside her. "That is how I came to meet Charlie. Poor Charlie is an orphan who only eats what he can steal. Charlie's parents passed away a couple of years ago from a plague, leaving Charlie homeless and having to take on the world on his own. I make a promise today to my kingdom's people, regardless of if I am crowned Heir, that children like Charlie will no longer be left in the cold to fend for themselves. These orphans will be cared for in a children's home funded by the royal family to protect and raise them into the leaders of tomorrow. These children are our future, and they desperately need our kindness and compassion. But there is more. As a mind conqueror I can undo the damage Agnes has caused this young boy. I can reconnect Charlie with his gifting, just as I promise to reunite everyone who has had the connection to their gifting severed due to Agnes's magical disease," Annie declared.

The guests gasped in awe and murmured loudly amongst each other in anticipation.

"Charlie, would you please bravely tell these people what your gifting was and try to use it please," Annie instructed the young boy.

"Before the magical disease was unleashed, I was a fire wielder," Charlie quietly explained. "I used to light fires at night to keep myself warm and cook my food. Now it's the middle of winter and I can't even light a candle to see at night," Charlie said as he tried to use his gifting, but not even a flicker of flame came to his fingertips.

"I am sorry for what has happened to you Charlie, but I can help you. Would you please take a seat in my throne?" Annie asked gently and Charlie eagerly did as he was asked.

"I want you to relax your mind and think about your fire wielding gifting," Annie instructed Charlie. "Try and recall what it felt like, what it looked like. I want you to picture it in your mind and while you picture it, I will help you with my gifting. Is that alright with you Charlie?" Annie asked.

Charlie nodded, his bottom lip trembling slightly from worry, but he closed his eyes to concentrate on the task at hand.

Annalyse took a deep breath and passed into his mind with her mind conqueror gifting, attempting to locate the young boy's gifting. Having found it after a few short minutes of searching, she repaired the broken connections separating his gifting from his mind, allowing Charlie once more to access his fire wielding powers.

Taking another deep breath, feeling unsteady from the intensely quick healing she had just performed, Annie withdrew from his mind and asked Charlie to attempt to use his gift. The crowd shot to their feet and applauded the Princess in awe and excitement, cheering triumphantly as Charlie was able to light a blazing purple flame in his hand. The young boy grinned with exhilaration.

The royal family and High Priestess all rose to their feet, applauding Annie's demonstration. Annalyse bowed graciously in thanks towards King Titian and Queen Amealiana before turning back to Charlie. Annie thanked the young boy for participating in the trial and Charlie surprised her by throwing his arms around her in a hug and repeatedly thanking her.

"It was my pleasure Charlie," Annalyse chuckled. "Now, if you go with this kind guard, he will escort you to the stables where you can learn to be a stable hand if you like? You will never have to steal food again and you will also gain an education. You will be able to live in the staff quarters with the other stable hands, where you will have a warm room and bed all to yourself. How does that sound Charlie?" Annalyse asked the young boy.

"I would like that very much!" Charlie cried, tears now trickling down his eyes. "Thank you, Princess Annalyse! Goddess bless you!" Charlie exclaimed, giving the Princess one last hug and gratefully following the guard out of the grand ballroom.

Princess Annalyse contently watched Charlie leave the room before collapsing into her throne, wholly fatigued from utilizing her gifting. The crowd continued their standing ovation for Princess Annalyse until the King moved to the center of the stage and signalled for the audience to resume their seats, which they did so after bowing respectfully for the King.

"Thank you, Princess Annalyse, for that wonderful demonstration on how you plan to care for our kingdom in the future. Thank you to all our potential Heirs for your wonderful, presentations. I am so proud of all of you. The future of Alearia is looking very bright indeed," the King stated warmly. "We will pause for a brief intermission while Queen Amealiana, High Priestess Elizabeth and I deliberate the results of today's event. Then we will resume the proceedings to announce the current placings in the Crowning Ceremonies. For family and kingdom," the King concluded, exiting the stage and ballroom, followed by Queen Amealiana and High priestess Elizabeth.

The Alearian rulers and High Priestess deliberated in the throne room for over two hours, before they returned to announce the revised placings on the leader board. During the intermission, the guests had been served refreshments and afternoon high tea by the palace staff. The potential Heirs had taken the opportunity to retire to their own suites to freshen up.

Princess Annalyse took the chance to have a rejuvenating rest after draining her gifting during the demonstration. Annalyse's Lady's Maid awoke the sleeping princess, who was now feeling much better after a doze, to help her promptly refresh her appearance so she was presentable for the results announcement. The potential Heir then quickly made her way to the grand ballroom, this time in much more comfortable shoes.

Queen Amealiana

'Why must the High Priestess be so difficult sometimes? We need to work together on this. The future of Alearia depends on who becomes the future Queen. Elizabeth shows little warmth towards Annie, though at least she applauded Annie after she healed the young boy. I suspect Elizabeth has an ulterior motive for not wanting Annie to be crowned Heir, though I am uncertain what it could be.

'Anastasia would make a wonderful Queen, but I feel in my heart that regardless of whether she is crowned Heir, she will do great things for the kingdom. Anastasia does not need a title to tie her to a destiny. Anastasia will change the world helping one person at a time, caring for those whom our society has neglected for too long.

'Alecia surprised me the most. Her idea of regular training sessions to nurture the peoples' gifts, whilst also considering the need for the kingdom to remain running was innovative. Alecia's proposal would benefit the kingdom immensely. Imagine what we could do as a kingdom if all our people were fully trained in their gifting. Envisage how many healers we could potentially discover if people had the time to advance their skills and giftings. We could nurture a new generation of healers; the rarest of giftings following Annalyse's mind conqueror gifting.

'What an incredibly difficult choice to make. I strongly oppose the High Priestess's verdict. I question if I should go against her and announce the results before she has the opportunity. Elizabeth could never attest that I had lied. I would only be acting in the best interests of the kingdom,' the Queen attempted to rationalize.

'What if the High Priestess uses my lie as an excuse to turn the religious sisters against the crown? Don't be silly Amealiana, she may be a little argumentative and outspoken, but she would never commit treason. Oh, my goodness Goddess, give me a sign as to what I should do," Amealiana internally debated, sitting in her throne atop the dais awaiting the remaining guests to take their seats.

Sir Corneal took his place once again in the center of the stage. "Welcome back your Majesties, High Priestess, potential Heirs, and distinguished guests. Now is the moment you have been waiting for; an update on the leader board. After our potential Heirs' inspiring speeches, I am glad that I was not the one having to decide upon the winner. Please welcome High Priestess Elizabeth to announce the current leader board positions at the end of day four of the Crowning Ceremony," Sir Corneal announced, beginning to clap, but the Queen quickly stood to her feet at the same time as the High Priestess.

"That's quite all right High Priestess, I wish to make the announcement today if that is permissible with you?" The Queen sweetly requested of the Priestess, knowing full well that to question the Queen in front of her subjects would not be appropriate.

The High Priestess's eyes flared in annoyance, but she quickly schooled her features into neutrality.

"As you wish Your Majesty," the High Priestess replied with a shallow bow, re-seating herself.

The Queen smiled sweetly in response before taking center stage. The guests stood and bowed for the Queen in respect.

"Good evening my people," Amealiana began her address. "There was much debate regarding the leader board today, but we have come to a unanimous decision. After today's Crowning ritual the scores from both challenges have been tallied, and our new potential Heir placings are as follows. Currently leading in first place in the Crowning Ceremony is Princess Annalyse." The guests applauded with excitement and Princess Annalyse blushed from embarrassment.

Queen Amealiana waited until the crowd had quietened before continuing her announcement. "Currently in second place, is Princess Alecia!" The crowd applauded and Alecia beamed with pride.

Anastasia grabbed Alecia's hand to give it an encouraging squeeze. Alecia squeezed her hand in return.

"Currently in third place is Princess Anastasia," the Queen announced confidently.

'*Please Goddess, let this not backfire on me!*' the Queen stressed internally.

The crowd cheered at the turn of events. All the Princesses beamed with pride. The King gave the Queen a look which said, '*we will talk about this later,*' and the High Priestess directed a stare that would make grown men cower, at the Queen.

The Queen inhaled deeply, masking her face with a serene smile.

"Please join me in one last applause for our three potential Heirs," Amealiana spoke warmly. "At this stage, whom will be crowned Heir only the Goddess knows. Thank you for joining us this evening. Tomorrow will be a day of celebration and rest. On day six of the Crowning Ceremonies we will have our final trial, and on day seven, one of these three Princesses will be crowned Heir and future Queen of Alearia. For family and kingdom, good night," the Queen declared before taking her leave.

"For family and kingdom," the people echoed.

47

Day Six of the Crowning Ceremony

High Priestess Elizabeth

"Your Majesties, esteemed guests, ladies and gentlemen, welcome to the final crowning ceremony ritual!" Sir Corneal announced. "Today is the day we have all been waiting for, the final challenge for our potential Heirs. Tomorrow at the final Crowning

Ceremony celebration, an Heir will be announced and crowned before our very eyes. What a highly anticipated couple of days we have ahead," Sir Corneal announced from the stage erected in the center of the training arena. "Today's final ritual is comprised of a series of interview questions. I'm sure you all have many questions regarding our potential Heirs. Well, do not fear people of Alearia, all will be revealed in today's interview!"

The Alearian castle training arena was packed to the rafters. Thousands of people had come to be a part of history and witness the last Crowning ritual of this generation of potential Heirs. Today was the final opportunity for the potential Heirs to prove their suitability for the crown. Behind the series of stands built for the Crowning Ceremony, people stood packed in against each other eager to listen to the day's events, even if they could not see the proceedings. The King and Queen of Alearia watched on from the royal viewing platform also playing host to the visiting royals and dignitaries for the day's event.

The sky was once again beautiful and clear; the perfect weather for today's ritual. Overnight it had snowed heavily, and the arena floor was once again blanketed by beautiful, gleaming fresh snow. The pure white powder was almost blinding due to the beautiful beams of light reflected from the sun. Upon the dais, two interview chairs were staged opposite three thrones. One for each potential Heir. The High Priestess sat confidently and comfortable in one of the interview chairs, with the other reserved for Sir Corneal.

The commentator stood in the middle of the stage, directing his attention towards the large crowd of spectators.

"For today's event, we are blessed to have our High Priestess interview each of our three potential Heirs," Corneal announced.

"High Priestess Elizabeth has only one question prepared for each potential Heir, meaning that each Princess only has one opportunity to impress us with their answer. Could you please rise and warmly welcome our three potential Heirs; Princess Alecia, Princess Anastasia and Princess Annalyse."

The crowd roared excitedly for their favorite potential Heirs as the three Princesses entered the arena. Each potential Heir walked along a snow cleared path before making their way up the dais and taking their designated throne in order of birth order.

The atmosphere in the training arena was electric. Sir Corneal took his seat beside High Priestess Elizabeth, utilizing his wind whisperer gifting to project each of the High Priestesses' questions and Princesses responses.

'Let's see how you handle today ladies. Your mother may have altered yesterday's results, but I will not let any potential Heir off lightly. As the potential future rulers of our kingdom, they need to be challenged and face some hard truths. As the Goddess's chosen High Priestess, I have a greater influence over the kingdom's people than even the King or Queen realize,' High Priestess Elizabeth mused to herself.

"Welcome Princesses, to your final day of ritual challenges," High Priestess Elizabeth said warmly. "As Sir Corneal has kindly explained to the crowd, today's ritual consists of an interview. A simple personalized question for each of you to help us gauge your suitability to become a powerful, kind, and compassionate ruler. Today's questions are designed to challenge each of our potential Heirs. Being a ruler is no easy task and therefore, to make sure the right Princess is chosen I must ask the hard questions. Before we get into today's interview questions though, I would like to lead us all in a prayer to the Goddess. Holy Goddess, we praise you. We thank you for your guidance and insight throughout the Crowning Ceremony process. Please reveal to us today whom you believe should be crowned Heir tomorrow. For family and kingdom, we thank you Goddess."

"For family and Kingdom," the potential Heirs and spectators echoed.

"For today's task, we will conduct the interviews in random order, to not allow anyone an unfair advantage of extra time to prepare their answer. Sir Corneal, will you please prepare the hat," the High Priestess requested.

Sir Corneal took the top hat off his head and placed three numbers inside, before swirling them around to mix them up. He then passed the hat to each potential Heir so they could draw a number, determining their interview question order. Princess Annalyse drew number one, followed by Princess Alecia, then lastly followed by Princess Anastasia.

'This could not have gone more perfectly,' Elizabeth smugly thought to herself.

"Congratulations Princess Annalyse, you are first," the High Priestess announced cheerfully.

"It would be my honor High Priestess," Princess Annalyse calmly replied.

"Very good," the High Priestess acknowledged. "Now a large part of being Heir is having to answer difficult questions, so consider this a practice for what may lie ahead for your future. Princess Annalyse, you say you were raised in Quillencia and taught your mind conqueror craft in secret by King Julian himself. Other than that, we know extraordinarily little about you. As an outsider, how can we trust you?"

The crowd gasped at the High Priestess' brashness but began murmuring amongst themselves in agreement.

The King stood from his throne and projected across the arena, "High Priestess, are you publicly questioning a potential Heir's integrity?"

The High Priestess feigned offense and distress, painting herself the picture of an elderly woman being verbally bullied by her ruler.

"Quite the opposite your Majesty. I do apologize for giving you the wrong impression," the High Priestess replied, allowing her voice to quiver. "I was merely trying to find out more about our new mystery potential Heir. I am sure the people of Alearia would like to know more about her as well. I believe the people are entitled to know who their potential future ruler is your Majesty. If the Princess has nothing to hide, then there is no harm in her answering the question is there?" The High Priestess asked innocently.

The King stared daggers at the High Priestess, but he was wise enough to recognize when he had been outsmarted and backed into a corner.

"Very well. Carry on High Priestess," the King reluctantly advised her.

"As you wish Sire," the High Priestess beamed. "Princess Annalyse I will simplify the question. What makes you a trustworthy potential ruler of our kingdom?"

Princess Annalyse took a deep breath to focus her thoughts. "I was raised in a small town called Lavender Grove. All my life I believed I was an orphan taken in by a healer to raise as an apprentice apothecary. I dedicated my life from a young age to serving my townspeople through sickness and health. I worked alongside my mentor, learning her craft so that I could better learn how to help my people. The leadership skills she taught me are transferable skills that I plan to use if crowned Heir, to help lead my people. Some people are suspicious of mind conquerors and rightly so," Annalyse agreed."

"The kingdom of Alearia was betrayed by Agnes," Princess Annalyse continued, "a mind conqueror, and that has only reinforced the peoples' fear in my gifting. However, I do not plan to use my gifting as she did. I will not use my gifting for personal gain of any sort. I plan to use my gifting for healing. A mind conqueror gifting works differently to how a traditional healer gifting works. My mind conqueror gifting can delve more deeply into the mind. I can identify each part of the mind like a road map interpreting signals and electrical activity, which will allow me to heal those who have had their giftings separated from them by Agnes. King Julian taught me how to repair the connections of the victims of Agnes's actions with their giftings. If you respect King Julian, then you would trust in his decision to train me and my mind conqueror gifting," Annalyse politely replied.

"Thank you for answering my question, Princess Annalyse. Forgive me, Princess, I did not mean to inadvertently question your integrity earlier, it was merely a line of questioning that needed to be pursued for the peoples' peace of mind. I'm sure you understand," High Priestess Elizabeth stated sweetly.

"Certainly, High Priestess," Princess Annalyse replied innocently.

"Terrific! Shall we move along? Princess Alecia, it is your turn," the High Priestess announced. "Princess Alecia, your behavior of late has been a little erratic, shall we say. What makes you fit to rule our kingdom?" The High Priestess questioned.

Alecia bit her tongue to hold back her retort and pursed her lips before replying.

"Thank you for your question High Priestess. It is true that I have not been myself lately. The pressure of the past year and the Crowning Ceremonies affects us all differently I suppose," Alecia pondered.

"I was raised to be a leader," Alecia continued. "I may come across as a little arrogant, however, people of great power are often falsely perceived as such. My gifting is the strongest of my generation. My demonstration in the first Crowning ritual proved that I will do whatever it takes to get what I want. How will that benefit our kingdom, you might be thinking? Well it's simple really. I will fight for my kingdom's best interest. I will be the strong powerful leader that the people need. I will not be meek or mild, but passionate and stand up for what I believe in. I will be a strong advocate for my people and if war ever finds our doorsteps, I will be on the front lines defending my people, because that is who I am. I am a strong capable leader just as my father King Titian has always been."

The crowd murmured their acceptance of the Princess's explanation.

"How gracious and humble of you Princess Alecia," the High Priestess replied passive aggressively. "I'm sure the people have no doubt that you will continue to be a strong, capable leader. Thank you for your time," the High Priestess concluded.

Alecia merely smiled sweetly in return, ignoring her attempt to criticize her.

"Finally, as they say, last but not least, Princess Anastasia," the High Priestess purred. "Princess Anastasia, you have been the darling of the Alearian people and up until recently our youngest potential Heir. Your speech in the second crowning ritual was inspiring. The way you talked about wanting to be a hands-on practical, caring leader, made my heart sing with pride. There was one tiny thing I need to ask you, however," the High Priestess smirked.

Anastasia held her breath preparing for the attack that was coming her way. The Princess nodded to indicate she was ready for her question. High Priestess Elizabeth transformed her face into a mask of concern and empathy.

"Princess Anastasia, I speak for all of the people of Alearia when I say how sorry we are for the loss of your brother. We all grieve in our own way. You yourself said you suffer from crippling anxiety. Are you fit to run our kingdom?" The High Priestess questioned seemingly innocently, but internally patted herself on the back for clearly striking a nerve with the Princess.

Princess Anastasia straightened her back.

"High Priestess, I can see your concern," Anastasia acknowledged, "but I want to reassure you and the Alearian people that I am fit to take my place as ruler of our great kingdom. Having feelings does not make me weak. Being aware of my struggles is a strength because it means I have been able to identify areas of my life that I need help with, and I will reach out for help as I need it."

Murmurs around the crowd increased as people empathized with the Princesses situation much to Elizabeth's frustration.

"I have a supportive family that will stand by my side whether I am crowned Heir or not," Anastasia continued. "I may not be perfect, but no one is. We all have our faults and burdens to carry. I did not choose to suffer anxiety, but I am learning to live with it and managing it in my own way, just as many people do in their day to day lives."

"Having anxiety does not define who I am or what I stand for," Anastasia spoke with conviction. "It is a condition that I battle every day, and that battle has grown me into the strong, independent leader I am today. I would be proud to serve my kingdom as their Queen. I care for my people and I would serve them whole heartedly. A wise leader once told me that: *'Magic is the happiness that we create when we give ourselves permission to follow our dreams.'* My dream is to serve my people wholeheartedly. For family and kingdom," Princess Anastasia concluded confidently.

"For family and kingdom," the crowd echoed, standing to their feet and applauding the young potential Heir's brave and honest response.

48

Day Seven of the Crowning Ceremony

Queen Amealiana

'Sixteen years ago, my family was completed and then torn apart.
In the last year, I have lost my son, and my best friend sacrificed

herself to save my long-lost child. Lily was loyal and generous to a fault, right until her very last breath.

'Oh, Lilianna, how I wish you were here with us today. You would see how much Annie has matured and blossomed these past months. It is as though a weight has been lifted from her shoulders, and she has finally given herself permission to be happy and dream her own dreams.

'Her twin Anastasia is a blessing to all who know her. Anastasia battles her own demons every day just as I do, but it never holds her back. She takes on the world with fierce determination. Anastasia has such an innocent joy about her that is infectious. She loves wholeheartedly and is so like you in that regard. Her unending hope, positivity, trust, and loyalty makes me so proud of her.

'Alecia has a will of steel and nothing will ever break her. Alecia has had her own challenges this year and I think temporarily losing her gifting was good for her in the end, as it allowed her to see what life is like for those powerless to defend themselves.

'Agnes remains in the dungeon. Tomorrow she will sadly meet the fate her dark choices led her towards. I wish there were another way, but what she has done is unforgivable. If we allowed Agnes to escape the consequences of her actions, we would be showing unfair privilege. Even royalty must be held accountable to the law of the people.' Queen Amealiana reflected to herself whilst standing upon the dais in the grand ballroom; the room bustling with a hive of activity as the palace staff attended to last-minute decorations and preparations.

White flowers and candles hung around the room. House colored banners of red and gold, hung proudly along the walls. The curtains were drawn fully back from the ornate floor to ceiling windows, revealing the winter wonderland of the Alearian mountain alps. The hearths around the room burned brightly, giving the room a comfortable tranquil ambiance. The lit candelabras added a sense of romance and intimacy to the room.

It was mere minutes until the guests were permitted to enter the grand hall for the final Crowning Ceremony event; the moment everyone was waiting for. The future Queen of Alearia would be crowned Heir today.

Guards were posted all around the room should security be required. One could never be too careful at formal political events such as these. The Queen took a deep breath.

'I can do this. Just a few more hours and the Crowning Ceremony will officially be over. Then I can visit Agnes and say my goodbyes in private.'

King Titian entered the ballroom from the royal family's private side entrance and approached his wife upon the dais.

"Are you ready my darling?" the King asked in a rare tender moment in public.

The King was always so determined to remain strong for his people that he rarely let his staff or the public see the other tender, gentle, loving side of him. The Queen nodded in affirmation, turning towards the King and embracing him.

"Yes, my love. Let us announce the good news. It is time to crown our Heir. I believe we have made the right choice for our family and kingdom," Queen Amealiana replied.

The King nodded in understanding. "Then let us proceed as planned."

The King signaled for the head guard, who came promptly over and stood at attention awaiting orders.

"Guard, please open the doors so that the guests may take their seats," The King ordered. "Can you please ask the High Priestess to join us on the dais? It is time to begin the ceremony. That will be all thank you."

"As you wish, my King," the guard bowed before taking his leave.

King Titian took his wife gently by the hand and led her over to her throne. They both took their seats but remained hand in hand for reassurance and support. The quartet began playing sweet traditional music, ready for the guests to arrive.

'Breathe Amealiana, only a few hours to go and it will all be over,' the Queen reminded herself, as she masked her face into a pleasant regal disposition as the three hundred royals, dignitaries and esteemed guests began to file into the grand ballroom.

Each guest approached the main aisle to bow respectfully to the King and Queen before taking their seats.

Once all the guests were seated, the herald announced: "presenting her holiness, High Priestess Elizabeth."

The two doormen held open the door for the High Priestess to enter down the main aisle, where she was directed by the guard to take a seat on the other side of the Queen.

The King stood from his throne and walked to the front of the dais, commanding the room's attention. "Welcome everyone, to such a historic moment in our Alearian history. Today, as you all know, is the final day of the Crowning Ceremony and an eligible Heir must be chosen as the Goddess and tradition demands. Not all has gone to plan this week but after much deliberation, the Heir and future Queen of Alearia has been chosen. After seeking guidance from the Goddess, we believe it is the Goddess' deigned will that this Princess should be crowned Heir of Alearia," the King stated as waiters started handing out glasses of wine to the gathered guests.

"Before we get underway with the official ceremony, I would like to make a toast," the King declared, raising his glass of wine that a servant had just handed him. "Life is precious, and we must treasure those we love. Life is too short for bitterness or hatred. As my wise daughter, Princess Anastasia reminded us yesterday; *'Magic is the happiness that we create when we give ourselves permission to follow our dreams'.* May all your dreams come true, and your lives be truly blessed with magical moments. May today mark the beginning of a new era of mighty Brandistone rulers. May our future Queen always place family and kingdom above all other things. For family and kingdom, please join me in a toast to our future Heir," the King declared.

"For family and kingdom," the people proudly declared toasting their glasses and taking a sip of the luxurious sparkling wine.

"Without any further delay, we will now commence today's celebration. I would like to warmly welcome High Priestess Elizabeth to the dais to lead us in our opening prayer," King Titian introduced the priestess.

High Priestess Elizabeth rose from her seat to lead the guests in prayer.

"Holy Goddess, we thank you for your continued blessing over our magnificent kingdom," she began. "We thank you for our allies in neighboring kingdoms and for the prosperity that our close ties bring. We pray that our future Queen is a blessing beyond measure to her people. We pray that you bestow upon her the wisdom of a thousand leaders, the courage of an army, as well as the kindness and compassion of a mother. Over the coming year, we pray that you prepare our new Heir for her future role as Queen of Alearia. For family and kingdom, may we always strive for greatness, kindness, and compassion. Thank you, Goddess," The High priestess concluded before resuming her place beside the Queen.

The King resumed his former position standing at the front of the dais. "Please stand to welcome our three potential Heirs," the King announced, smiling broadly as the people rose from their seats to bow in honor of the Princesses as they entered the grand ballroom one by one.

"Proudly presenting Princess Alecia, the mighty fire wielder," The King announced. "Next, we have Princess Anastasia, a talented fire wielder in her own right, and finally, presenting Princess Annalyse, a gifted sage and mind conqueror. Please congratulate them all on their efforts this past week during the Crowning rituals," the King requested, leading the gathered guests in a round of applause for the three Princesses as they took their places in the thrones allocated for them along the left side of the dais facing the guests.

"Today marks a new era for our people. For many a generation, we have not seen a female crowned Heir of Alearia. It is with great pride that the Queen and I would like to announce the Alearian kingdom's crowned Heir. Queen Amealiana, would you like to do the honors?" the King kindly offered.

The Queen smiled warmly in return and removed her crown, holding it preciously in front of her as she walked to the front of the dais to address the room.

"It is my greatest honor and privilege to announce to you today, Alearia's new Heir and future Queen," Amealiana warmly declared. "This Princess demonstrates kindness and compassion in everything she does. This empathetic Princess embodies all the virtues and values our mighty kingdom stands for. Please bow in respect for our new Alearian Heir, and our future Queen," the Queen spoke solemnly as a tear of pride trickled down her cheek, turning to face her daughters and placing the crown upon the future ruler's head.

"Presenting Princess Annalyse Brandistone, Crowned Heir of Alearia, sage, mind conqueror, and our future Queen."

Epilogue

Queen Amealiana

The kingdom's people were overjoyed with the announcement of their new Heir and future Queen. As was to be expected, some of the nobility were overheard gossiping amongst each other and questioning the decision, but that was always bound to be the case. Princess Anastasia was incredibly excited for her sister, though Alecia appeared rather sullen and disappointed by the announcement, which was also to be expected.

Queen Amealiana felt exhausted from the Crowning Ceremony events, but she wanted to take this time while everyone was preoccupied with the celebrations, to visit her eldest daughter in private to say her final goodbye. Queen Amealiana had changed out of her formal gown from the Crowning Ceremony and now wore a simple black day dress with a woollen cloak, reflecting her feelings of grief and devastation.

'Am I wrong to come and visit Agnes?' the Queen worried as she walked down the dimly lit passageway towards the dungeon's quarantine room. *'What if she doesn't want to see me? I'm sure Agnes must feel as though I have committed the ultimate betrayal as her mother, allowing her to be sentenced to death. And she is right. No matter what Agnes has done, as her mother I should stand by her. I can't help but love her no matter all the poor choices she has made.*

'Every time I feel tempted to beg my husband for mercy on our daughter's life, I remember the poor families of the guards she killed in cold blood. Agnes burned those brave guards without a second thought. We must all face the consequences of our actions. In these, her final hours of life, I need to make peace with her. I need Agnes to know before she passes from this world into the next, that I love her, and I always will. I need Agnes to know that regardless of all she has done, I am still her mother and I will always love her.'

Queen Amealiana approached the door to the quarantine room, which was strangely left unguarded.

'Perhaps I have arrived at a guard changeover time or possibly the guard is inside the room giving Agnes her final dinner. Very strange indeed,' the Queen thought to herself as she pulled out the key to the quarantine room door from her pocket.

Queen Amealiana took a deep breath.

'*Be strong Amealiana, Agnes needs your strength right now. My poor daughter must be terrified knowing what lays ahead for her tomorrow.*'

The Queen turned the key and pushed the door open gently. Beholding what lay inside the room, the Queen dropped to her knees and screamed. The guard was lying face down, unconscious in a pool of his own blood.

Agnes had escaped.

Acknowledgements

Thank you, reader, for taking this journey with me.

Thank you for supporting me as an Indie author.

Thank you to my husband Joel and my daughter Lily, for your unending support. Thank you for believing in me. Thank you for supporting me and pushing me to see this book through. Thank you for valuing my dreams and pushing me to fulfill them. Joel, you are my rock and I could not have finished this without your help and support, thank you. I love you.

Thank you for pushing me to be a better writer Andy.

Thank you for your thorough revisions, Chloe Hodge.

To my friend and neighbor Brooke, we have not known each other long, but I feel like we have been friends for forever. You have been a constant support and cheerleader from the side, thank you for being my first reader.

Thank you to my family. Clare, Josh, Marie, Mum, and Dad, thank you for your continuous encouragement. It means so much to me, dad and mum, that you are proud of me for seeing this through.

Thank you to my amazing friends new and old, who have encouraged me along the way. To all the mums, for anyone out there who thinks it is too late to pursue your dreams, I want to tell you it's not!

Thank you to my fellow writers who have supported me on my journey. Thank you to the my bookstagram friends for all of your support. Special mention to my Perth book loving friends, life wouldn't be this much fun without you.

Thanks Jess for doing one final proofread for me to make this new edition the best version it can be.

"Do what makes you happy," as my brother Josh wisely told me once. Make your dreams come true everyone.

Live the life you have always dreamed.

About the Author

Nattie Kate Mason is an independent self-published author from Australia. Mum to the gorgeous Lily and wife to supportive husband Joel. Nattie works as a nurse in her day job, but her passions are reading and writing. Nattie has traveled around Australia with her little family of three and their pets, living in various towns and cities for various periods at a time. Life is never dull for Nattie and her unique little family. Nature, life and reading help to inspire Nattie's creative side. You will often find her reading a good book outdoors, enjoying the peace and quiet, drinking an endless amount of exotic tea.

Nattie's books can be found in many independent bookstores throughout the Perth region, through most online retailers or via her website nattiekatemason.com

Titles by Nattie Kate Mason

The Crowning young adult fantasy series:

The Crowning

A Queen's Fate

Heart of a Crown

Chapter Books by Nattie Kate:

Lily Rose and the Pearl Crown

Lily Rose and the Enchanted Fairy Garden

Visit nattiekatemason.com to stay up to date on the

latest new releases from this author.

Follow Nattie on social media

IG/FB: @nattie.kate.mason.writer

www.ingramcontent.com/pod-product-compliance
Lightning Source LLC
Chambersburg PA
CBHW030349120726
47901CB00007B/1964